Kasey Michaels

dial M for Mischief

ISBN-13: 978-0-373-77291-9
ISBN-10:   0-373-77291-2

DIAL M FOR MISCHIEF

Also available from
Kasey Michaels
and HQN Books

Dear Reader,

Ex-cop turned private investigator Teddy Sunshine raised his daughters to be tough and resilient, and to depend on themselves even as they'd always been able to depend on each other. And then Teddy died, supposedly committing suicide after strangling the wife of Philadelphia's top mayoral candidate.

Jade, the eldest of Teddy's three girls, who worked with Teddy, summons her movie-actor sister, Jolie, and investigative cable news journalist, Jessica, home for their father's funeral. Together they vow to prove their father had not been a murderer.

The men in their lives are sympathetic, yes, but not at all happy to have the girls digging around in Teddy's cold cases from his days on the police force, looking for the reason Teddy was killed.

Four unsolved cases had haunted Teddy.

The case of the Vanishing Bride.

The shooting death of a Scholar Athlete.

The Fishtown Strangler murders of six prostitutes.

And, lastly, the Baby in the Dumpster, a case that still held the attention of all of the cops in Philly.

Somewhere in one of these cases, all recently worked yet again by Teddy, lay the answer to Teddy's death.

Somewhere, in the emotional turmoil of lovers past and present, the Sunshine girls hope to find some healing, some answers and a return of some sunshine to their lives.

And somewhere out there, somebody should be very, very afraid that old crimes and new crimes are about to be solved!

Oh, and one thing more—it would seem that two of the men in their lives are descendants of Ainsley Becket, patriarch of the Beckets of Romney Marsh, and heirs to the infamous Empress, a priceless uncut emerald that remains hidden two hundred years later, waiting for its "bad luck" to wear off so it can be found.

I hope you'll enjoy Jolie Sunshine and Sam Becket's story, and then watch for Jessica's and Jade's stories in the months to come.

Happy reading!

Kasey Michaels

dial
M
for
Mischief

To Diana Ventimiglia
Onward and upward, baby!

CHAPTER ONE

THE SKY WAS UNUSUALLY bright the day his daughters buried Teddy Sunshine, the sun a big yellow ball chasing away all the early-morning clouds, if not the chill temperatures.

Jolie Sunshine, when she noticed the sun, wondered whether her father had ordered it up or if it was some sort of sick joke dealt them by fate.

In contrast to the brightness of the day, the small crowd around the grave site resembled nothing more than exotic black crows beneath the blue canvas canopy with Fulton Funeral Home stamped on the overhang. The only other colors were those of their pale faces and the blanket of bright red roses draping the bronze casket.

When I kick off, I want to go out like a Kentucky Derby winner—draped with roses. Big red ones. Don't you forget!

"We remembered, Teddy," Jolie whispered under her breath, earning her quick, inquisitive looks from her sisters, which she ignored.

Roses they could do. What his daughters couldn't do was to have their father buried with a full police funeral. Murderers didn't get that kind of honor.

Jolie swayed slightly between her sisters as the priest read a final prayer. The three held hands as they stood in their birth order: Jade to Jolie's right, Jessica, the baby, to her left. Teddy's Irish setter, Rockne, reclined stretched out at their feet, wearing his Notre Dame Fightin' Irish kerchief around his neck.

They were quite the dazzling trio, Teddy Sunshine's girls; Teddy's Angels, he'd only half-jokingly called them, harking back to the days of that old television show, *Charlie's Angels,* which Teddy said the movie couldn't really hold a candle to for sheer enjoyment.

Jade could almost be typecast in the role Kate Jackson had played in the mid-seventies. Beautiful, refined and all business.

Jessica could be a fresher, more lush and wholesome Farrah Fawcett, with brains as well as looks. Although, as Jessica had pointed out more than once, her teeth weren't as big.

But Jolie? Jolie didn't fit Jaclyn Smith's role, the one heavy on brains and beauty but also on sex appeal. Jolie was brunette; she was always told she was photogenic, but she had also spent most of her life believing herself to be too tall, too thin, too angular. Her mouth was too wide, her lips too full, her hair too straight, her hands and feet too long.

Hell, she'd spent most of her teenage years carrying the nickname Jolly Green Jolie.

Whenever she stood between her sisters, taller than either Jade or Jessica, she felt plain beside Jessica's almost too-perfect beauty and stupid when compared to Jade's quick, incisive brain—a living, breathing example of middle-child syndrome.

It was only when she was in front of the cameras that Jolie didn't feel awkward, inept, a giraffe in a field full of graceful gazelles. When the lights came on, all her self-doubt disappeared and she could be anyone she dreamed she could be.

How she longed to be somebody else today, rather than a grieving daughter. How she longed to talk to Teddy Sunshine just one more time, watch as his big Irish smile lit up a room brighter than any Hollywood klieg lights and made her feel so very special, so very loved.

Most of all, she wanted to hear his laugh, a laugh that could fill her world.

But now—in the shade beneath the blue canvas tarp, except for the droning voice of Father Sheehan and the sobbing of two maiden aunts from Buffalo Jolie would have been hard-pressed to name correctly—silence, cold and uncomfortable, was all around them.

There should be a Philadelphia Police Department honor guard in attendance, at the very least. Taps played. A salute fired. A flag ceremoniously folded and presented to Jade, as the oldest.

But the Sunshine daughters had to make do with a priest who had never known Teddy, filling in for Father Muskie, who was on his annual vacation in the Canadian north woods and out of touch, unknowing that his good friend and gin rummy partner had died in disgrace.

What the Sunshine funeral did have was press. Lots of it. Print and television news, along with about two dozen dredges of the tabloid-journalism pool, paparazzi hoping for a few good photographs, and some Mary Hart look-alike from one of the evening celebrity-magazine shows.

The local reporters had shown up to put a fairly boring cap on the Teddy Sunshine story: the ex-cop turned P.I. who'd eaten his gun after squeezing the life out of mayoral candidate Joshua Brainard's beautiful wife.

The rest were here for Jolie Sunshine, movie star—and may they all go straight to hell.

Rockne slowly clambered to his feet as the priest walked past, shaking hands with all three Sunshine daughters, and then collapsed onto his belly once more, raising his sad brown eyes to Jolie. He hadn't eaten anything for the past two days, even when she had gotten down on the floor early this morning and gone face-to-face with him, one of his favorite treats clamped between her teeth as she'd mumbled, "Yum-yums. 'Ook, 'Ock-nee, yum-yums."

Now *there* was a picture for the tabloids: Movie Star Fights Pooch for Doggy Treat, Fears Rise Over Mental Collapse of Fan-Fave Sunshine.

Like she'd give them the satisfaction. She'd get through this. They'd all get through this.

"Okay, it's over, Jolie. Time to say our last goodbyes," her sister Jade told her quietly.

Jolie felt her knees threaten to buckle once more but steeled herself to remain upright. When they left the grave site, the workmen standing under those trees over there would come back, lower Teddy into the ground, locking away all the real sunshine in her life forever. She wasn't ready for that. "No, not yet. Please, not yet."

Jade sighed, squeezed Jolie's hand. Jade, the oldest and, even now, in the midst of their nightmare, the practical one. The one who had stayed with Teddy, worked with Teddy in the Sunshine Detective Agency. The one who had come home to discover Teddy's body and then called her sisters, broken the news to them without tears, without hysterics. Just, "Daddy's dead—I need you here. Now."

"Honey, we have to face the cameras. One last time, and then we can go home, begin to figure this thing out. Okay?"

"Come on, Jolie, Jade's right," her sister Jessica urged. "We'll face them together. Just ignore the slimy bastards, say 'No comment' if you say anything at all as we keep moving toward the limo. You know the drill."

Jolie looked wryly at her sister, the blond bombshell who was currently on sabbatical from her own job as an on-air investigative reporter. "Slimy bastards, Jess? Aren't they your comrades-in-arms?"

Jessica rolled her huge sherry-brown eyes even as she tossed her head, her long blond hair falling forward once more to frame her face. "Puh-leez. I'm the real deal. What's waiting on the other side of the road are the dregs of humanity. Entertainment reporters? Bottom-feeding, scum-sucking dirtbags, that's all they are. But we're not going to let them get to us. Right?"

Jolie nodded. "Right. Just give me another minute. Just…just one more minute."

Jessica looked past Jolie to Jade, who only shrugged her shoulders and left the two of them standing where they were while she retrieved a trio of long-stemmed red roses the undertaker had provided. "Here, one for each of us. Jolie? Come on, honey. Follow me, do what I do."

"Yes, Mother," Jolie said, smiling for the first time in days as she took the rose. She was an actress. She would act. The grieving daughter approaching at the graveside, kissing the petals of a drooping rose and then placing it on top of the casket that was really empty, a prop, a part of the scene, that's all. She was the Mafia wife bidding farewell to her mobster husband, gunned down as he ate his favorite pasta in his favorite mobster restaurant. The sweetheart of a fallen World War I soldier who'd perished somewhere in France. The sister of a frontier sheriff ambushed on the streets of Laredo.

Her hand barely shook as she gently laid the bloom on top of the blanket of roses. She was acting. It was all a sham. This wasn't real. Teddy wasn't dead. Her daddy wasn't—

"Oh, God, I'm sorry I'm being such a jerk. Let's just get out of here before I lose it," Jolie whispered as she stepped back from the casket and bent down to grab Rockne's leash. She pushed past Jade, who had been stopped by one of the anonymous, interchangeable aunts.

"What's the rush? Oh, you want to leave now, Jolie? What a fantastic idea," Jessica muttered, following after her. "Jade and I would never have thought of that on our own—you long-legged dork-stork."

"Stuff it, Barbie doll—if you don't already—and go rescue Einstein from the aunts, will you? I'll go ahead to the limo, keep the cameras off you guys if I can." Jolie squared her shoulders. They were the Sunshine girls. They'd hung in this long and they were going to get through this!

None of them had cried throughout the funeral mass or the short ceremony at the grave site; they wouldn't give anyone that satisfaction. All Jolie wanted now—all she was sure the three of them wanted now—was to get this done, get this over and go back to the house Jade had shared with their father.

The house where he had sat in his study, surrounded by a lifetime of achievements nailed to the walls, and used his service revolver to blow his brains all over those signed photographs and commendations.

Jolie looked across the cemetery with its flat bronze plaques fairly hidden in the well-manicured grass, giving the area the appearance of a wide, green park. Pretty, even peaceful, if not for the crowd being held behind rope barricades on the far side of the macadam roadway that wound through the center of the cemetery.

As she and Rockne moved toward the limousine, eager arms were raised and she could hear the whir and snap of two dozen cameras, had to blink at the sharp shafts of sunlight reflected from many of the telephoto lenses pointed in her direction.

Her mouth went dry. Her heart pounded with pain and anger. She wanted to run, longed to run. Felt her hands bunching into fists at her sides because she wanted to hit someone, shake someone, demand to know if they really believed the "public's right to know" extended to being voyeurs at a funeral.

But she knew she had to keep walking slowly, at an unhurried pace, her head held high, her face shielded somewhat by the large, round sunglasses.

Jolie swore she could hear her father's big, encouraging voice whispering in her ear.

That's the way. One foot in front of the other, Jolie, baby, and soon you'll be walkin' right out that door....

She was almost there, almost at the limo. She had to hang on just another minute, and they would be out of this madness.

There were a half dozen rent-a-cops on the scene for crowd control, and yet someone wasn't on the job. One of the paparazzi slipped through the line to do an end-run around the hearse and toward Jolie, snapping his camera as he approached.

"Jolie! Look here! Look over here! Toss the glasses, babe! Let's see those big baby blues! Come on, honey, you owe your fans something, right?"

Steady, girl. One foot in front of the other...

The rent-a-cops stood back as the photographer edged closer. He dropped to one knee to get a good shot, the telephoto lens still in place. Jolie madly wondered if her fans really needed a close-up of the hairs in her nose.

"Hey, Jolie! What's it feel like knowing your daddy was a murderer? Gotta be tough, right?"

Something inside her snapped, actually went *br-oi-i-n-g*. She took a step toward the photographer.

"That's it, Jolie—nearly perfect. Now ditch the glasses."

"Don't do it, Jolie," Jessica called out, jogging toward her as quickly as she could in four-inch heels. "Don't react. Just let it go."

"The hell with that. Come on, Jolie. Look this way. You smile for us when you want us around. Smile for us now!"

Aw, the bloody blue devil with it, sweetheart— go give him a good conk!

Jolie would probably never remember how she got from point A to point B, but she was suddenly there, looking down on the son of a bitch who was still shooting frame after frame up into her face. She'd rather not remember grabbing the camera from him even as she kicked front with one foot, connected with his chest and sent him sprawling on his back on top of Bertha M. Pierce, 1917– 2003, beloved wife of Henry.

Yanking open the back of the camera, Jolie ripped out the film, exposing it to the sun, and then pulled back her arm, ready to throw the camera in the photographer's face. She knew the other photographers and video cameramen were having a field day from their vantage point across the road, but she didn't care. She'd needed a target for all her anger, her grief, her frustration, and this bozo had volunteered for the job.

And then she heard the scream.

Turning, with the camera still in midair, Jolie saw the interchangeable great-aunts ten yards behind her.

One of them—Aunt Marie; or maybe it was Aunt Theresa—had her right leg jammed up to the knee in a hole in the ground. She wasn't screaming, even though her mouth was open and moving. She was white-faced with terror.

"Help! Help!" the other aunt, the screamer, cried hysterically. "Somebody's trying to pull her down!"

Jolie let the camera fall to the ground as Jade and Jessica joined her, the three of them now staring at the aunts. "What in hell…?"

"Gopher hole," the undertaker explained quietly as he walked past the girls. "Happens a couple of times every summer, and they always think one of the dearly departed is reaching up to get them. I'll dig her out. I keep a shovel in the hearse."

Jolie forgot about the cameras, forgot about the reporters, even forgot her anger. She involuntarily drew in her breath, air sucking in so long and so hard she thought she might have forgotten how to exhale. And then, when she believed she might faint, something inside of her released. She let loose with a fountain of laughter that had built up inside her and now exploded from her, totally beyond her control.

She laughed until she had to bend over, brace her hands on her knees. And still she laughed.

She laughed until the laughter turned to tears. Hard, racking sobs that sent her down to her knees, because Teddy would have loved the gopher hole *so* much and then later woven the incident into a huge story twice as funny as what had actually happened.

"Come on, baby, showtime's over."

Jolie stiffened at the touch of hands closing around her shoulders, pulling her to her feet. She turned around slowly…to look up into a face she hadn't seen in five long years.

"Sam? Oh, God…Sam…"

"Yeah, Sam. We've got that covered," Sam Becket said as he slid a protective arm around her shoulders and guided her away from the limousine and toward a sleek black Mercedes parked at the bend of the macadam road. "Your sisters can manage, but we've got to get you out of here."

Jolie tried to slow her steps, but Sam kept a strong grip on her as he hastened her across the grass. "I can't just leave them to—"

"You can, you are, and for once in your big, in-dependent life you're going to let someone else take care of you, damn it," he told her. He opened the passenger door and all but folded her in half to shove her into the front seat as the bottom-feeders stampeded in their direction, cameras flashing and whirring. They plastered their cameras against the side window and windshield, and Jolie covered her face with her hands.

Sam opened the driver's-side door, pausing a moment to say, "You've got three seconds to back off, people. Move it or lose it."

One of the reporters, microphone in hand now, pushed even closer. The guy had bottle-blond hair, an indoor tan and too-white capped teeth that might make him look good on television but up close and personal he looked a little like a beaver. "Oh, yeah?" he yelled the challenge. "And who are you? Who the hell are you!'

"Me? Well, I'll tell you, Bucky—I'm the guy who's leaving now. Two seconds. Which one of you losers wants to be my new hood ornament?"

"You won't do that. We have a right to—"

Sam's door slammed. He shoved the key in the ignition and put the transmission into Drive. One quick warning tap on the horn and the large car moved forward.

"Sam, you can't just run them down," Jolie warned him, at last realizing what she'd done. "I shouldn't have snapped like that. I know the drill, I know what they are. I— Sam, don't!

Outside the car, someone yowled in pain and the rest of the barracudas scurried to safety.

"Oops. Guess I might have rolled over a foot or two, huh?" Sam said, smiling at her. "Yeah, well, it wasn't as if they weren't warned. Duck your head, Jolie, we're almost out of range."

"My publicist is either going to hug you or shoot you. Me, too, come to think about it," Jolie said as the Mercedes came to a halt just past the wrought-iron gates, then turned out onto the highway.

"Do you care?"

She looked at him, seriously considering the question. "No, I don't think I do." She searched in her pocket and came out with a wad of tissues to wipe at her eyes. "Thank you, Sam. You didn't have to do this."

"What can I say? *Underdog* to the rescue?" He flashed a quick grin at her, and Jolie's stomach executed a small but powerful flip. How did men do it? Women just got older—and quickly, especially in Hollywood. But men? Men aged, like wine. Sam Becket, she should have realized, could be considered nothing less than the finest vintage.

"All the superheroes to choose from, and you chose Underdog?"

"I guess I'm just a sucker for long, floppy ears."

"Oh, my gosh—Rockne! I let go of his leash!"

"Jade has him," Sam said as he moved into the passing lane, one eye on the rearview mirror. "Hold on, we've got a tail."

"No, *you* have a tail. You're Underdog, remember?" Jolie turned around on the seat and looked out the rear window. "So can this thing outrun a news van with a honking-huge satellite dish on top?"

To answer her question, Sam put the pedal to the metal, so that Jade had to hold on as she tried to turn around in her seat once more and buckle herself in tight. "How could I have forgotten what a show-off you are?" she asked him, leaning her head back against the headrest as he cut in and out of traffic, the speedometer edging past eighty in the thankfully thin late-morning traffic.

He was all concentration now, and Jolie took the opportunity to look at him more closely. His profile was still sharp, his nose straight and perfect, his cheekbones high, his brow smooth and unlined, his chin rock-solid as he edged past the sunny side of thirty. Thirty-three? Thirty-four? She should probably remember that, but she didn't.

What she remembered was the thick, dirty-blond hair he wore shorter than the last time she'd seen him, and rather tousled—the kind of tousled that probably cost two hundred bucks a haircut. His fine, unblemished skin was a golden tan, although his right hand was a bit more pale, proving that he'd found time to get in a few rounds of golf while running Becket Imports, one of the many holdings of the embarrassingly rich Becket family.

Mostly what she remembered was how her body fit so well against Sam's long, lean frame, the top of her head coming up to his chin, when she seemed to tower over most men. The way his hands had moved over her skin, the taste of his mouth, the intense, soul-exploding look in his green eyes as their two bodies merged…

"Where…uh, where are we going?"

"It would be rather senseless to lose the press and then go straight back to your father's house, don't you think?"

She nodded, biting her bottom lip. "True. So where are we going?"

"My place," he said, dipping his head and looking across at her above the silver rims of his sunglasses. "Do you mind?"

Jolie shook her head, ignoring another quick stomach flip. "I don't think I'm ready to go back home yet, so, no, I don't mind. You know, I was so busy trying not to look at anybody that I didn't even see you this morning. Were you at the church?"

"Sorry, no. I was out of the country until late last night and only saw the newspaper clippings my secretary put on my desk when I got to the office this morning. And since I haven't said it yet, I'm really sorry about Teddy. He was a hell of a guy."

"He always liked you," Jolie said, blinking back tears again.

"Not always."

She turned to look at him. "Excuse me? It was always Sam this and Sam that and 'Sam is a helluva guy, Jolie.'"

"That probably was before he warned me to stay away from you or he'd rearrange my face."

"He—oh, he did not. Did he? Omigod, he did! When did he do that?"

Sam looked at her, doing that head-dip thing again so he could hit her with those green eyes of his above the sunglasses. "Do we really want to go into ancient history right now, when we're getting along so well?"

"No, I suppose not," she said as she slid down onto the base of her spine and watched the scenery that consisted mostly of enormous cement sound barriers erected to protect the mansions on the other side from the sights and sounds of the highway.

Ten uncomfortably silent minutes later Sam eased onto the Valley Forge exit, and she knew they were now only minutes away from his home in Villanova. Too soon, he turned onto the familiar long, winding lane leading toward his house. His mansion. His humungo—ridiculously humungo for one person, in any case—house that stood at the rear of a cul-de-sac, behind high stone walls, huge wrought-iron gates. And a gatehouse, for crying out loud. Sam's house made ninety-nine percent of the mansions in Beverly Hills look both insubstantial and faintly tacky.

That was one of the differences, Jolie had decided, between old money and new money. New money shouted. Old money whispered.

"Again, I'm sorry I got to the cemetery so late, although it turned out I got to park close enough to do my Underdog-to-the-rescue bit. I'd expected more of a crowd."

Jolie was grateful for the change of subject. "There was a crowd, lookie-lous outside of the church. But only the press followed us to the cemetery. And," she added, sighing, "I guess you really know who your friends are when you're accused of murder. I can think of at least two dozen faces I should have seen there today and didn't. They'll not be welcome once Jade and Jess and I figure out who killed Teddy and that woman, let me tell you."

He stopped in front of the closed gates. "You're kidding, right?"

She looked at him levelly, which wasn't easy to do as she'd raised her chin a good three inches higher into the air. "Do I look like I'm kidding?"

"No. I remember that determined look. I think

I still get nightmares, as a matter of fact. But we're not going to talk about any of that now, right?"

Jolie knew what he was saying without really saying it, and since the last thing she had energy for was a five-year-old fight, she sat up straight as the gates swung open. Sam eased the Mercedes through the opening and stopped.

"Isn't that—"

"Carroll Yablonski, yes. Although the last person who called him Carroll is probably still in traction," Sam said as the human fireplug lumbered toward the window Sam was lowering. "Bear Man? No visitors, okay? I'm not home to anybody. Oh, and if any reporters show up and try to give you a hard time, you have my permission to eat them."

"That'd be fun. Got the choppers for it now, thanks to you." Carroll grinned, showing off a too large set of obvious dentures. Then he leaned his head in low and looked across the interior of the car at Jolie. "Hullo, Miz Sunshine. Love your movies. Seen 'em all. Tough break about your daddy."

"Thank you Car—Bear Man. I appreciate that."

Bear Man stepped back a pace, banged the flat of his hand on the roof of the car to give the all-clear, and Sam continued up the curved driveway.

"Well, I'm waiting," Jolie said quietly.

"He needed a job."

"I thought he was a professional wrestler in one of those W-W-W-W thingies. And a star, too."

"He was—until he had his head run into the turnbuckle a few too many times. They may fake that stuff, but people still do get hurt. Bear Man needed a job that didn't tax his scrambled brains too much. He needed somewhere to live. I just happened to be able to help him out, that's all."

"The quarterback taking care of his offensive linemen," Jolie said, smiling at him. "Did Carroll—Bear Man—ever graduate? I don't remember."

Sam stopped the car at the top of the circular brick driveway, just in front of the arched wooden door that, Jolie knew, was so thick it could probably withstand a battering ram...or a bazooka. "No. He just couldn't keep up his grades. Probation for one semester, and then he lost his eligibility and dropped out. But we kept in touch."

"More than can be said for you and some other fellow grads of good old Temple U. Not that we attended the same years. All I got to hear about back then, though, was Sam Becket, the scholar, the quarterback, the legend."

"Meaning?"

"Meaning nothing," Jolie said, unbuckling her seat belt. "I'm saying all the wrong things. I just buried my father, for God's sake. Forget I said anything."

He put his hand on her forearm to keep her in her seat. "I've missed you, Jolie."

She looked down at his hand, willing him to

remove it, wishing he had put his arms around her. "Not enough, Sam."

He moved his hand. "Let's go inside and find you something to drink. Find us both something to drink."

She didn't wait for him to come around and open the door for her but stepped out into the now warm June sun to stand looking at the house she'd visited a hundred times. They'd made love in most of those rooms. Twenty-three of them. Including one memorable interlude in the barrel-vaulted formal dining room that had involved the genuine Tudor-era table, a pair of sturdy, low-hanging wrought-iron chandeliers and the cream puffs that were supposed to be their dessert.

Which they were. Sort of...

Her cheeks had been flushed with embarrassment the entire next evening as she'd sat at the bottom of the table, playing hostess, while Sam had entertained the mayor and his wife to help launch the man's reelection campaign. Especially when dessert had been served. Cream puffs. Sam had winked at her as one was set in front of her on a Rosenthal dessert plate. He'd then told the mayor how the chandeliers in the room were rumored to have been an acquisition of his notorious ancestor Ainsley Becket in the late 1700s, back when privateering was an acceptable way of life.

And why did she have to think about all of that now?

Her cell phone rang, shaking her out of her un-comfortable thoughts, and she rummaged in her bag, glad for the interruption.

"Hello?" She looked at Sam, mouthed *Jade*. "You and Jessica want to what? I know nobody knows about him, but what does that have to do with—I don't know, I'll have to ask him. But won't you be followed?" She listened a moment and then rolled her eyes. "Mea culpa. How could I ever even think the great Jade Sunshine couldn't elude a—hey, Secret Squirrel, I said I'll ask him. Give me a minute, all right? Munch on a walnut or something."

She pressed the open phone to her chest and looked at Sam, who was smiling at her in a way that told her he still enjoyed listening to the Sunshine sisters bicker like little children. "Jade and Jess want to come here, talk, maybe spend the night until the last of the press takes a hike from our front yard. I'll tell them no."

"No, don't do that. If the press is still bothering you at the house, it seems logical to bunk here, at least overnight. I've got plenty of room."

Jolie put a second hand over the phone. "But I don't *want* them to come here. Say no, Sam. Be a beast."

He reached for the cell phone, and since she was holding it between her breasts and the contact was a little too intimate, she let him take it from her.

"Jade? Hi, it's Sam. Good to hear your voice

again, too. No problem, somebody had to do it. Hysterical?" He grinned at Jolie, who glared daggers back at him. "I wouldn't say exactly *hysterical*. But you know how she is…yeah, right. Sure. See you then."

"You know how she is *what?*" Jolie demanded, following him up the three shallow steps to the front door. "How is *she,* Sam?"

He placed his thumb against a small, discreet panel cut into the woodwork of the doorjamb, and the door swung open soundlessly. "How she's prone to be a bit dramatic at times," he said as Jolie stared, bug-eyed, at the panel. "But that probably comes with the territory with actresses, right?"

Jolie pointed at the panel. "It beats being paranoid, Chester. And why not a retinal scan? Or didn't you want to be seen as going overboard? Jeez."

"Ah, that brings back memories. I haven't been Chester for a long time. And I took the security system in exchange for a pair of Ming-dynasty floor vases I'd been trying to unload for two years. I don't even need to key in a code once I'm in the house, thanks to the thumb pad. Clever, yes?"

"Uh-huh," Jolie muttered vaguely as she entered the large flagstone-floored foyer, mentally throwing away the key to Sam's front door that she'd refused to part with for five long years. She stopped to take a look around, wondering what else had changed in her absence.

But she should have known. Furnish your house in antiques and you don't exactly go running out to JCPenney every couple of years for a new pseudo-suede lounge chair with built-in cup holders and a pocket for the TV remote.

She removed her sunglasses and walked straight ahead, into the living room that stretched nearly across the entire rear of the house. A person could bowl in Sam's living room, which he sometimes called "the lounge" or "the salon." But only when trying to impress somebody who wanted to be impressed, as she recalled. "How long before Jade and Jessica show up?"

"Two hours or more, I guess. They're going to go out for lunch once they can get shed of the aunts—Jade's words, not mine—and then they have to give the reporters the slip. That reminds me—I have to call down to Bear Man and alert him that they're coming. Why do you ask?"

He asked the question from only a foot or two behind her, so that Jolie found herself beating a retreat to one of the sets of French doors that led out to the flagstone terrace and the Olympic-size reflecting pool that stretched lengthwise away from the house between two rows of slim, tall Italian something-or-other evergreens. *We made love in the pool, too…more than once….*

When she turned around, it was to see that Sam had also removed his sunglasses. And loosened his tie, unbuttoned the top button of his crisp white dress shirt. How she longed to feel his arms around her, to feel something other than grief.

Distance. She needed to put some distance between them. Fast.

"I just…I feel grubby. Do you mind if I take a shower?"

Sam bowed his head slightly and waved her toward the foyer and the wide circular staircase that led upstairs. "Be my guest. You know where everything is. Oh, and I think there's still a few pieces of your clothing in a bottom drawer in my dressing room."

"You think?" she asked, her heart beginning to do its pounding-too-hard thing again.

"All right, Jolie, I *know.* I had the bathroom and dressing room remodeled last year, and Mrs. Archer asked me what to do with a few things."

"And you told her to put everything in a bottom drawer? Why, Sam?"

He looked at her levelly, a muscle working in his cheek. "Just go take your shower, Jolie, all right? I'll find Mrs. Archer and have her make up some sandwiches for us before she leaves for her sister's anniversary party."

She caught her bottom lip between her teeth as she nodded. It took everything she had not to run from the room but to only walk away and not look back.

But that wouldn't work. It hadn't worked then, it wouldn't work now. She'd been looking back for five long years....

CHAPTER TWO

SAM PLACED THE TRAY OF sandwiches on the round table in the alcove in front of the windows and turned to look across the large room. Jolie's slingback heels sat on the floor at the bottom of the bed, her black silk dress spilled across the burgundy and gold striped raw silk coverlet.

He fought the urge to pick up the dress, hold it to his face, breathe in the scent of the perfume she always wore. Amazone. He'd bought it for her, and she still wore it. There should be a law that no other woman could ever wear that fragrance. It belonged to Jolie.

"Keep it up, Sam, and soon you'll be writing bad poetry," he mumbled beneath his breath as he slipped out of his suit jacket and settled it over the back of a chair. He was just sliding his tie out from beneath his collar when the door to the bathroom opened and he turned, his hand still gripping the tie, to see Jolie standing in the open doorway.

She was wrapped in a large white, monogrammed Becket Hotels bathrobe belted tightly at her waist, and was rubbing at her wet head with a matching white towel. "Oh, you're up here. That's some bathroom you've got. It took me five minutes to figure out how to work the shower," she said, dropping the towel. She then bent at the waist so that her shimmer of medium brown hair hung down as she ran her long fingers through it. When she stood up once more, giving her head a quick backward flip, every last damn strand of hair fell away from her face and sleekly to just beyond her shoulders, as if styled by a master.

God, she was gorgeous. Tall and slim, her beautiful face bare of makeup. Not the movie star. Jolie. She reminded him of a young thoroughbred. His lovely, vulnerable, always skittish Jolie.

She leaned against the doorjamb and returned his look.

Just looked at him, her eyes so incredibly sad.

"Are you all right, Jolie?"

"No, Sam, I'm not. I'm not anywhere close to all right," she said quietly, her hands untying the sash as she walked toward him. "Make me all right, Sam. Don't talk, don't say a word. Just make love to me. Please."

Her sea-blue eyes were turning liquid, and he could drown in them, if he let himself succumb. He caught her at the shoulders, holding her at a distance.

"I'm going to hate myself for this. No, Jolie, we can't. It's not a good idea."

"Why not? Why, Sam?"

He pulled the lapels of the robe together as she retied the sash. "You just buried your father, sweetheart. You're going through hell. I don't want you to do anything right now that you might regret in a few days."

Jolie's bottom lip began to tremble as a single huge tear rolled down her cheek. She wiped it away with the back of her hand, as if ashamed of her show of weakness. Which, she couldn't realize, only made her seem that much more vulnerable. Sam had to look away from her or else pull her close, comfort her, do anything she wanted him to do.

And then, in a few days, he'd also probably regret what they'd done.

She stepped away from him. "You're probably right. What I don't need in my life right now is another complication. I've only got two weeks here before I have to go back to California."

"You're beginning a new movie?"

She shook her head, cinching the sash tighter before sitting down at the table. "I don't go on location for nearly a month. This is promo for *Small-Town Hero*. It premieres then, with the usual round of talk shows, interviews. I'm dreading them."

Sam pulled out the facing chair and sat down. To him the answer seemed simple. "So ban all questions about your father. You can do that, can't you?"

Jolie held up a finger as she chewed on a bite of ham-and-cheese sandwich, her favorite. Everyday American cheese, the sort that comes individually wrapped, and sliced boiled ham from a local butcher shop on white bread. He doubted she'd had either while in California. "Oh, this is *so* good. This ham is from Harry's, isn't it? His special wedding ham? It has to be. And we can't do that, Sam. Make not talking about Teddy a deal breaker and it assures us that someone will bring it all up. Hell, they'll make a story about how I don't want to make Teddy a story."

"Is this where I ask *Why don't you just tell them all to go screw themselves and walk away?* and you say *What, and give up showbiz?*"

She smiled around another bite of her sandwich. "I really have missed you, Sam. Even with all this—" she indicated the room, the house, Sam's whole world, he imagined, with one graceful sweep of her arm "—you're still the most sane and normal person I've ever known. Well, normal multimillion-aire anyway, I guess. I, uh, I'm sorry I sort of *pushed* myself at you there a minute ago. It wasn't fair of me."

"Good. Now do something about that gaping

neckline or I might forget how normal and sane I am," he told her, and she quickly pulled the lapels of the robe together across her magnificent breasts. He got to his feet. "Did you find the clothing I told you about?"

"I did, yes, and I can take a hint. I'll finish my sandwich, get dressed and meet you downstairs, all right? Better yet," she added, putting down the sandwich and getting to her feet, "I'll go get my clothes and get dressed in another bedroom, because you probably came up here to shower and change into something more—Sam?"

He'd closed the gap between them before he could think of any good reason not to, and cupped his hands on her shoulders. He began to knead at the hollows beneath her shoulder blades with his thumbs, vaguely aware that the terry cloth was damp, that she must have used the robe in lieu of a towel. More than vaguely aware that the robe was all she wore.

"Sam…?"

There had been other women since Jolie. He wasn't a saint, and she'd been gone for five long years. But none of them had ever been allowed here, in his house, in his bedroom, naked beneath his robe. He'd reconfigured the master bathroom with her in mind, knowing that was insane. But a man without hope might as well just pack it in and start collecting stamps or something.

"You were wrong a while ago, Jolie. I did miss you enough. For the first year I believed every day that you'd be home again. For the second, I told myself you were just trying to build up the courage to admit you'd been wrong, that Hollywood wasn't the place for you. And then…and then the movie came out and I knew. You had only a couple dozen lines of pretty lousy dialogue and appeared in only three scenes—I counted. But when you were up there on the screen, nobody else was there, nobody else mattered. You were magnificent. That's when I knew, Jolie. That's when I knew you weren't ever coming home."

She lowered her gaze. "I got lucky. I *was* ready to come home by the end of that second year, my tail between my legs, when that horrible movie came out. Walter put me in his next movie, and I've been working steadily ever since. Things…things happen the way they're supposed to happen. If I'd come home a failure I wouldn't have been worth anything to anybody, Sam, not to you, not even to myself."

As she spoke, he was using his massaging thumbs to slowly push aside the lapels of the robe. "And you did it your way."

"Meaning not your way?" She put her palms against his chest and slowly eased them lower until they rested at his waist. "But that's all over now, Sam. I didn't take your money, I didn't take your help. I could sing fairly well, I knew I could dance. I had to know if I could act. I had to, Sam, and I had to do it myself. So I waited tables, I sold shoes, I bagged groceries, asked if people wanted fries with their order. I did it on my own. I somehow finally nabbed that one role in the worst slasher movie ever made and I got lucky. I can't believe you even saw it. The studio pretty well buried it once they wanted me for the new girl next door."

Now it was his turn to avert his eyes. "Somebody mentioned seeing you in the movie. I'll admit I had to hunt for it."

"It nearly went straight to the video stores," Jolie said, and now her fingers were busy, working at loosening his belt even as he was backing up, backing the both of them toward the bed. "Sam? Are we going to keep talking or is this going anywhere?"

Sam knew their conversation wasn't going anywhere near the truth, that was for certain. Not if he could help it. So why didn't he just let it go where they both wanted it to go?

His thumbs had done their job, and now his fingers were touching smooth bare skin, even as he felt the back of his thighs touching the heavy footboard of the bed. "Is that your way of saying you're hungry and you want to finish your sandwich?"

She looked up at him from beneath her remarkably long lashes. "I am feeling…hungry."

He skimmed his fingertips down the front of the robe and found one end of the sash, pulled it. The robe fell open.

"God," he whispered, drinking in the sight of her long, achingly perfect body.

She shrugged her shoulders and the robe dropped to the floor, pooling at her feet, so that she stood there completely nude, completely un-ashamed, diligently working to open his belt, his button…his zipper. Then, with one swift move-ment, he was naked from the waist down, his slacks and boxers tangled around his ankles.

He knew Jolie. He knew her moods, her signals.

There wasn't going to be anything gentle about what happened next.

Sam closed his eyes for a moment, then looked past her, to the expanse of mirrored doors that con-cealed a small wet bar and entertainment center. He watched, bemused, as he saw his hands go around her back, cup her firm, high buttocks. Watched himself pull her closer, watched as her hands came up to balance herself against his shoulders.

Watched as, lithe, limber dancer that she was, she bent one leg, gracefully hooked it up and around his waist.

"Hold me, Sam," she whispered, nipping at his earlobe as he braced himself against the bed. "Help me."

Did he have any choice? His hands still cupping

her buttocks, he spread his legs as best he could to support her as she lifted her other leg, wrapped it around his back.

He couldn't stop watching the two of them in the mirrors. Even as he licked at the side of her neck, pushed his tongue into the curve behind her ear. Even as she slipped a hand between them. Found him. Helped him. Settled herself around him, over him. Drawing him in. Deeper. Deeper.

"Yes…yes…Sam, *yes.*"

This was need, simple and basic. Animal instinct.

She wanted to forget. He longed to remember.

He realized that at this moment in time he had all the control of a teenager unable to master his own raging hormones. He moved into her as she dug her long fingernails into his back. Once, twice, pulling her against him as he thrust, before something inside of him snapped, broke free, and he was convulsing inside of her, spilling himself inside her, giving himself over to her completely, absolutely.

He selfishly took.

She selfishly took.

And then they were on the floor, Sam on his knees, still inside her, still with her wrapped around him like the dancer she was, the two of them breathing fast, saying nothing, for there was nothing to say.

But there should be something to say, shouldn't there?

What in hell had happened? They hadn't even kissed.

"Jolie…sweetheart…"

"No, Sam, don't. Please don't. A mistake…this was a mistake. I'm sorry," she said quickly, just as gracefully disentangling herself as she had wrapped herself around him. She reached for the robe and held it in front of her, searching for the neckline as she got to her feet. Then, with a swirl of terry cloth that would do a caped superhero proud, she settled the robe over her shoulders and quickly padded back into the bathroom, shutting the door behind her.

The dramatic exit. Jolie was the master of dramatic exits. He should know.

Sam stayed where he was, his feet still tangled in his slacks, damn it.

That's why she was the queen of Hollywood, while he, at the heart of it, bought and sold used furniture….

After a few moments spent mentally kicking himself for having made the first move—Jolie would be quick to point that out if the subject of the last minutes ever came up, which he decided it wouldn't, not if he could help it—Sam got up and headed for one of the guest room bathrooms to take his own shower.

He was downstairs in the living room once more by the time Bear Man sounded the musical chime that alerted Sam that his guests had arrived. By the time he got to the foyer, Jolie was coming down the stairs. She was barefoot and dressed in a thin sleeveless navy pullover that didn't quite meet the waistband of the white shorts topping her mile-long legs. Her long hair, still damp, was tied back in a ponytail, and she hadn't reapplied her makeup, not even lipstick.

There were women—legions of them he was sure—who could cheerfully kill her for being so beautiful.

"You found the clothes," he said unnecessarily.

She looped a finger in the waistband of the shorts and pulled it away from her body. "I've lost weight in five years. Here's hoping they stay up."

And then she bit her bottom lip before she smiled, shrugged. "Sorry."

"I didn't think it was an invitation," Sam told her, once more heading for the door. "Jade, Jessica, good to see you," he said as the two women stepped into the foyer, both of them kissing him on the cheek before putting down their overnight bags. Rockne entered behind them, padded straight to Jolie and lay down at her feet.

"It's really great of you to let us barge in on you like this, Sam," Jade said. "I've got one more trip to the car, and then we can all get reacquainted."

Jessica lifted her hands to her neck and gave her blond hair a quick flip as she grinned at Sam. "Ever notice how Jade takes charge? Do you want to get *reacquainted*, Sam? Maybe you'd rather go to a movie or take a nap or play a game of strip Ping-Pong. But Jade says we're to get reacquainted, so that's what we're going to do. She doesn't even realize she's arranging everyone else's lives."

"Have you two been fighting?" Jolie asked as she picked up Jade's overnight case and put it at the bottom of the stairs. "Again?"

"Don't be silly," Jessica said, rolling her eyes at Sam. "I'm never combative—it's not in my nature."

"Right. Which explains why you're on suspension from your network." Jolie looked at Sam.

"I was asked to take an extended bereavement leave. That's different."

"The *extended* part sure is," Jolie said, winking at Sam, who was beginning to feel he was a spectator at a tennis match.

"Did you see the interview she did with that poor Willie somebody-or-other?"

"Cartwright," Jessica said, turning the name into a dirty word. "New York's own Willie Cartwright. And I only asked him a few questions."

"She asked him questions, all right, Sam. *But how?* she kept asking him whenever he said what he would do if he's elected to the U.S. senate. He'd clean up crime in the streets. *But how?* Jess asked.

He'd secure our borders. *But how,* Jess pushed him. He'd balance the budget, reduce the trade deficit, improve education, provide health care for all. *But how? How? How you gonna do that, sir?* She kept at him and at him until I thought the poor guy was going to have a stroke—Jade sent me a tape of the whole thing. And then—bam—our little Barbie doll zings him with a quick question about some by-the-hour motel just across the line into Jersey and how he was seen there the previous week with a woman not his wife."

"So what's the big deal? The guy deserved it." Jessica gave her hair another flip. "He was using *my* airtime to make a campaign speech, and I wasn't going to let him get away with it. I wouldn't have zinged him if he hadn't been so damn determined to stay on his talking points and not say anything concrete. That's all. Who knew he'd go so ballistic with my bosses?"

"Right," Jade said from the open doorway. "Shame, shame on poor old Willie. And it's really not her fault, Sam, she's right about that. Most times the men she interviews take one look at that hair, that face—the *girls*—and say oh, please, please, let me tell you all of my most embarrassing secrets."

"I'll have you know, Jade, I don't appreciate you saying that the only reason I'm on-air is because of my hair and face."

"And the girls. Don't forget the girls."

Sam might have been embarrassed, except he'd heard all of this before, a dozen times. They'd soon be doing a verbal tag-team match, with everyone changing sides every few minutes just because it was fun. He looked to Jolie, waiting for her to chime in, wondering whose side she'd take. But she just held up her hands in a sort of surrender and shook her head. She'd taken her shot, bringing up Willie Cartwright, and now she'd retired to her corner.

Jessica appealed to him, explaining, "Jade's chest somehow missed out on puberty, and she thinks it's my fault that I got her share. Isn't that right, Jade? Hey, you want help with those brief-cases?"

"No, I don't," Jade said tersely, and Sam belatedly noticed that her trip back to the car had been to retrieve two ancient, battered tan briefcases, the sort that actually had straps on them to hold them closed.

"Good," Jessica said, "because I wasn't planning on helping you anyway. Bar still in the same place, Sam?"

"Straight ahead and then to your left," he told her before helping Jade by taking the briefcases from her. "Wow, you brought me bricks, Jade? Really, you shouldn't have."

Jolie seemed to have changed allies and was

now targeting Jade. "You're right, Sam. She really, really shouldn't have. Jade, this could have waited until tomorrow, when we're back home."

"Not really, sis," Jade told her as they all headed for the living room. "If nothing else, we had to bring Rockne over to see you. He still hasn't eaten anything, although he did drink some water—thank God—so we might want to take him outside later if he starts looking for doors."

Jolie bent down to give the setter a hug. "Why don't you and I go into the kitchen and see if there's anything there you want to eat, hmm?"

"We've offered him everything from cold spaghetti to doughnuts, Jolie—he won't eat. You can try again later, all right? The sooner we get started, the sooner we clear Teddy's name. Jess," she called out as she headed for the large round topped coffee table flanked by curved tapestry couches done in the Empire style, "get me a soda, too, while you're at it. Diet, please. And ask Jolie and Sam what they'd like to drink."

"Jessica is right," Sam said, grinning. "Jade really does give orders."

"She's the oldest, remember, even though she and I are Irish twins, only eleven months apart. After our mother took a hike, Jade elected herself mama duck, with Jess and me as the baby ducklings she had to keep marching all in a row. That, and she's just basically bossy. Court used to tell her she'd make a fine prison warden," Jolie told him as Rockne nuzzled his head against her knee, nearly knocking her over.

"I saw him last week, you know, in London," Sam told her, referring to his cousin, Courtland Becket, once Jade's husband. Sam, for his sins, had introduced them. The marriage had lasted less than six months. But Court still should be told about Teddy. "Damn, I should have called him as soon as I heard about your dad."

Jessica approached carrying a tray with ice-filled glasses and cans of soda on it, offering them their choice. "Court? Oh, he whose name cannot be spoken? What's he doing in England?"

Sam chose a glass and a can of ginger ale. "Thanks. Visiting our relatives at the ancestral manor, I guess you'd call it. Becket Hall. It's a huge old pile located in Romney Marsh, right on the Channel. Our cousin Morgan got in touch with him a few months ago about something, and he decided to accept the invitation to come see the place."

"Morgan? Yet another handsome guy, right? Nice to know there's one left for me to romance and then toss away," Jessica said, toasting Jolie with a can of Coke.

"Children should be seen and not heard," Jolie warned her tightly.

"Sorry, Jessica," Sam told her. "Morgan's a girl.

Morgan Becket Eastwood. Her branch of the Beckets has been living at Becket Hall since a bunch of the family emigrated to America nearly two hundred years ago. Court and I had a bet going as to how drafty the old pile has to be."

"If it's two hundred years old, it probably has a bunch of ghosts, too," Jessica said, raising her eyebrows. "I'm surprised you didn't go with Court. Even if there aren't ghosts, think of all that moldy old furniture. You'd have been in heaven."

"I thought about it, but as it turns out, I'm glad I decided to come home instead," Sam said, looking at Jolie. "At any rate, I really should go call him. He should know about your father, decide whether or not he wants to cut short his vacation."

"Jade won't thank you for it," Jolie pointed out. "And Court will go nuclear when he hears what Jade and Jess and I are going to do."

"Yes, what you three are going to do," Sam said, looking across the room to see Jade unloading fat manila file folders on his antique table—after pushing a delicate Sevres porcelain bowl to within a half inch of the edge. He wasn't a stickler, he really wasn't. Still… "Jolie? Pretend I'm Jade, issuing orders. Rescue that bowl, find coasters for your glasses in that drawer next to the couch Jade's sitting on and let me go call Court. I'll be back in five minutes."

Well, that settled it. He was now officially old. And boring. Although he hadn't been all that old and boring an hour ago, upstairs. Maybe there was hope for him yet....

CHAPTER THREE

THEY WERE SITTING around the coffee table, Rockne, having walked in a circle three times in front of the fireplace, now soundly asleep in front of the cold hearth.

They were not, basically, a jolly group.

"And that's it, a thumbnail sketch. Business has been slow, as it usually is around Christmastime, and then it tails off again a little in the summer months."

"Maybe all the adulterous spouses are too full of holiday cheer in December, and on vacation in June?" Sam suggested, and Jolie covered a laugh with a cough.

"We do more than divorce work, Sam," Jade told him tightly. "Background checks for corporations, for instance. That's really the bulk of our business. We've had nothing new open this past month except, okay, a few run-of-the-mill divorce cases, and they're already wrapped up except for the paperwork. Nothing out of the ordinary there, unless Teddy was hiding something from me."

"Not out of the realm of possibility," Jessica said, popping a pretzel nugget into her mouth. "If it was a dangerous case, that is. His little girl and all that—oh, stop glaring at me, Jade, you know I'm right."

"I know," Jade said, sighing. "He's hidden a few things from me before, but I always found out eventually. So we work the case Teddy may have been working when he died—as soon as we figure out what the hell it is. In the meantime, we work these four old cases that have been driving him crazy for years, hoping one of them may be the right case and lead us to the true killer. He had all four cases out on the desk in his bedroom, so I know he was checking into them again. As I said, it's been a slow month."

Jade looked all business, as she always did, Jolie thought, watching as her sister straightened the pile of manila folders, unaware of the picture she made in the afternoon sunlight streaming in through the French doors. She was really pretty— elegant actually. The one who most favored their mother in appearance.

Although Jade had never played up her good looks. She wore her light brown hair straight and long from a center part. Her hair was naturally streaked with gold, because Jade would consider hours spent in a stylist's chair, her hair separated and wrapped in tinfoil, to be a total waste of valuable time. At least she wore black mascara on her lashes, highlighting her sherry-brown eyes, and she occasionally remembered to tint her wide, full lips a soft apricot.

And Jessica was wrong. Mother Nature hadn't overlooked putting Jade through puberty; she'd just employed defter strokes, so that Jade was slim, slightly curved, not voluptuous.

Again, like their mother. Maybe that's why Jade had never played up her looks. For Teddy. Because seeing her might then bring back the pain of his wife's defection. Was that the reason? Was that why Jade stayed, worked with Teddy in the agency? Did her big sister still long to go to medical school, as she'd talked about years ago, in junior high school —before their mother left?

That was a hell of a depressing thought on a generally depressing day. Jolie wondered if she might run it past Court the next time she saw him. A self-sacrificing Jade might explain a lot of things to her ex-husband.

Jolie shook herself back to attention when, after having remained silent for several minutes as Jade stated her case, Sam finally spoke. "You're kidding, right? You three can't really, seriously be considering playing at private detectives."

"Playing? Jade has a *license,*" Jolie pointed out, wishing he didn't sound so incredulous and she didn't sound so defensive.

"Yeah," Jessica added as she popped another pretzel nugget into her mouth. "Go ahead, Jade, whip it out, show Sam that big bad boy."

Jolie covered another involuntary smile with her hand, wondering if it might be possible to muzzle her baby sister. But Jessica got away with outrageous statements. Maybe it was the blond hair. Maybe it was the innocent tilt of the head and the fairly bemused look. Maybe it was all a carefully orchestrated act....

"All right, Jolie. So Jade has a license. And yippee for her," Sam all but barked, getting to his feet and heading for the wall of Chinese cases that served as a concealed wet bar. "However," he said, turning his back to them, "you do not have a license or any training, Jolie, and neither does Jessica. It's a bad idea. A really bad idea." He opened the doors, pulled out the stopper of a crystal decanter almost as if he planned to drink some of its contents without wasting time looking for a glass before plunking the decanter down on the bar and facing them once more. "A really, really *bad* idea."

Jessica looked at Jolie. "Funny. I always used to like him. Oh, Sam-u-el—I'm a journalist, remember? An *investigative* journalist? And Jolie's a...um...Jolie, you want to help me out here?"

"I'm a quick study," Jolie gritted out from between her clenched teeth as Sam rejoined them.

"And now yippee for you," Sam said tightly. "But in the real world, sweetheart, the bad guys don't use blanks."

"Nobody's getting shot at," Jolie protested, thinking it might be time she headed for the wine decanter herself. "Why are you always such a pessimist? No, Rockne, lie down, sweetie. You can bite him later."

"A pessimist? You want to enlarge on that, Jolie?"

She closed her eyes, took a steadying breath. Now was no time to remind him that he'd said only one of every ten thousand hopefuls who flock to Hollywood in any given year ever end up with even a small part in a movie. "Never mind. Jade, let's hear about the cases. You know you're dying to tell us."

"No. Don't do that, Jade. You're not going forward with this, so we don't need to hear about any old cases," Sam said quickly. "Look, I know the three of you are devastated by what's happened. I would be, as well. I mean it. It's a tough pill to swallow—that Teddy would ever hurt anyone or that he'd kill himself. But you can't do anything about it. You just can't."

Jade sniffed—actually snorted. "Because we're women, right?"

Sam rolled his eyes. "That has nothing to do with—okay, all right, so it has a lot to do with it.

You want someone to investigate, I'll hire someone. I'll hire a whole team of someones."

"Who died and left you boss? You're not in charge of either Jade or me. And don't look now, Sam, but you don't own Jolie. She proved that when she left."

Now Sam turned to glare at Jessica.

"Sam, no, please. And Jessica, I can fight my own battles, thank you," Jolie cut in before there could be actual bloodshed.

"It's all right. I am coming on pretty strong, I guess. No wonder they called you the pest," Sam said, his smile helping to soften his words as he ruffled Jessica's hair.

Jolie had been watching Sam's face as her older sister had explained their plan and she'd known he wasn't going to stand up and applaud. But he seemed genuinely angry—which might be flattering, if her sisters wouldn't kill her if she said so. If Jessica's nonsense had made him smile, at least for the moment, she'd be an idiot not to take advantage. "Sam, look, it can't hurt anything to just *talk* about it. Teddy's been working these cases on his own since he left the force. Cold cases, they're called. We probably won't get anywhere with any of them. Lord knows he never did."

"Unless he did and that's why somebody framed him for murder and then killed him, making it look like a suicide. There is that. Besides, we've got to do something. We can't let this stand the way it is now. Teddy would never forgive us and we'd never forgive ourselves. Fighting is better than crying any day," Jessica pointed out, picking up one of the file folders and reading the words on the tab. "The Fishtown Strangler. Juicy. I think I want this one. Jade? Do you know what it's about?"

"Slow down, Jessica. First we'll discuss all of them, then pick one and work it together," Jade told her.

"Why?" Jolie asked her sister. "Three of us, four cases. Whoever solves theirs first, or runs into a definite dead end moves on to the fourth one. I can only be here for another two weeks, remember? Going one by one makes no sense."

Jade looked at her levelly for a moment and then nodded. "All right. But we discuss each case every night. Together."

Sam looked at each one of them in turn. "I can't stop you, can I? No, I can see I can't. All right, all right, then I'm in. My house, my coffee table, my booze—I'm in."

"Not with me, you're not. As long as we're dividing things up here, I prefer to work alone," Jade said quickly. "It's bad enough I have to keep an eye on my sisters, I'm not taking responsibility for you, too, Sam. We said three cases. Jolie, he's all yours. You watch him, he watches you, and that's one problem solved."

"Two amateurs do not one professional make," Jessica pointed out but then waved off her words. "It's all right, a fair division of labor. Forget I said anything."

Jolie was about to protest but then realized she had no good argument to offer. She and Sam weren't a couple anymore and hadn't been for five long years, that embarrassing interlude of two hours or more ago notwithstanding. And if she said no, Jessica would probably ask why, and then they'd go round and round and...no, she wasn't up to it. "Okay," she said at last. "If I have to, I suppose it's all right."

"It's so wonderful to be wanted. I feel like the last kid on the playground to get picked for kickball," Sam said, mockingly toasting them all with his wineglass. "Now, before I give in to the urge to get royally drunk, let's hear about these cases."

"Do the Fishtown Strangler first," Jessica pleaded. "Some headline writer came up with that name, right?"

Jade took a sip from her soda glass and then carefully replaced it on the coaster. "The Fishtown Strangler wasn't the Fishtown Strangler until the third murder. And nobody probably would have noticed someone was out there strangling prostitutes if it hadn't been for that headline—Fishtown Strangler Strikes Again. By the time the fourth body showed up the mayor had set up a task force. It was an election year, you understand. Concerned citizens, some higher-ups from the mayor's political party, a couple of pastors, that sort of thing. But after the sixth body there weren't any more and the trail went cold. If there ever was a trail—and I don't think there was."

"So why was Teddy involved?" Sam asked, finding a seat on the couch next to Jolie.

"He caught the second murder," Jade told him. "He couldn't stay the primary because of the task force and the detective who'd caught the first murder, but he got involved with the victim's mother and young daughter." She turned to look at Jolie. "You know Teddy—always leading with his heart. Funny, they weren't at the funeral. I would have thought they would be after what Teddy did for them."

"And what was that?" Jolie asked before Sam could open his mouth again, establish himself as the leader of their two-person team. Really, he was only hearing any of this because he was here. And it was his house. Jolie inwardly winced. Maybe she should take the chip off her shoulder.

"He moved them out of some condemned building in Fishtown," Jade told them as Jessica began paging through the manila folder in her lap. "And he's been checking up on the daughter all these years, the same way he's done with Jermayne."

Jessica looked up from the page she'd extracted and was holding in her hand. "Who?"

"Jermayne Johnson." Jade looked at Sam. "Sam, maybe you remember this one. Terrell Johnson? The high school basketball player who was found shot on a city playground about ten years ago?"

"Yes, I think I remember that. He was just about to sign a letter of intent with one of the top Division One schools and then he was gone." He shook his head. "A real waste of a good kid. Scholar-athlete, wasn't he?"

"He was going to use his talent to get his grand-mother and brother out of the city—that's what the grandmother told Teddy. So Teddy got them out. He wiped out more than half of his savings doing it, but that's Teddy." Jade shrugged her shoulders, sighed. "That *was* Teddy…."

"Were the Johnsons at the funeral?" Jolie asked, as long as they were all descending into the maudlin again.

"Mrs. Johnson passed away sometime last year," Jade told them. "But, you know, I don't think I saw Jermayne. Not that that means anything. I really wasn't looking around, counting noses."

"It wouldn't have taken you long," Jolie muttered, and Sam covered her hand with his. She didn't pull away. The man was offering her comfort and she was grateful for the gesture. But that didn't mean she was going to make any more mistakes. In two weeks, no matter what happened here, she would be back in Hollywood for the premiere and then off to Ireland to film a new movie two weeks after that. That's just the way life was for her now, for both of them.

"All right," Jessica said, still holding up a page of Teddy's precise notes. "This could be interesting. Teddy has notations on two of the four strangling victims, made in the last three weeks. A Tarin White and a Kayla Morrison. Are either of these two the one with the daughter?"

"Kayla Morrison. Her daughter's name is Keely. Now put that away because we're not finished yet."

"The warden has spoken," Sam whispered to Jolie, and once again she had to bite her bottom lip to keep from smiling. What a strange day she was having. Tears, yes, and also laughter. And a mistake…

"Case number three," Jade said, pulling another manila envelope onto her lap. She opened it, frowned. "Oh, this one. Another catchy headline. This one was called the case of the vanishing bride."

"Jolie and I will take that one," Sam volunteered much too quickly, and Jolie pulled her hand out from beneath his as if his skin had just turned white-hot. "You could say I've got experience."

"Not funny, Sam," Jolie said, absently rubbing

at the ring finger of her left hand until she realized what she was doing and stopped. "Not even remotely funny."

"Oh, I don't know, Jolie," Jessica said, finally closing the folder she'd been paging through for the past several minutes. "Jade? Was the bride one of Teddy's cases or someone else he just took a shine to?"

"It was his case. But as to why it haunted him?" Jade turned a few pages and pulled out an eight-by-ten photograph, turning it so everyone could see it. "You tell me."

Jolie's jaw dropped slightly as she looked at the photograph. "That could almost be Jess, just with shorter hair," she said, her stomach knotting. "How old is that picture?"

"About twelve years," Jade said. "Our Jessica was still in junior high when the bride disappeared, I think. But it's amazing, isn't it? Cathleen Hanson was about as old as Jess is now when this photograph was taken, and the resemblance can't be denied."

Jolie felt tears threatening again. Something about this one touched her, the fact that her father had seen his own daughter in the vanished bride. "All right. Sam and I will take this one."

"Deal," Jade said, closing the folder and replacing it on the table. "And I'll take Terrell Johnson. Leaving us with the fourth and last case. I don't think we have to concern ourselves too much about it, either, because this is one cold case that gets worked every year. These others? The cops assigned to them after the primary has retired must pull the cases out once a year, look them over…and that's about all they do with most of them. And since a homicide was never proved, the vanishing-bride case doesn't get looked at at all. She's just one more missing person. But it's different with this fourth case. In fact, this one was just on the news again last month."

"Let me guess," Sam said, actually raising his hand as if hoping to be called upon to answer. If Jade wanted to give up her job as warden, she'd be a great high school principal. "The baby in the Dumpster. A real heartbreaker."

"You've got it right in one," Jade said, grabbing the thickest folder. "This one hurt everyone, not just Teddy, who happened to catch it late one rainy night. He isn't—wasn't—the only active or retired cop who kept a personal file on the Dumpster case. A baby, only a few months old, thrown away like garbage. It hit everyone—bad. The skull was kept, forensic artists update what the boy would have looked like if he'd lived, there's DNA just waiting to be matched to someone out there. But nothing. Back when he was still on the job, Teddy would get reporters calling him every year on the anniversary of discovering the body. Which, by the way, were the only times I ever saw Teddy drunk. That he was drunk the night he died just screams to me that he'd discovered something he really didn't want to know."

"Which is why we're going to work these cases," Jolie said firmly, getting to her feet. "Is anyone hungry? I seem to have missed lunch."

"Most of it, anyway," Sam said, also getting to his feet. "We'll be in the kitchen."

"Why are you following me?" Jolie asked him once they were out of earshot. "I remember where the fridge is, you know." God, she was a bundle of screaming nerves, ready to explode. Didn't he know that? Surely she couldn't be that good an actress.

"True, and I don't think you're planning to pocket any of the silverware," he said, moving ahead of her to push open the service door to the kitchen. "We need to talk."

"No, we don't. What happened upstairs was a mistake. You know it, I know it. It was...it bordered on disgusting, frankly. I attacked you. I have no excuses, but I will say I'm sorry. But that's it. Discussion over."

"Agreed."

Jolie whirled around to goggle at him. "Agreed? You agree with what? That the discussion is over? That I should have apologized? Or that it was disgusting?"

Sam held up his hands, making a T, signaling time-out. "I agree it was a bad start, probably due to a bad ending five years ago. I also apologize and don't think we'll gain anything by having a postmortem, okay? Although I will say it's nice to know we're both so limber five years later—uh-uh, no hitting."

"Then stop tempting me," Jolie said, sure her cheeks were growing pink.

"If I might continue? I do *not*, however, agree that it was disgusting. If anything, it was a little like old times...at least some of the old times. Now, white bread or rye?"

"Neither, thank you," Jolie said quietly, feeling she'd been rightly chastened. They may not have actually swung from those chandeliers in the dining room that long-ago night, but it had been a close-run thing. And then there was the night they'd discovered the joys and varied interesting applications of the nifty pulsating hose sprayer on the kitchen sink just behind her. They'd nearly flooded the place. And that time she'd come straight to Sam's from dress rehearsal at the local theater, still in full makeup and wearing her black wig and Velma Kelly costume from the final scene of *Chicago,* and Sam had taken one look at her and...

"You don't want any bread at all?"

"Huh?" Jolie snapped herself back from the

movie reel of bordering-on-the-lascivious memories. "No. I'll just make up a small plate of ham
and cheese. They practically had to sew me into my
gown for the premiere at my last fitting. If I gain
an ounce anywhere, I could sneeze and end up
with the seams exploding in front of a million
cameras."

"Film at eleven," Sam said, smiling.

"Yes, and the cover of every trash magazine out
there," Jolie told him as she grabbed a plastic bag
filled with ham slices from the meat drawer of the
industrial-size stainless-steel refrigerator. "Where's
the cheese? I really need something that wasn't
free-range-bred or organically grown or certified
to be healthy for you while only tasting a little bit
like soggy cardboard."

Sam reached past her to retrieve the package
and then retired to one of the stools placed at the
large granite-topped breakfast bar that might, Jolie
had once remarked, be used to land a 747. He
turned over the package and squinted at the fine
print. "Let's see, how many calories in a slice of
cheese? Hmm, how about that? More than I
thought. You may have one slice, Ms. Sunshine, no
more. Break it into little pieces—it'll last longer.
I always wondered what the big time felt like. Now
I know. Slow starvation. You know, Jolie, you get
famous enough and you could just disappear alto-
gether."

"Funny man." She grabbed the package from him and pulled out a single wrapped slice. Then she thought about that for a moment and extracted a second one. Near-constant dieting was one of her least favorite things about the movie industry, and wasn't it just like him to zero in on that fact. "You know, Sam, if you're just going to take shots at me, we can end this right now. Jade and Jessica shouldn't have come here, and it wasn't my smartest move either, when you get right down to it."

"You want to go home now, run that gauntlet of reporters again? Be my guest."

"And don't *dare* me!" Jolie turned away from him, pinching at the bridge of her nose as she mentally counted to ten, trying to calm her temper. "I haven't slept in days. I hate staying in that house. Jade had some disaster-recovery company come in, promise to make things right again, and I guess they did—as much as they could, at least. Jade stays there with no problem. Jessica is back in her old room, surrounded by cheerleading trophies, stuffed animals and that frilly lace canopy over her bed. The princess back in residence, as if she'd never left. But I still know what happened in Teddy's study, right below my bedroom, and whenever I walk past that closed door I—"

"That settles it, Jolie. You're staying here with me. No more talk of leaving. And I won't pressure you for anything else, I promise. I won't turn you down if you offer. I'm not a monk, Jolie. But there will be no pressure, I promise. And no more arguing, either. I just want to make things easier for you."

"You know," Jolie said, slowly turning back to face him once more, "we never used to fight. I thought it was strange, actually, how well we... how well we got along. Slightly crazy but compatible. What happened to us, Sam?"

"We could only remain stagnant for so long before we came to a fork in the road? We got to it and I wanted to go one way, you wanted to go another. I lost. And," he ended on a wry smile, "it turns out I'm pretty damn lousy at losing."

"Oh, Sam," she said, collapsing onto the stool next to his. "I had to try, I had to know if I was good enough. If I hadn't..."

"It would have come back to bite me in the ass, I know. The road not taken, the wondering what might have been. You'd have grown to hate me, or at least resent the hell out of me. You left, you did what you had to do and now you know. You're wonderful, Jolie. Looks, talent, the camera loves you— the whole package, I think it's called. For a while there," he added, grinning, "I was wishing you'd been born with a big wart on the end of your nose."

Jolie laughed and the tension was broken. "My first agent wanted me to get my nose fixed— shorten it, thin it out a bit. And get implants, teeth caps, liposuction. I look back on that now and wonder if I would have done what he said, if I'd had the money. Now I'm the sexy but wholesome girl next door, so it's a good thing I didn't have that money."

Sam reached out to run his index finger down the side of her nose. "I'm crazy about that nose. And what you're saying is that if you'd agreed to let me bankroll you, that nose might be only a fond memory?"

"Yeah, but think about this one, Sam—the boobs would have been *spectacular,*" she teased, grinning at him before filling her mouth with a big bite of rolled-up boiled ham.

"Have I ever complained about that area?"

Jolie coughed, and a bit of ham stuck in her throat. She grabbed the glass he'd brought with him into the kitchen, taking a huge gulp. She shivered, a full-body shiver, and quickly put down the glass. "Eeww, how can you drink this stuff?"

"You have the palate of a plebeian, Jolie Sunshine," he told her, pulling a glass from the cabinet beside the sink and filling it with tap water. "Real wine isn't supposed to taste like some sweet, fizzy kids' drink."

"It does when somebody turns his back and somebody else slips a teaspoon of sugar into the glass," Jolie reminded him, grinning at the memory. "How old was that wine I did that to?"

"Old enough to have been treated with more respect." Sam turned his back to the sink and leaned against the edge of the counter.

Jolie caught her breath. Movie stars were handsome, granted. Although she'd often wondered about the offspring of all those gorgeous faces born with Mommy's original nose and inheriting daddy's original receding chin. But Sam? Sam was just Sam, and he was the real McCoy. He also didn't throw a hissy fit if she accidentally moved into his camera line during the filming of a love scene.

"Are we good now, Sam? There was hurt on both sides when I left, I know that, and I caused most of it. But have we agreed that what happened is in the past and at least now we can be friends? Can we move on now?"

"Friends? Maybe you could clarify that." He looked at her for a long moment, slowly measuring her from head to toe and back again with his gaze before seeming to concentrate on her mouth. "What level of friends are we talking here? Good friends? Very good friends?"

Her bare toes were trying to curl themselves into the coolness of the tile floor. "Good friends. Older. Wiser. Less inclined to be selfish, self-centered—and I'm speaking of myself, mostly. How's that?"

"It'll do. For now. And I take full blame for my

part in what happened back then—even more than you know. Shall we seal the bargain?"

"You never give up, do you?" Jolie said, laughing. And then she held out her right hand just to see what he'd do.

He did what she'd wanted him to do. He ignored her hand to slide his arms around her and lowered his mouth to her own.

For the first time since Jade's call at midnight four days earlier, Jolie let herself feel. Really feel, react, instead of just acting and hoping for something to fill the sudden hole in her heart. But what she felt when Sam kissed her wasn't passion. Nor was it the momentary escape she'd insanely hoped to find in their desperate coupling of only a few hours ago. Not lust, not even love. What she felt was this enormous *sorrow* welling up inside her. Filling her, crushing her, yet leaving her unbearably empty.

So many chances lost. So many missed moments that could never be recaptured. Choices made. Paths taken…and those not taken. But there was time; there had always been time—that's what she'd told herself.

And now she was out of time.

She couldn't go back, change anything.

Even Sam's strong arms around her couldn't change anything….

When she broke the kiss, it was to press her

face into Sam's neck, her voice catching on a sob. "He's gone, Sam. Teddy's gone."

Sam held her tight, mumbling words she couldn't quite make out because the hurt was swallowing her now, pulling her down into that black hole of misery and loss she'd been fighting any way she could, calling on every acting skill she might possess in order to hide her tearing grief. Her guilt.

"I phoned him once a week, Sam, faithfully. I invited him out to the coast a million times, but he always said he was too busy. And so was I. First working three part-time jobs to feed myself and then I always seemed to be shooting somewhere in the world. Six movies in three years. Once…once he visited me on location in South Dakota, but we were behind schedule, and I was almost always on the set and…"

She swallowed down hard. "A year, Sam. I hadn't seen Teddy in an entire year, not even on Christmas. The big movie star, always too busy even to come home to see her own father. And now I'll never see him again. We couldn't…we couldn't even have an open casket, not the way the bullet tore through…oh, Sam, this hurts. Just hold me, please. I hurt so bad."

CHAPTER FOUR

SAM WALKED INTO THE living room after an hour spent holding Jolie in the privacy of his bedroom suite. He'd taken her up the back staircase from the kitchen to avoid the living room and her sisters. She'd cried and apologized for crying and then cried some more. When he'd left her, she was in the bathroom, washing her face and applying makeup. He believed she was putting her mask back on but didn't think he should point that out to her, poor kid.

"She was crying about Teddy, not you. Right?"

He looked at Jade, one eyebrow raised at her sharp tone. "I beg your pardon?"

"Jade sneaked upstairs and listened at the bedroom door," Jessica informed him. "We wondered if we should knock, come in and check on her, make sure she was all right. We took a vote and it was a draw. I voted to leave the two of you alone, and Jade...well, you know how she voted. But that's to be expected. Jade's off men right now, especially Becket men."

"I think the day finally hit her," Sam explained as he retrieved his car keys from a small table just inside the door. "The finality of it."

"Exactly what I told Jade. Is she all right now? She probably needed a good cry, Sam. Me, I think I'm all cried out for now, but I cried buckets. God only knows what Jade did until we got here. Jade doesn't *share* easily, do you, Jade?"

Jade pointedly turned her back to both of them, picking up a small silver bowl and turning it over, examining the maker's mark—or pretending to so that she could hide her face.

Leaving Sam to wonder why women always said things like that, that someone *needed* a good cry. The statement had never made any sense to him, but Sam only nodded, sure it was a female thing men weren't meant to understand. "Jolie will be downstairs in a couple of minutes. We're going to go over to the house to pick up her clothes. She can't stay there anymore, at least not yet. She hates that she can't, but I think I convinced her that people handle things differently. There is no right or wrong way to grieve."

Jessica, who had gone back to reading one of the files, looked up at him, a pencil caught lengthwise between her teeth. "I erk," she said, nodding. "Alwus id."

"She works. She always did," Jade translated. She put down the bowl and turned around when

Jolie joined Sam, once more clad in her simple but elegant black dress. "I turn into a monster and go looking for a fight. Sorry, Sam. Do you remember the alarm code, Jolie?"

Jolie nodded, wiping at her eyes one last time with the increasingly large wad of crumpled tissues she held in one hand. "Teddy's birthday. One—two—four—three. I'm sorry I'm bailing on you guys...."

"You're not bailing," Jade assured her. "We know where to find you when we need you. Besides, you and Sam are going to work the bride case together, right? We'll meet here every night to talk over what we've done each day—eight o'clock good for everyone? Good," she said, not waiting for anyone to answer. "So just go now and get your clothes. I'll wait until five and then call for a pizza delivery at six, so be back by then. Sam? Does the guy at the gate like pizza?"

"Probably. With or without the box," Sam said, visions of Jade running his life poking at his brain and making him spare a moment's pity for his cousin Court. Then again, Courtland Becket always liked to be in charge, the go-to man. It might be considered a success that his and Jade's marriage had lasted a full six months. "Do either of you want anything else from the house while we're there?"

"See if Teggy as marcus." Jessica removed the

pencil from her teeth. "Sorry. Could you check in Teddy's office, see if he's got markers? You know, highlighter pens? Stupid, but I have a system when I work, and that includes highlighters. Pink would be nice, but I'll use yellow in a pinch."

"Pink highlighters," Sam repeated. "Got it." He put his hand on Jolie's waist. "Ready to go?"

But Jolie just stood there, staring into the middle distance, every muscle in her body taut. "Jade?" she asked quietly. "When you got home the night you found—when you got home? Was the alarm engaged?"

Jade shook her head. "Sorry, honey, I see where you're going, but that won't work. We need the code to shut off the alarm after we enter the house, but anyone can just push the set button on the way out and arm the alarm again. The cops say suicide in a locked house. We can say Teddy let his murderer in and the killer just set the alarm again before he left. We can say Teddy turned off the alarm, which he's been known to do, so that the killer entered the house without Teddy knowing it. Face it—a man who insists on using his birth date for a code isn't really taking the alarm system seriously in the first place, as I always told him. Any scenario works, but the cops bought the suicide version."

"You should change the code in any case," Sam pointed out, feeling himself being drawn into this whole murder/suicide conspiracy thing. Much against his will, not to mention his better judgment. "If you're right, that is, and Teddy let his murderer into the house that night. Even if you still need a key for the front door, the guy could—"

"The perp," Jessica interrupted brightly. "If we're going to play private dicks, let's use the snappy lingo, okay? You're a guy, Sam. The killer is a perp." Her smile faded slightly. "Besides, I'm having trouble thinking *Teddy* and *killer* in the same thought. Somehow *perp* is easier."

"All right, the perp," Sam conceded. "*If* there was a perp, and Teddy admitted said perp to the premises, said perp may have seen Teddy punch in the code. In other words, ladies, change the damn code, all right?" He looked to Jade because he wasn't stupid, he recognized the pecking order in their little group: Jade, Jessica, Jolie and, fourth, finishing out of the money, himself. "Jade? We agree on this?"

"Hmm?" she said, blinking as she looked at him. "Sorry. I was trying again to remember if the alarm was on or not that night or even if the door was locked. Teddy was so lax about setting the alarm. In fact, to get real about the thing, if it was on, that alone would be unusual. I just can't remember if it was engaged or not. As for the front door lock? I always use my key, but that doesn't mean the door was locked when I put the key in, you know? I think I'll take Rockne for a walk in the garden, if nobody minds. I have to go think about this, mentally retrace my steps. If it *was* on, that might tell us for certain that Teddy was killed—not that I'm questioning that…."

Sam looked at Jessica, who was making notes on a scrap of paper and totally ignoring everyone, and then glared at Jolie. "Humor me. Change…the damn…code."

"We will," Jolie promised as she headed for the front door. "You want to explain to me why you'd think the murderer would come back?"

"If I had all the answers, sweetheart," he told her as he opened the car door for her, "I'd be king of the world. I'm basing my concern solely on books and TV shows wherein the murderer—excuse me, the perp—always returns to the scene of the crime. Like it's part of their job description."

Jolie buckled herself in as he started the car. "So you're going along with us? You're willing to believe Teddy was murdered?"

Sam put the transmission into gear and the car pretty much on autopilot as he headed toward the Sunshine family home in nearby Ardmore. "I just walked in on this earlier today, Jolie, and haven't had much time to think about anything but the moment following the one that just preceded it."

"Our fault, I know. The Sunshine girls invaded, and you haven't had much chance to do anything but listen to us rant and rave. So think about it now, Sam. Do you think Teddy was capable of suicide—for any reason? I really do want your opinion."

"Okay, I'll think about it."

A minute later Jolie gave him a soft punch in the arm. "Out loud, Sam. Think about it out loud."

"All I seem to be doing today is taking orders. All right. Teddy was one of the most *alive* people I ever met. That's one. He loved you three girls more than anything else in the world, and I can't see him taking the coward's way out of trouble, leaving you three behind to clean up his mess—and I mean that in any way imaginable. Whatever trouble he might have been in couldn't have been more important to him than…well, he had to have known Jade would be the one to find him. So, no, Jolie. I can't see Teddy doing something like that to Jade, no matter how much distress he might have been under at the time."

Jolie nodded, clasping and unclasping her hands in her lap. "That's what Jade kept telling the police. Teddy wouldn't have done that to her. He would have gone somewhere private, away from the house. Somewhere someone else would find the…find the body. And he would have left a note, too. Explaining what he did, why he did it. He would have apologized, told us that…told us that he loved us."

This was something new to Sam. He looked across the car at Jolie. "He didn't leave a note?"

"No. Nothing. Jade said there was an almost empty bottle of Irish whiskey on the desk. An overturned glass on the floor across the room, as if he'd flung it away from him. That's how Jade described it, anyway. The case Teddy kept his old service revolver in was on the desk, too, open, the key beside it. The gun was on the floor next to him, two shots fired."

Sam nearly ran off the road as he looked over at Jolie. "Two? Two shots?"

Jolie sighed, nodded. "According to the police, the first was a test shot to see if he really had the nerve to pull the trigger. A lot of people do that, supposedly. They dug that shot—slug?—out of the floor. But there was no note. Not in his handwriting, not on his computer."

Sam turned onto the street where the Sunshine family lived in a small Georgian-style brick two-story house and slowed the car to a crawl when he saw a nondescript blue van parked at the curb.

"Only one still sticking around, Jolie," he said, looking at the blond man sitting on the second of two steps that led up to a long cement walkway and another half flight of steps that ended on the front porch of the house. He had one shoe off and was rubbing at his foot. "Looks like my new friend from the cemetery. And he's trespassing. What do you want to do?"

Jolie leaned forward in her seat, lowering her

sunglasses and squinting into the sun. "Oh, God. It's Gary Tuttle."

"I should recognize the name? I mean, I did run over his foot."

"Nobody should know him. He should live under a rock. Maybe Gibraltar. Tuttle works freelance, which means he'll do anything for a photo, a story, and then sell it to the highest bidder. He's been sued at least three times and got out of it each time, claiming he was just trying to make a living and the person he was harassing was a public figure and not entitled to privacy. Whoever thought up that law also should be living under a rock."

"So Tuttle's not destined to be one of my best friends." Sam pulled to the curb behind the van, more than ready to take out his frustrations on the so-called reporter. "You stay here. I'll get rid of him."

"No, Sam. You've already done enough, more than enough. We'll be happy if he doesn't sue you for pain and injury." She pulled down the sun visor and turned her head side to side, practiced a smile. "How do I look? My eyes are sort of puffy, but if I keep the sunglasses on it shouldn't be too bad, right?"

"You're going to *pose* for the bastard?" Sam felt his temper climbing.

"The proverbial performing seal, yes." She shoved the visor back up and put her hand on the door handle. "It's the easiest way, and Tuttle knows it, which is why he stuck around. Three seconds to make up your mind, Sam—do you want to be in the photos or not? Because we're going to give Tuttle a cover shot that should make his day. And make him go away."

"I don't freaking believe this," Sam said, pushing open his door and walking around the front of the car, glaring at Gary Tuttle the entire time, his left arm out, warning him to keep his distance. "I'm beginning to have a lot of sympathy for anybody who ever popped one of these guys in the nose with his own camera."

Jolie turned on the seat, her long bare legs exiting the car first. She took his hand and allowed him to help her and then touched at her sunglasses once more and began walking down the sidewalk. To the idle observer, Sam thought, she looked the picture of calm, of confidence. More than ever he longed to run over Gary Tuttle's other foot. With a tank.

Gary Tuttle was already on his feet, his open cell phone aimed at them, snapping pictures. "Call off the muscle, Jolie, sweetheart. I don't want any trouble from him," he shouted, backing up a few paces even as he kept snapping photos. "A man's gotta eat, Jolie, you know that."

"I know that, Mr. Tuttle," Jolie said, linking her arm through Sam's. "Just as you know that I've just buried my father this morning. Now, we're going to keep walking and you snap as many pictures as you can, and we'll call it a victory for both of us, all right?"

Tuttle held on to the camera phone as he pulled a notebook and pen from his pocket. "You've always been the best, Jolie. Abso-toot-lee aces! Give me a name, okay? Who's the hottie? Been a while since we've seen you with anyone special. Guess Mick's been replaced, huh? He know it yet? He will tomorrow when my photos hit the papers, right? Give us a smile. Hey, how about a kiss while we're at it?"

"Sam, don't," Jolie whispered as Sam growled low in his throat. "Michael Carnes is on location in Australia, Mr. Tuttle, as you know. My old family friend Samuel Becket was kind enough to offer his comfort and support in my time of grief. That's Becket—one T, Mr. Tuttle." She stopped in front of the first short set of steps, turned with Sam, tilted her head intimately toward his shoulder as she squeezed his arm and looked into the camera one last time, her expression unreadable.

"Careful, Mick will be jealous," Sam whispered, actually beginning to get into the ridiculousness that surrounded Jolie Sunshine, movie star.

"Shh, don't ad-lib," Jolie warned before addressing the news hound once more. "We're also,

you might want to know, investigating the circumstances surrounding my father's death. We're confident, my sisters and myself, that we will soon be
able to prove that he had nothing to do with the
murder of Melodie Brainard and in fact was a
victim of murder himself. You have that, Mr.
Tuttle? I'm not speaking too quickly for you?"

"Got it, got it," Tuttle said, still scribbling.
"Comfort, Jolie? What kind of comfort is he
giving you?"

"Okay, that's it, Tuttle, quit while you can still
chew soft foods," Sam said, tugging on Jolie's arm
so that she had little choice but to follow him up the
cement path to the house. "I never knew you were
a masochist, Jolie. You live with that crap all the
time?"

She stepped forward with the key when he
pulled open the old wooden screen door. "It comes
with the territory. I've learned to go along to get
along, unfortunately. And Tuttle's right. There are
times we're more than happy to have guys like
him around. So it cuts two ways."

She opened the door and moved inside, going to
the security panel and punching in the code: 1243.

"Don't forget to change that," Sam said,
standing in the small foyer and looking around, beginning to reacquaint himself with the house he
hadn't seen in five years. "Doesn't look as if
anything's changed. Not even the smell."

"What smell?"

"You don't smell that? It always smells like roast beef in here for the first few moments. I get hungry every time I come into the house."

Jolie smiled, but the smile was sad. "Pot roast, Teddy's favorite. He also said it was the only thing he knew how to cook. We ate a lot of pot roast growing up, even after Jessica took over kitchen duty while she went through her wanting-to-be-the-next-Martha-Stewart phase." She put her hand on the newel post and hesitated, one foot on the first step leading up to the bedrooms. "Sam? Mick Carnes was my costar. We made appearances together for publicity, and that's all. He's dating a script girl, but he knows if the press finds out, they'll shred her, so I agreed to be his cover. Not that I should have to tell you that."

"I didn't ask," he reminded her.

"No, you didn't. Thank you for that. You, um, you can wait here. I'll be just a few minutes. Oh, and we should pack up some of Rockne's toys and some of his food if I'm staying with you. I'm sure I can get him to eat something soon. If not, we'll have to take him to the vet tomorrow."

Sam walked into the living room that also hadn't changed since the last time he'd been invited into the house. Not that he'd been there long—just long enough for Teddy to warn him off Jolie. *Let the girl have her head,* he'd said. *She's young, and she's chasing her dream. If it's you she wants, she'll be back on her own.*

Sam had agreed but only because he'd had a plan of his own. The one that had backfired right in his face.

He spent a few moments looking at a collection of photographs of the three Sunshine sisters and then could no longer avoid the door on the far wall. The door to Teddy's office.

"Pink highlighter," he muttered as his excuse and turned the knob, entered the room where Teddy Sunshine had died.

Knotty-pine paneling out of the sixties or maybe the fifties. A huge oak desk strangely clear, as it had always been littered with files, with the humidor containing Teddy's favorite cigars, with at least one family-size box of Tastykake chocolate cupcakes. And photographs of his girls. You couldn't walk more than five feet in any direction in Teddy's house without running into photographs of his girls.

The commendations Sam was used to seeing hanging on the wall behind the desk were also gone, lighter rectangles visible on the aged paneling showing where they had once been displayed. The desk chair, a massive piece of cracked burgundy leather, was also missing, as was the carpet. There was a raw hole in the floor, probably where a bullet had been pried out and removed as evidence. The entire room reeked of cleaning materials, and the smell burned at Sam's nose, the back of his throat.

Teddy simply wasn't in this room anymore, wasn't a part of it. And yet his ghost was also everywhere in the room.

"We'll stop at a store, get Jess's damn highlighters," Sam told himself, told Teddy's ghost, leaving the room and softly closing the door.

With nothing else to do, he climbed the stairs to offer to carry down Jolie's suitcases.

"Oh, you startled me," Jolie said as he knocked lightly on the doorjamb and she turned around to face him, holding several hangers in her hand.

"I thought I could help," he explained, looking about the room. There were movie posters tacked to all four walls, her degree from Temple University almost lost among them, the furniture merely dark and old rather than antique. Funny, he'd never seen her childhood bedroom, had never been upstairs in the Sunshine house. Which gave him an idea. "Did the police search up here that night?"

"Up here?" Jolie frowned as she carefully laid the blouses, hangers and all, in the suitcase opened on the bed. "I don't know. Why would they search up here?"

"Isn't Jade's office up here?"

"Yes, but—oh. You're saying that someone might have come here to demand something that

Teddy had and then somehow shot him with his own gun and left before he found whatever it was that he wanted?"

Sam didn't say that he found it difficult to believe that Teddy could "eat" his own gun unless he'd done it himself. He certainly couldn't say that he was just plain nosy, even if he was. "Anything's possible," he said, shrugging.

"We'll have to ask Jade."

"True, but she's been under a strain these last days. You all have. Plus, Teddy might have hidden something in his bedroom rather than keep it in his office if he was worried about something."

"I didn't think of that. We only went into his room one time, to get clothes for the burial."

"Maybe if I took a quick look around?"

"I can't go in Teddy's room again, Sam. Not yet. You do it while I finish up here."

He didn't need a second invitation or even bother to ask Jolie which room was which.

The first door he opened had to be to Jessica's room. Pink and white, complete with a canopy bed littered with stuffed animals and a half dozen huge cheerleading trophies lined up on wall shelves. The huge wall poster of Dan Rather during his years of reporting in Vietnam would have seemed out of place expect for the career path Jessica had chosen.

He opened the other door on that side of the

large, square hallway and stepped into Teddy Sunshine's bedroom. It was a small room, clearly not designed as the master bedroom, and held only a single bed, a large dresser that was probably the companion to the one in Jolie's bedroom and a small desk on the far wall. The only thing on the desk was an ancient twelve-inch television set.

Sam opened the door to the closet and smiled at the colorful array of Hawaiian-print shirts and a short row of identical khaki slacks. Teddy's post-cop uniform. Sam wondered if he'd been buried in his only suit and then wondered if Teddy had even owned a suit.

"We buried him in his blues," Jolie said from the doorway as if he'd spoken out loud. "Even as a detective, he had to keep a set of blues for certain occasions. He was so proud to have been a cop. And then to be denied a cop's funeral? Right now we should all be crowded in down at Shandy's Pub for one hell of a party, laughing, telling stories about Teddy, listening to more outrageous stories, all while lifting pints to his memory. That's the way he wanted to go out, Sam, he always said so. No tears. Laughter."

Sam closed the door on the Hawaiian shirts. "Jade's room is across the hall?" he asked, feeling stupid because he had nothing to say that could make up for the honors Teddy had been denied.

"She won't like us looking around in her room,"

Jolie said, leading the way. "Just look at her desk, Sam, that's all."

He waited for her to enter the room and then followed after her to see that Jade had the largest bedroom.

Once again Jolie seemed to be reading his mind. "When Mom left, Dad took over Jade's room and gave her his. He just couldn't stand being in the room anymore. Jade was the oldest, so she got it. I don't think she wanted it, to tell you the truth. But it worked out in the end, because it's large enough to also serve as her office."

Sam looked around the room, one word repeating inside his head: *spartan.* No photographs, no prints or paintings, no knickknacks on the furniture tops, just an alarm clock next to the bed and a single lamp. The space was as impersonal as a hotel room, maybe even more so. And the empty curio cabinet and wall shelves seemed almost ominous.

"What did Jade do in high school and college?" he asked.

"Do? What do you mean?"

"I'm not sure. You've got movie posters on your wall, Jessica's got her cheerleader trophies and stuffed animals—I'd mention Dan Rather, but I'm not sure I want to go there. Jade's got nothing here, nothing of herself. It just seems strange, that's all."

Jolie looked around the room. "You're right. I

guess I wasn't paying attention. She used to collect Belleek china. You know, that china made in Ireland? Oh, of course you know what I mean. Teddy brought her a few pieces back from a trip he took to Dublin years ago, and she added to it a lot over the years. Pretty pieces, mostly with little green shamrocks on them. I wonder what happened to it all."

While Jolie spoke, Sam made himself busy walking around the room, inspecting the areas around the locks on the filing cabinet and the desk drawers. Everything seemed neat, with no signs of tampering. As a private eye, he was pretty much striking out. Hell, as a nosy snoop, he was also batting zero, less than zero. Then he opened the door to Jade's closet.

"Omigod! Oh, Jade…"

Sam caught Jolie's arm as the two of them looked down at the floor of the closet, littered with shards of once-treasured Belleek china. He pushed aside the clothing, exposing gouges in the back wall of the closet where the pieces had hit, shattered and fallen to the floor. Pieces thrown in rage, grief—what?

When presented with her father's death, Jolie had held it together as long as possible, denied her grief until the floodgates opened on their own. Jessica had "cried buckets" and then gone to work.

And Jade? Sam could see her in his mind's eye.

All alone in this house, waiting for her sisters. Unable to cope with the horror of what she'd seen, Teddy's body being taken away in a body bag, listening to people telling that her father was a murderer and, worse, a coward who had killed himself knowing his oldest daughter would find his body.

She hadn't cried. No, not Jade. She'd come up here and taken out her anger, her grief, her rage, by methodically smashing her beloved collection against the back wall of her closet.

And then she'd closed the door on what she'd done and taken charge because she was the oldest and everyone expected her to be the strong one, the sane one, the one they could look to for guidance. For answers to seemingly unanswerable questions.

A person who can hold on that tight was bound to break, and break badly, at some point. Just like that Belleek china, shattering into pieces too many and too small to be repaired.

"We've got to get Court back here, Jolie," he said at last. "Fast."

CHAPTER FIVE

JOLIE, NOW CLAD IN SOFT cotton sleep pants and a cotton knit sleeveless top, sat cross-legged on one of the couches in Sam's magnificent living room, forcing down a last bite of warmed-up pizza, still marveling that she had any appetite at all after the events of this never-ending day.

At least she felt a bit better about Rockne, who'd shown no interest in any of his own food but who had finally eaten a slice of pepperoni pizza and was once again sleeping on the hearth.

She'd kept sneaking looks at Jade ever since they'd come back to Sam's house, but she really couldn't see a single crack in her older sister, not as they'd shared their dinner and not now, three hours later, while waiting for Sam to return from a quick trip to his center-city office. She was still all business, extremely focused, very much in control. As always.

And Court would soon be on his way across the Atlantic in the Becket family jet. He'd arrive in

Philadelphia by tomorrow morning, their time, and drive directly to Sam's house.

Jolie wondered if anyone would mind if she took a short trip to the North Pole, just to be out of the way when Jade first caught sight of her ex-husband.

"So I've decided, Jolie. That's what I'm going to do first. Jade says I'm crazy, but who listens to Jade, right? Jolie? Did you hear me? I said I'm running away with the FedEx guy from my office. He's married and has six kids, but what can I say, I'm a born home wrecker. Jolie?"

"Hmm?" Jolie turned to her sister. "I'm sorry, Jess. What did you say?"

"Nothing, forget it. No, don't forget it. I said I'm going to retrace the steps of the murdered women, check out where they used to work, talk to some of the other prostitutes. Ladies of the evening, I mean. Those women might not talk to the cops, but almost everyone talks to me. So what do you think?"

"That depends," Jolie said, wiping her hands on a paper napkin. "Are you going to Fishtown dressed for the occasion?"

Jessica frowned. "Dressed for the—oh. You mean am I going to hit the street corners looking like an investigative journalist or a hooker? I was sort of thinking hooker. That's when Jade started making faces."

Jolie looked across the coffee table at Jade, who looked a warning at her, one Jolie found easy to read. "I think I'm siding with Jade here, Jess. As a hooker, you'd sort of be invading their territory, so why would they talk to you? Better if you went as a reporter—sorry, journalist. How long has it been since the last murder?"

"Well over ten years. A dozen years? I don't remember. All these cases we're looking at are from around then, if you haven't noticed. All of them pretty much right before Teddy got hurt and had to take early retirement. Why?"

"Because none of the women you meet might even remember the murders. But if you're lucky and someone does, that person might be angry that the killer hasn't been found. You might be welcomed with open arms if you promise you're going to give the case national publicity, all that baloney."

"True. Very good, Jolie," Jessica said, pointing a finger at Jade. "And one of you can come along as my cameraperson if you think I need a chaperone, which I don't. You, Jade, because you're so darn worried. We've got a sister station here in Philly, so I know I can scrounge up a camera and a mic, anything I need, from somebody down at the station."

"You're on suspension, reluctant as I am to point that out," Jolie reminded her.

"Extended bereavement leave. Sort of." Jessica rolled her eyes. "And, yeah, like that's going to stop me. I'll take care of this first thing tomorrow morning. Jade, be ready to roll—when—about ten tomorrow night? Once it gets dark, at least."

"Did I agree to this?" Jade asked Jolie, who merely smiled at her because they both knew she would do it. Neither one of them was crazy enough to let Jessica out on her own, not on the seamier streets of the City of Brotherly Love. "Never mind. No matter what, I've had it. I'm going up to bed. I want to get an early start tomorrow morning. I only hope Jermayne hasn't moved since his grandmother died. I want to know why he wasn't at the funeral today, and if Teddy had been in contact with him lately, which we know he was."

"A logical place to start," Jessica agreed, also getting to her feet. "And wait for me. I'm going to go take a nice, long bubble bath. Sam has the most interesting bathrooms. Did you know mine has a copper tub? Maybe tubs are a fetish with him? But you'd know that, Jolie, right?"

Jolie smiled, shook her head. "You're wrong, Jess, not *everyone* tells you all their secrets. And don't forget we're pretty much locked in here until Sam lets us out, so don't open any outside doors tomorrow morning and set off the alarm."

"Rats," Jessica complained. "I'll have to call my FedEx guy and cancel."

"Huh?"

"Ignore her. It's easier," Jade said, yawning. "You should come upstairs and get some rest, too, Jolie."

"I'll be up soon. I want to wait for Sam just a little longer,"

"Good idea. He's been waiting for you long enough."

"And that means…?" Jolie asked, glaring at her younger sister.

"It means it's time for me to go to bed," Jessica said, wincing. "Definitely."

"Sam and I are…we've…he's just being…" Jolie shoved her fingers into her hair. "Oh, God, what am I doing here?"

"Happy now, Jess?" Jade asked, grabbing her sister's arm. "Jolie, Sam's a friend, a good friend. What you two had five years ago might be gone, but the friendship stayed, even though you may have, well, parted in anger, and even if you haven't seen each other in all of that time. Yes?"

"Yes, of course. Sam's a good man. A good friend." Jolie tried to block out what had happened in Sam's bedroom, but it wasn't working. She could feel her cheeks growing hot and quickly bent to begin gathering up the plates from their snack.

What *was* she doing here? Jolie asked herself again as she carried plates and glasses to the kitchen. Would she have stayed here if Jade and

Jessica hadn't barged in on them, asking sanctuary for the night? And why had she agreed to stay here instead of going to a hotel because she couldn't stand being in her childhood home right now?

Sam.

The answer was Sam. She wanted to be here with him.

And that was selfish, because she'd soon be back in California and then off on location for a good three months, and he'd still be here. That fork in the road he'd mentioned had come along five years ago, and they were both now five long miles down very separate roads.

Jolie rinsed the glasses and put them into the dishwasher, then reached for the hose to rinse the plates and quickly changed her mind. She finished up, running the plates under water from the faucet, and headed back into the living room.

"Sam!" she said, startled. "I didn't hear you come in. What do you have?"

He was crouched down in front of Rockne, his right hand outstretched, a paper bag in his left. "I stopped at a supermarket for some meat chunks."

"You're feeding him raw beef? That isn't good for him."

"It's eighteen dollars a pound choice filet," Sam said as Rockne got to his feet and began to eat out of Sam's hand. "I asked the guy behind the counter

to chop up a pile of the stuff. Look—he's eating."
He got to his feet, holding out the open bag. "Come
on, champ, let's adjourn to the kitchen, set up a
dish for you, all right? I'll be right back, Jolie."

She rather vaguely waved him on his way,
shaking her head to think that Sam would make a
special stop—at a supermarket, no less, and she
was sure he'd had to hunt to find one, as Sam
Becket wasn't the push-the-cart-down-the-aisle
type. He was a good man, such a good man.

And he'd just laid another such huge guilt trip
on her, whether he'd meant to or not.

She fished in her purse for her lighter and a
single cigarette—her last, damn it—and stepped
out onto the back terrace to have her third smoke
of the day, the cigarettes taking the place of snacks
when she felt hungry between meals. She didn't
really like cigarettes, but everyone said smoking
was a great diet aid, and lately she'd begun to want
one when she felt stressed. That couldn't be good.
She tucked the unlit cigarette and the lighter behind
a planter, took ten deep breaths in through her nose
and out through her mouth instead.

Much better for her lungs, she supposed, but not
nearly as satisfying.

When she reentered the living room, Sam was
sitting in the seat recently occupied by Jade, one
of the manila folders in his lap. "I thought you'd
gone to bed. I was just choosing some bedtime

reading for myself that might make me forget you were sleeping just down the hall."

"Aw, Sam," Jolie said, sitting down on the facing couch, careful to keep the coffee table between them. He looked tired, and she remembered that he'd told her he'd just flown in from England the night before the funeral. He had to be jet-lagged, at the very least. "We really shouldn't be here. It isn't fair to you."

"I admit it, I'll wave goodbye to your sisters with a happy heart tomorrow. This is a big house, but Jessica could probably hunt me down in a place twice this size. And Jade...well, I think Jade needs to go home, where she can feel private again."

"Which will be a neat trick with Jess there," Jolie said, smiling slightly. "So maybe Jess could stay here?"

Sam rubbed at the back of his neck, his exaggerated frown widening Jolie's smile. "I don't know. Do you have an extra leash for her? Maybe a muzzle?"

"I'll tell her in the morning. I was going to tell you that we'd all leave, but I really don't want to stay in a hotel with leeches like Gary Tuttle knowing where I am. And giving Jade some space by having Jess here, too? Plus, Court will be here tomorrow, and he'll keep an eye on Jade—unless she shoots him, of course. Are you sure you don't mind?"

"Oh, I mind," Sam said quietly, looking at her from beneath lowered lids. "I mind that you think you have to ask. I mind that you're keeping Jessica around as a chaperone so that you're not tempted to share my bed. But I'd mind it a hell of a lot more if you left."

Jolie didn't know what to say, so she lowered her head, said nothing.

"Come over here, Jolie. We'll read Teddy's file together, plan a strategy for tomorrow."

She was quick to agree, partly because she had yet to look at the file she'd chosen, while her sisters were already working, but mostly so that she could sit next to Sam. And wasn't that pathetic?

She sat down close beside him and reached toward the file. "Flip to the back, Sam, like Jessica did with hers. Teddy made notations every time he read the file...or something like that."

"'Progress notes,'" Sam said, holding up the last sheet of paper in the file. "He titled the page that way. Hmm, he seemed to have been very orderly in his updates. Twice a year, mostly December and June. See? His last note was dated three weeks ago. *Contacted A. P. No changes.* Well, that's succinct. I wonder if he kept the same schedule with the other cases he was still working on."

"Jessica said Teddy had written a note in the Fishtown Strangler folder three weeks ago, remember." Jolie leaned in closer to read her father's note. "You know, I thought Jade was crazy when she said we should work on these cases, but if all four of them have updates in them in the past month, maybe she's onto something. Unless it's just that summer lull in the business thing. There's that, too."

She pulled her head back, nearly colliding with Sam's chin. "Oops, sorry. But I just thought of something. What if someone Teddy spoke to is— well, is our bad guy? Even with Court keeping an eye on Jade, she'll still be alone in the house. She has to stay here, too, Sam, or we all have to stay at the house." She rubbed at her bare forearms. "This is silly. I've got goose bumps all of a sudden. Maybe we shouldn't have started this."

"It's not too late to let me hire someone," he told her, slipping his arm around her shoulders so that she could lay her head against him, which is what she'd wanted to do ever since she'd come into the living room to see that he had come home. "I'd say let it go completely, accept the conclusions the police came to, but I know none of you will do that. I don't blame you."

"Teddy did not strangle that woman. He would never hurt a woman. And he'd never commit suicide. He just wouldn't, and you know it."

Sam pressed a kiss against her hair, squeezed her tighter. "I looked into his office," he told her quietly. "I don't have the best imagination in the world, but I think I could pretty well picture what Jade came home to that night. Teddy would have had to have been past rational thinking at that moment, that's the only other explanation."

Jolie pushed slightly away from him. "And he was drunk," she said flatly. "Now you sound like the police report. Look, Sam, if you don't want to do this, say it now. Unless you believe what we believe, there's no point in even discussing anything with you."

"Just say it, Jolie, all right? Clear the air. You want to know if I'm pulling some cheap trick, if I'm only stringing you along, being helpful, offering my house and my assistance in order to get in your—"

She raised her hand, and then stopped, shocked. Dear God, she'd almost slapped him! Was she out of her mind?

"Sam!" She gently laid her hand against his cheek, as if that could take away the sting of what she'd almost done. "Oh, Sam, I'm sorry. I'm so sorry."

He covered her hand with his own. "So am I, sweetheart," he told her quietly. "I'm sorry that what we once had has gotten so screwed up. I'll bet," he added, smiling slightly, "you could really pack a wallop."

Jolie let out a breath that was half sob, half sigh

of relief, and then leaned in to kiss him. She meant it to be a short kiss, an I'm-sorry kiss, maybe even a let's-be-friends kiss.

She should have known they could never be friends.

He opened his mouth beneath hers, and she responded just as she'd always done, following his lead and then anticipating his next move as they melded their bodies together.

The open manila file slid soundlessly to the floor, pages scattering unnoticed.

She'd been the aggressor that morning, so she let him lead the way, turned herself boneless in his arms as he lowered her onto the soft down cushions of the couch. His hands were beneath her ribbed cotton top now, inching the material up and over her breasts.

Her nipples grew taut in anticipation even before he closed finger and thumb around each one, his eyes watching hers.

She knew what he was looking for. He'd told her, a lifetime ago. He was watching for her pupils to go dark and unfocussed. He'd told her how the sight of her arousal only increased his.

So she looked at him as he touched her, gave him what he wanted, until the sensations rippling through her forced her eyes closed, her head arching back as she bit on her full bottom lip, every nerve in her body attuned to his touch.

She knew what came next. Knew his moves just as he knew hers.

Even so, when it came, when his mouth closed around her nipple, she could not hold back a quiet moan of pleasure. She clasped her hands around his neck, using her thumbs to trace the shape of his ears, press into the hollows behind them, and then slid her hands down onto his shoulders, digging her nails into his taut muscles.

He was kissing her all over now, his fingers busy with the front buttons on her sleep pants, and Jolie could no longer count the moves, plot them. She simply gave over control to her body, disengaging her mind even as her fingers were somehow between them, loosening his belt, easing down his zipper.

"No," he whispered, stilling her hand with his own. "Tonight's for you, Jolie. Just for you…"

She lifted her hips in protest, hoping he could not resist her as she pressed against him. But Sam Becket was a stubborn man. He pushed himself up on his knee. His green eyes turned dark as night as he looked down at her, as he removed her sleep pants, lifted her legs up and onto his shoulders.

Lowering his head, he found the heart of her.

"Sam…"

Once again she closed her eyes and let the sensations wash over her. Lift her, take her, narrow her world to a place where only she and Sam mattered, where only the two of them existed. Together. As they should be…

He took her up, took her over, held her so she wouldn't crash on the rocks below, let her shudder against him, again and again, until she could only hold up her arms and cry out his name. Then he was with her, holding her, taking in all of her pain and her hurt and her tearing grief and smoothing them all away.

She calmed slowly, still holding on to him as if he was the one sure anchor in her world. "Are you all right?" she asked him, not unaware of his sacrifice.

"I'm fine," he said, stroking her hair. "Just give me a minute for my eyes to uncross, and I'll get up, give you some breathing room."

His words struck Jolie as being the funniest thing anyone had ever said, and she began to giggle.

"Uh, God, Jolie—don't move."

"I'm sorry," she managed, burying her head against his shoulder as her giggles intensified. "It wasn't that funny."

"Good. So stop laughing. You're killing me here."

"I…I can't help it," she said as she braced her hands on his shoulders and pushed him up so that she could roll out from beneath him, landing facedown on the floor. This set her off into another round a giggles. "At least…at least I'm keeping my promise to myself," she said, trying to catch her breath. "I'm not muddying the waters by sleeping with you. *Ouch!*"

Sam had swatted her bare backside, which she probably deserved, and she rolled over, shifted her tank top back down over her breasts and struggled to pull her sleep pants on once more. Luckily, one leg had caught around her ankle, so she didn't have to go searching for them.

When she looked up again, Sam was fixing his belt buckle and looking down at her.

"I owe you, Sam," she said sincerely.

"I know, I'm keeping a tab," he said, his grin close to evil. "And now, not to ruin your fun or anything, but you're sitting on our vanishing-bride case. Fingerprints, people will understand. Even a smudge from a candy bar you might be eating while reading the file or a stain from spilled coffee. But a butt print on the bride's face?"

"Oh, God," Jolie exclaimed, looking around her at the two dozen or more sheets of paper. "You know what, Sam? You're a corrupting influence on me. Now get down here and help me put this file back together."

"Yes, ma'am," he said, going to his knees and picking up the folder, then beginning to pile pages inside it while she handed him other pages. "These pages aren't numbered, Jolie. We're going to have to figure out how to separate them by year, topic, whatever. Like, this page is typed and this one is handwritten and—hey, I know them."

Jolie scrambled to her knees and looked over his shoulder. "Who? You know who?"

"Whom," Sam said absently, now searching for whatever page might follow the one he was holding in his right hand. "Angela and Timothy Lutton."

"Friends of yours?"

"Not really, no. Acquaintances. Brother and sister. Tim was a library trustee the year I first came onto the board. That was during my do-gooder days—before you ask what I was doing on a library board. It was his final year, so I really didn't get to know him well. That was, what, eight years ago? Angela is his sister. I ran into them a few times at social affairs. But she's not Angela Lutton. Now she's Angela…Pierce, I think? That might be it. They're older, maybe midforties. Maybe he's in his early fifties." He looked at Jolie. "Exactly how long ago did this bride disappear?"

Jolie was busy trying to push Rockne away, while the now happily fed dog was attempting to do his three-times-in-a-circle routine before lying down on the scattered pages. "I don't know for certain. We'll have to hunt for that, too—Rockne, stop it. Bad dog."

Rockne dropped his head and pushed it into Jolie's chest as if trying to hide his shame.

"Now you've done it," Sam told her. "Apologize, Jolie, or we'll never get these papers back in order."

She put her cupped hand beneath Rockne's muzzle and lifted his head so that they were eye to eye. "Rockne, be a good dog. Jolie loves you, but she's busy now and—oh, ick!" She rubbed at her face, trying to wipe away the effects of Rockne's tongue. "I forgot he does that. The only dog in the world that likes to French kiss. *Bleech!*"

Sam had managed to retrieve the rest of the pages and now sat on the couch once more. "And I'd forgotten how *varied* my life is when you're in it. So far today, I've run over a reporter, had vertical sex—it's been a long time since I've done that, and I thank you very much—posed for that same reporter like some dumb trained monkey, been recruited as a private eye, eaten pizza in my living room, shopped in a supermarket, had sex again, this time on a twenty-thousand-dollar antique couch that may or may not have once belonged to Cardinal Richelieu, so we might both be going to Hell, and now I'm being upstaged by a dog. And you ask if I've missed you, Jolie?"

She patted Rockne's head and pushed him away before collapsing onto the couch beside Sam once more. "Twenty thousand dollars? Two couches equals forty thousand dollars. And you let us sit here and eat pizza? How much is this huge coffee table worth? I mean, you did ask me to pass out coasters."

"You don't want to know," he told her. "Besides, I'm a dealer, remember? I pay wholesale."

"So what you're saying is that these pieces are really bargains?"

"I'd call them *steals,* except I actually did pay for them, unlike my ancestor, who just took those chandeliers in the dining room, for instance, and called them the spoils of war."

Jolie nodded, understanding that Sam wasn't ready to talk about Angela or Timothy Lutton yet, for some reason. Perhaps he was still trying to refresh his memory of the brother and sister. "The privateer—I remember. I wonder if Court will come back with juicy stories to tell, since this distant cousin of yours lives in the house where he once lived."

"He mentioned something when I called him, but only in passing. He was too concerned about Jade. Okay, I remember now—Angela Lutton's married name is Pearson, not Pierce. At any rate, she's written up here as Angela Lutton, so this case has to go back maybe ten years or more. Really cold. Do you think we'll actually be able to do anything to warm it up?"

Jolie had taken several of the pages from him and was looking them over as he played at pessimist again—not that she'd point that out to him this time, either. "I think I've found a photocopy of the original report…or docket or whatever it's called. See? There's Teddy's signature at the bottom."

Sam took the page and scanned it quickly. "It's a Missing Persons report. Twelve years, Jolie. Our bride vanished a dozen years ago. Cathleen Hanson, age twenty-six, did not show up at the appointed hour for her marriage to one David Pearson—whoa!" He sat up straight, began reading more slowly and, this time, out loud.

Jolie listened as he read her father's words, trying to imagine him as he'd been: the Philadelphia detective, asking questions, seeking clues, writing down the facts, adding his observations.

Cathleen Hanson had been employed as a waitress at Thompson's Diner in Kensington, her last day that of the day before her marriage to David Pearson, only son of one of the most socially prominent if not the wealthiest men in Philadelphia. Cathleen had worked her final morning shift, been the guest of honor at a small combined farewell party and wedding shower at the diner and had then supposedly walked home to her second-floor apartment in a nondescript converted row home two blocks away.

She had next been seen at the rehearsal at the Ridings Country Club, followed by a large dinner for members of the wedding party and about two hundred other close friends. As her groom had been drinking heavily to every toast offered—and there were many—Cathleen reportedly had begged him to ride home with his parents and left the club herself in a Philadelphia taxicab. When she didn't return to the club the next morning for their noon wedding, the groom first phoned her and then went to her apartment when she didn't answer, but Cathleen was not there.

"Teddy wrote that David Pearson called all the local hospitals and then the police, asking if there had been any accidents, any unidentified victims— and nothing. She was just gone," Sam said, putting down the page. "You have anything?"

Jolie nodded. "I found the page with Angela Lutton's name on it. Teddy wrote that he interviewed her—she was supposed to be the maid of honor—and that Angela did call Cathleen rather late on Friday night to be sure that she'd gotten home safely and because she was worried that Cathleen might have been angry with David for getting shit-faced. Hey, that's what Teddy wrote. *Shit-faced.* She said that Cathleen told her she wasn't upset, and that was that. So Angela Lutton— Pearson—was the last person to speak to Cathleen before she disappeared."

She squinted at some small writing at the bottom of the page. "Oh, I've got it. Teddy wrote that phone records confirm Miss Lutton's story. She called at 12:46 a.m. It was the only call on the luds? Leds?

Maybe lugs? It's one of those. I had a line like that in *Cooper Heights,* as Detective Eve Riker. 'We checked the leds, Captain, and...' That one stupid line took five takes before I got it right, and I still don't know if it's lugs or luds or something else. Anyway, the only other phone calls were from David Pearson, Friday afternoon, and then a bunch of them beginning around eleven o'clock Saturday morning."

By now, Sam had gotten most of the file back in chronological order. "This isn't good," he said, tapping another sheet of paper. "Teddy wrote here that a young, pretty blond woman pawned a diamond ring and necklace that same Saturday morning at a pawnshop about a mile from Cathleen's apartment and then asked the owner the most direct directions to the bus terminal. David Pearson and his mother, Althea Pearson, both individually identified the two pieces of jewelry as gifts to Cathleen. I don't know, Jolie. It sure sounds like our bride took a hike."

"That's sad," Jolie said, looking at the photograph of Cathleen Hanson. "Do you suppose something happened the night of the rehearsal dinner? Something that made her think she was making a big mistake?"

"I don't know," Sam said as Rockne, who must have thought he'd assumed his look-ashamed pose long enough, plunked his head down on Sam's lap.

Sam absently began rubbing the dog behind the ears, so that Rockne now wore his I-adore-you-beyond-all-reason face. "So how do you want to attack this? According to his notes, Teddy pretty much wore out his welcome with the Pearsons, mother and son—and wife."

"Angela Pearson. The maid of honor. Sam? Doesn't that strike you as sort of…convenient? That Cathleen disappears and Angela's right there to console the jilted groom, step into the bride's shoes? I wonder when she and David Pearson got married."

"Well, I guess that answers my question. We start with Angela Pearson. That's whom your father spoke to a few weeks ago—A.P., remember? Unless it was her mother-in-law, Althea Pearson. It's a shame Teddy was writing these notes just for himself. But we'll start with Angela. I'll call her tomorrow morning, see if she'll meet with us."

"At least she can tell us what she told Teddy, I suppose. I think I'd also like to stop by Thompson's Diner and ask a few questions there. I know it has been a long time, but somebody might remember Cathleen. You know, maybe the owner? I mean, they gave her a bridal shower and all, so they must have liked her."

Sam closed the folder and replaced it on the table as he stood up. "That'll work. Jolie Sunshine, movie star, showing up in some family diner, signing autographs and asking questions."

Jolie glared up at him and then likewise got to her feet. "My sunglasses wouldn't be enough?"

"I doubt it, no." He slipped an arm around her shoulders. "Maybe you hadn't thought of that yet, but I have. It's not going to be easy, Jolie, going out in public, trying to ask questions. Maybe you could don your *Zorro* mask or something?"

"You're right, Sam. Thank you! I need to call Smitty."

"Okay. You're welcome. Who's Smitty?"

"Never mind," Jolie said, standing on tiptoe to plant a quick kiss on his cheek. She'd have to make this all up to him another time—the investigation came first. "It's only ten o'clock in California. I'm going to go upstairs and call her. Good night, Sam. Oh, and I think Rockne needs to go out. You'll take care that, right?"

"Sure. Lucky me. Perfect host, sex machine and dog walker. A hell of a combination, Jolie—think about it. I'm either the greatest catch or the most pathetic jerk in the world," he called after her jokingly, and she could feel his gaze on her as she half walked, half jogged out of the room. She smiled as she headed up the steps. She didn't know how Sam had done it—oh, all right, so she had a pretty good idea how he'd done it—but she felt alive again. Able to think, able to feel something other than the overwhelming grief that had consumed her since Jade's phone call.

Maybe A.P. was the one. Angela Pearson, the no-good who'd offed the inconvenient bride and then moved in on a grieving groom and married him. Oh, didn't that sound like a made-for-television movie? Sure did. And if Angela Pearson had thought that Teddy also thought that and finally had some proof? Wanting the man for herself was a motive for murder, right? Or had she been reading too many bad movie scripts?

Jolie entered the guest room she'd chosen and dug the small address book out of her carry-on bag even as she picked up her cell phone. Here's hoping Smitty didn't have an early call in the morning and hadn't yet taken her sleeping pill....

CHAPTER SIX

SAM WOKE TO THE LESS-than-pleasant buzz of the internal phone system and grappled for the receiver. "Bear Man?" he mumbled as he sat up and attempted to rub the sleep from his face. "What's up?"

"There's a guy down here who says he wants in, and he's not being real polite about it. You want I should get rid of him?"

"Yes...no—wait. Blond guy, and I'm beginning to think he wears a rug, big teeth, obnoxious personality?"

"No, sir. Tall guy, black hair—and pissed off. I think I probably could take him, but he looks pretty, you know, fit?"

"Court," Sam told himself, throwing back the sheet and getting to his feet. "Didn't he give you his name, Bear Man?"

"Well, yeah, but anybody could say he was a Becket, right? Gotta protect Miss Jolie from all those pat-parazzis, that's what I figured, so I beeped you. You want I should let him in?"

"Yes, please, do that. Uh…good work, Bear Man."

"Thank you, sir! I do what I can."

"We all do, Bear Man, or at least we try," Sam muttered as he grabbed the slacks he'd worn yesterday and pulled them on, pushing his arms into his wrinkled dress shirt as he headed for the stairs. If Jade was already awake, already downstairs, he didn't have time for the niceties of brushing his teeth, buttoning his shirt or even finding his shoes. Not if he was going to avert World War III.

Court was leaning on the bell by the time Sam's bare feet hit the foyer tile. He hurried to disengage the alarm and open the door. "Christ, Court, why not just break it down?"

"Where is she?" Court said, waving a folded newspaper in Sam's face. "Where the *hell* is she? Is she nuts? Are they all nuts? And *you?* What in all that's holy were you *thinking?*"

"Have a good flight? I'm fine, by the way. You're looking…harassed."

"Oh, shit. Sorry, Sam," Court said, heading for the living room and, of course, expecting Sam to follow. He and Jade could both use a refresher course in Diplomacy 101. "The woman drives me out of my mind, I swear to God."

Sam took the newspaper Court was now holding out to him. It was either that, he figured, or have it shoved in his face.

"Front page of the national section—God help us—just below the fold," Court told him, sitting down on one of the couches and then just as quickly standing up again. "You have any coffee?"

Sam glanced at the mantel clock. "I asked Mrs. Archer to have a breakfast buffet served in the dining room at eight. We're a little early, but she probably already has coffee set up. Now what am I supposed to be looking at here—hmm, maybe not my best side, huh?" he asked, looking at the photograph of himself standing just outside his car at the cemetery, supporting a distraught Jolie as he helped her into the front seat.

"Don't worry about it," Court told him as he led the way to the dining room. "There's four more pictures on page two. And it has gone from the wire services to the cable news stations. I saw your pretty face staring out of every last damn street corner newspaper box and newsstand on my way in from the airport. If you're lucky, maybe you'll bounce Britney Spears off the cover of *People* next week. Cripes!"

Court was right. Jolie's friend Gary Tuttle had gotten off some good shots. But Sam knew it was the headline that had set his cousin off into the stratosphere. Sunshine Daughters Vow to Clear Father's Name.

He read the first few paragraphs, quickly locating a direct quote from Jolie: "We're confident, my sisters and myself, that we will soon be able to prove that he had nothing to do with the murder of Melodie Brainard and in fact was a victim of murder himself."

"He didn't screw up the quote, at least. Swear to God, Court, I didn't know Jolie was going to say that. It's probably why she was so nice to Tuttle in the first place—she even told me it goes both ways, the press using the celebrities and vice versa. I really didn't think much about it at the time, but I believe I see your problem. If they're right and there is a murderer out there, Jolie just invited him to go after them. Damn."

"It's Jade's fault. Her idea, I just know it. Teddy could never do anything wrong, not according to Jade. Christ, Sam, I don't want to believe he murdered that woman. I *liked* Teddy. But facts are facts. Did you read the rest of the article?"

"No, not yet," Sam said, sitting down at the table. "Thanks," he said, accepting the cup of hot coffee Court put in front of him. "I really don't know much more than what Jolie and her sisters told me. I left you in London, crashed at home, got to the office, saw the clippings my secretary had put on my desk and took off for the cemetery. Everything that's happened since then has been sort of a blur, to tell you the truth. Teddy Sunshine raised three very determined daughters. Should I read this or do you want to fill me in on the official version?"

Court held up a hand to hold Sam off as he took a drink of his coffee. "One more cup of this stuff and I might have been able to fly here without the plane. All right, the capsule version, most of it found on the *Inquirer*'s Web site while we were waiting for clearance at Heathrow. Teddy had been harassing the Brainard's for about three weeks. Calling, dropping by the Brainard estate unannounced and even stalking them at campaign events. The wife, mostly."

"Campaign stops, because Joshua Brainard is running for Mayor. And now he gets to cash in on the pity vote, I imagine, since I can't see him dropping out of the race," Sam said, thinking about the murder of Melodie Brainard seriously for the first time. "Wow, I'm a cynic. Who knew?"

"You're talking politicians now, Sam. When it comes to politics, you either become a cynic or you're just not paying attention. In any case, security cameras on the grounds recorded Teddy showing up there the night of the murder-slash-suicide. The cameras caught him arriving, leaving, but not in between because the security camera out at the pool was mysteriously nonfunctional. That's where they found Melodie Brainard, remember, strangled and facedown in the swimming pool."

Sam sat forward in his chair. "So the murder itself wasn't recorded? The cops can't know for sure that Teddy killed her—just that he was there that night?"

Court nodded as if conceding the point. "But the cameras were working everywhere else, Sam. Teddy was the only person to show up on any of the tapes that night until Joshua Brainard arrived home from some political prayer meeting in the city and discovered his wife doing the dead man's float."

"Nice, Court. You've got a really sympathetic way of saying things. But I can see how the cops would be so ready to pin the murder on Teddy."

"Right. And then Teddy goes home, gets royally plastered because of what he's done and then eats his gun. Oh, and something else, Sam. Melodie Brainard struggled, so there were marks on her body. There were also bruises on his body, and you don't get bruises in a suicide. Case closed."

"Of course it is, Courtland, in your closed mind," Jade said from the doorway.

Sam turned around quickly, wondering if he should be giving instructions about a three-knock-down rule and retiring to neutral corners, but Jade didn't seem in a huge hurry to actually come into the room.

Court was on his feet now, but he made no move to close the distance between his ex-wife and himself. "I'm sorry about Teddy, Jade. I got here as quickly as I could after Sam called me."

"Sam should mind his own business," Jade said. "And so should you, Court. But as long as you're here, let me fill you in a bit on what's not in the newspapers and is being ignored by the police. One, if the cameras were not working in the pool area, anyone could have come and gone without being seen, not just Teddy—who was seen, and who had to know there were surveillance cameras as part of the security at the Brainard mansion. My God, Court, he was a cop."

"Unless he hadn't gone there planning to kill her and it was a crime of passion," Court shot right back at her, surprising Sam with his quick—and polar opposite—interpretation of the facts.

"Highly unlikely. Unless you're suggesting that Teddy and Melodie Brainard were having an affair—and if you are, I'm wasting my time here, because you should be on a couch somewhere, having your head examined."

"Gosh, I can't see how you two lovebirds ever broke up," Sam said, buttoning his shirt. "You get along so well."

"Shut up, Sam," Jade said without taking her eyes off Court. "Two, the Brainard house backs up on a wooded area and a creek, and there is no fence, which means the cameras out front could have been avoided with little problem. Which makes me think the cops should have been looking closer to home for her murderer—someone who knew the camera was broken or maybe even broke it himself."

"Oh, wait," Court said, holding up his hands. "Don't tell me you're going to start stalking Joshua Brainard at his rallies, accusing him of murdering his wife."

"Hardly. But we are going to take a close look at our fair-haired candidate. And three, Teddy had no scratches, only bruises. Melodie Brainard might have put up a fight, but there were no skin scrapings beneath her fingernails. She put up a fight, Teddy put up a fight—as best he could if he was drunk and his attacker was a much stronger man. Teddy had arthritis in his hands, Court, and there were days when he had trouble making a fist, let alone pulling a trigger—or strangling a relatively young, strong woman, an athlete who swam every day. Oh, and one more thing, Court. Where's Teddy's motive? Not even the cops could come up with a motive that made any real sense, which is why they kept calling him *distraught* and *unhinged,* like he was some sort of mad dog. Not that you care about any of that."

"Ball's in your court, Court," Sam said, unable to resist. What the hell, as long as he was going to have a full house, he might as well enjoy himself. Ah, and here was Mrs. Archer, carrying in some of their breakfast. "Good morning, Mrs. Archer. How was your evening?"

The older woman answered as she shifted her gaze from Court to Jade and then back again, obviously not unaware of the tension in the room. "Fine, er, just fine, Mr. Becket, thank you. I'll…uh, I'll just take this back in the kitchen for now."

"Good idea," Sam said, pushing back his chair. "I'll join you. Fight nice, children, and remember that this was my great-grandmother's china, please," he warned as he grabbed his coffee cup and made his escape. He was immediately sorry for that last little bit that he'd added, thinking back to Jade's closet, but there was nothing he could do about that now. Later, he'd tell Court about the Belleek and let him handle it.

Sam sat at the large counter and ate the bacon and eggs Mrs. Archer served him, making calls to his office and showroom to give a few orders and say he would not be in but could be reached on his cell. It was still too early to phone Angela Pearson, but he could at least try to track down her address and phone number. "I'll be in my office, Mrs. Archer. And thank you, everything was delicious."

"Yes, sir. Should I take food into the dining room now, do you think?"

"Good question. I'll go check and get back to you, since I don't think hazardous-duty pay is figured into your salary."

He headed back through the large butler's pantry to the dining room and pushed open the swinging door an inch, listened. When he didn't hear either raised voices or the smashing of china, he figured it was safe to enter the room. Court was alone, nursing his cup of coffee. "Jade left?"

"She went out for a run," Court told him. He shook his head. "I haven't seen her in a year or more, and we just took up where we left off, sniping at each other. I can't even tell her I think she made some sense, ticking off her reasons the way she did, because she not only wouldn't believe me, she wouldn't listen to me in the first place. She's going to move back to the house, by the way, so that I can stay here with you, she said. I think she believes this place is now contaminated by my presence. I'd kiss it all off, go home to Virginia, but that won't solve anything. Do you mind if I bunk in with you, at least for a few days? Or I could just go to the hotel."

"I hear the Becket Hotels are pretty decent," Sam said, grinning. "But it's a big house, Court, and I did call you. Let me tell Mrs. Archer the coast is clear, and while you eat we can talk about something Jolie and I saw yesterday. Something I think you need to know."

Forty-five minutes later, with a damn worried-looking Court installed in one of the guest rooms, planning to take a shower and catch a nap until noon, Sam at last headed for his office to search for Angela Pearson's phone number.

Jolie had beaten him to it. He entered his office

to see her sitting at his desk, rummaging through his Rolodex.

"I have my little black book computerized now," he told her, smiling as she visibly jumped in the chair at the sound of his voice. "You'd want to look under B, for Babes."

"Very funny," she said. "You did say B, didn't you—for Bimbos?"

"Court's here," he told her, figuring they'd taken the B joke as far as it could do without getting into dangerous territory. "Jade saw him and she's decided to move back to the house."

Jolie pulled a face that, on her, was rather appealing. "Is that a good idea? You sort of spooked me with that talk about the alarm code and the bad guy returning to the scene of the crime."

Sam reached past her and woke up his computer. "And I sort of spooked Court when I told him about the Belleek. I don't know how he's going to handle that one, but since neither of us knows how to keep Jade from doing what she wants to do, we've agreed to put Bear Man outside your father's house in my SUV, to watch the place."

"Carroll?" Jolie tipped her head to one side, a habit she had when she was considering something. "That seems a good solution. But he can't be on duty all day and all night. Even bears sleep sometime in the summer, don't they?"

"Bear Man told me not to worry. He's already

called one of his friends to take up the slack. I'd ask him who the guy is, but then I might have to worry. Plus, Court's probably going to stick close to Jade, even if she threatens him with a Taser."

"I don't think she has a Taser. Isn't that illegal, for civilians to own Tasers? But I do know she carries pepper spray. And her gun, of course."

"Of course. We might want to warn Court to pick up a bulletproof vest. Get up, Jolie, please, and let me check my address book. I might still have Pearson's number somewhere from when we were on the library board together. He's old money, and old money is both ex-directory and stays where it is, so I doubt he's moved."

Within the hour they were in Sam's car and heading for Bryn Mawr. Jolie had downed a glass of orange juice and a single slice of whole-wheat toast before her longing looks at the platter of bacon pushed Sam into wrapping two pieces in a napkin and taking them with them.

She was munching on one of those pieces now and making rapturous sounds with each small bite. "I haven't had bacon in months. Well, not real bacon. You ever eat turkey bacon, Sam? Trust me—it's an experience devoutly to be missed."

"I don't want to push, Jolie, and you look great. But do you ever eat? I mean just pick something from a menu because it appeals to you and then eat it?"

"No, Sam, I don't. The camera zeroes in on any extra ounce. And I can't begin a shoot as a size two and end it as a size four, now can I? I've told Rose—my agent—to try to find me a role where I have to gain weight. But, for the most part, only men get parts like that—DeNiro, Tom Hanks. For women, they prefer to use padding. I'm healthy, Sam, I really am. And I'm usually not tempted by bacon and pizza because I try to stay away from occasions of sin and just graze the salad bar."

"I understand sex works off a bunch of calories," Sam suggested, sneaking a look at her while they were stopped for a red light.

"Let me take a wild guess here. You're volunteering your services, right?"

"What can I tell you? I'm generous that way. Okay, only a few more blocks and we'll be there. Do you have a plan, Sherlock?"

"Not really, Watson," Jolie said, sighing. "I wanted to ask Jade how I should do this, but she'd already packed and taken off before I got to her. How bad was it seeing Court?"

"She left, didn't she?"

"True. It's so sad, Sam. They really loved each other. But Court couldn't stand that she insisted on working with Teddy even after they were married. Court in Virginia all week, Jade flying back and forth to Philly? And when she got shot at, Court gave her an ultimatum—him or the detective agency."

"And she chose the detective agency, I know."

"I think now that she chose Teddy," Jolie said as he eased the car around a curve in the narrow macadam road and then turned in between two stone pillars. "I think Jade believes she had a responsibility to him. Maybe even felt she should be around to protect him. Mom really screwed us all up there for a while when she left. But Jade most, I think."

"And Court never should have given her an ultimatum," Sam said, pulling the key from the ignition. "I don't think Beckets are really good at compromise."

"No," Jolie said, blinking at him. "I don't they think are." Then she turned away, looking up at the large fieldstone Colonial that could have slept Washington and all of his troops. "Ready?"

"As I'll ever be," Sam told her, opening the door and stepping out onto the patterned concrete driveway he believed to be a bad match for the old fieldstone. Jolie joined him at the front door, standing just behind him as he rang the bell.

He could hear the chimes. "Lara's Theme" from *Doctor Zhivago*. That was fairly pathetic.

"Yes?"

Sam looked at the middle-aged woman in the maid's uniform as the door was opened. "Good morning," he said pleasantly. "Samuel Becket to see Mrs. Pearson."

The maid looked past him, toward Jolie and her huge, concealing sunglasses. The no makeup and simple ponytail were other nice touches. But he, for one, would have recognized her in an instant. Then again, he could recognize her in the dark.

"And my associate," he added. "We don't have an appointment, but I did phone earlier. Mrs. Pearson is expecting us."

"Then please come in," the maid said, stepping back from the door. "Mrs. Pearson is out at the pool. If you'll follow me?"

Jolie leaned close to him as they trailed the maid through the foyer and down a wide hallway lined with paintings. "Your *associate?*"

"I don't think the name Sunshine would have gotten us through the door."

"Oh. Right. Would you look at these paintings? So many—and they're huge. It's like a mini art gallery. Lots of money here worth killing to get, Sam."

"And very little taste, unfortunately," Sam told her, eying the paintings as they walked past them. "A quick lesson, Jolie—big doesn't always mean better."

"I get a lot of spam e-mail that says differently," Jolie told him, giving him a soft shove with her shoulder. "Sorry, couldn't resist. I'm really nervous. We probably should have planned what we're going to say. You know, a script? I'm good with scripts."

"Just follow my lead," Sam told her, squeezing her hand for a moment as the maid stopped in front of a set of French doors leading out into the sunshine once more. "Thank you, we'll take it from here," he told her and then waited until the maid nodded and walked away.

He opened the door and motioned for Jolie to precede him and then joined her on the patterned cement expanse that seemed to reach from one end of the house to the other. Someone must have gotten a good discount on cement, he supposed, and then remembered that the Lutton family owned a large cement company. Which still didn't make it right, Sam decided, also deciding that he was a bit of a snob when it came to maintaining a house most probably built in the early 1800s.

He and Jolie walked down the wide expanse of steps to the large pool and then waited until Angela Pearson finished swimming a lap and gracefully pulled herself up on the pool surround. She knew they were there—her body language told him that—and he barely resisted a smile as she carefully removed a tight-fitting racing cap and shook her black hair free to fall around her shoulders.

"A candidate for skin cancer if I ever saw one," Jolie muttered, for Angela Pearson's skin was a deep bronze. "If she's forty-five now, by the time she's fifty-five she'll have skin like a lizard. And, yes, I'm being catty. I don't know the woman, but I don't like her just on general principle. So there."

"Well, as long as you're thinking like a private detective and not subjectively," Sam teased her, and Jolie sniffed, adjusted her overlarge sunglasses. "Mrs. Pearson? Angela?" he then called out, rounding the side of the pool, his right hand extended. "Samuel Becket. So good of you to take time out of your morning to see me."

Angela took his hand and allowed him to pull her to her feet before smoothing her hands down the sides of her French cut white bathing suit that was more than considerably see-through—which the woman had to know. "How could I resist," she said in a smoker's deep voice, "when you sounded so mysterious on the phone. Let me slip into my wrap—I feel absolutely naked standing here with you two all dressed like that."

"*Definitely* don't like her," Jolie whispered. "And I *am* being objective. There's not a female in America who would like this woman."

Sam wondered briefly if Jolie ever thought that other women might hate *her* because she was beautiful, talented and a movie star. But he knew that wasn't true. Jolie was real, for all that she was a star, and people liked her. They'd probably like her even more if they knew how insecure she was, how unaware of her beauty—and, more than anything, how she probably hadn't been able to scarf down a hot fudge sundae in five years.

"There, much better," Angela said, having tied a pink-and-black capelike thing at her waist, leaving little of her breasts to the imagination—or the fact that the pool water must be cold this morning. "It's been years, Sam, since I've seen you, and then only in passing at one event or another. And you haven't introduced your companion. Odd, she looks familiar...oh! Jolie Sunshine! Sam, you brought *her* here? How could you do that? Haven't I been put through enough?"

Sam put out his hand to hold Jolie back, but Jolie didn't move. Nor did she say anything. That probably wasn't good, because when she did let loose—which he was pretty sure she would if Angela Pearson kept up her little game—he'd be stuck with the job of referee. Some men might enjoy a catfight, but he wasn't one of them. He was probably getting old.

"Been put through enough, Angela?" he asked, following the now flouncing woman to a nearby round table and chairs shadowed by a large umbrella. "Are you referring to Jolie's father? We know he paid a call on you a few weeks ago."

Angela reached for a pack of cigarettes and a silver lighter that were on the table and lit up, blew out a thin stream of smoke before answering him. "Twice a year for, what, a dozen years? If he'd only kept his *visits* to spring and fall, I'd know when to adjust the clocks for daylight savings time. The man was *obsessed*. Didn't surprise me a bit that he killed poor Melodie if he was hounding her the same way he hounded me. I'm just lucky he didn't kill me. He was insane, just like the papers said," she ended, looking at Jolie. "There's no other explanation."

"He was investigating the disappearance of your husband's former fiancée," Jolie said, speaking at last, and Sam relaxed, pleased to hear her even tone. "If you did nothing wrong, you had nothing to fear, did you?"

Okay, Sam thought, he was pleased at first. Now he wasn't so sure he should have relaxed so quickly. "What Jolie's trying to say, Angela—"

"Jolie can say for herself," Jolie said, cutting him off. "As you may have read in this morning's newspaper, my sisters and I are conducting our own investigation into our father's death. That includes, Mrs. Pearson, tidying up after him, tracing his movements in his last weeks, during which time he was catching up on the old, unsolved cases he continued to work in his spare time. Among others, he visited you."

"There's nothing unsolved about Cathleen Hanson's disappearance," Angela said, fidgeting with her cigarettes, carefully rounding off the lit tip in the ashtray. "She left David at the altar. He was devastated. I thought he'd had a lucky escape, frankly."

"And you were there to console him. Some might say that was lucky for you."

"I don't think I like your tone, Ms. Sunshine. Cathleen Hanson was a gold digger, plain and simple. Certainly not one of us. My God, she worked as a waitress. Slinging hash! Personally, I believe she finally realized that she was out of her league the night of the rehearsal party. No one actually *shunned* her, but it had to be obvious to her that Mother Pearson and others were not pleased with her. So she cut her losses and ran. Taking two extremely expensive pieces of jewelry with her. That necklace has been in the Pearson family for over one hundred years. We got it back, of course, but I can't ever wear it. It would upset David. Cathleen cheated me of that necklace."

"And yet you were going to be her maid of honor."

"Yes, Ms. Sunshine, I was, at Mother Pearson's request. Jesus, did you think we could have one of Cathleen's waitress friends standing up for them? There are limits, you know." Angela crushed the cigarette in the ashtray and immediately lit another one. "I tried to be her friend, I truly did—for David's sake. But Cathleen was cold, hard. She rebuffed my every overture."

Sam was pretty sure they were listening to revisionist history, a juggling of facts that flattered Angela and condemned Cathleen. "You know, Angela, I was reading the file Teddy Sunshine kept on the case and I noticed something odd. Cathleen left without her clothes, her toiletries, without anything but the clothes on her back, it would seem. Don't you find that to be a bit strange?"

Angela snorted—not a flattering habit. "Are you kidding? Why would she want any of those *rags* she wore, insisting that David not buy her a thing until after they were married. She played the little shop girl so well, she really did. Butter wouldn't melt in her mouth, as my mother would have said. And then she pawned the ring he gave her and the necklace and then she left town ten thousand dollars to the good. A pittance, but it must have seemed a fortune to someone like her."

Jolie took off her sunglasses and laid them on the tabletop. "Teddy's report says you were the last person to speak to her before she disappeared."

Angela rolled her eyes. "She *left*, Ms. Sunshine. She did not disappear. I can see I will be forced to either have you escorted out or else answer your questions so you just go away. Very well, Ms. Sunshine—Jolie. Yes, I may have been the last person Cathleen spoke to, at least on the telephone. David was quite angry with Mother Pearson that night—the night of the rehearsal dinner. She wouldn't speak to Cathleen, really wouldn't acknowledge her at all, and everyone noticed. It was very uncomfortable. There were whispers, giggles. And David kept drinking."

"He got shit-faced," Jolie offered, and Sam coughed into his hand to hide his smile.

"He was rather drunk, yes," Angela said, putting out her second cigarette. This time she did not light another one. "Cathleen begged him to go home with his mother and to try to come to some sort of understanding with her and then she left. I personally called for a cab for her when she refused my brother's offer to drive her back to her apartment, which just proved how ungrateful she was, as Timothy certainly didn't have to offer any such thing. Later, I phoned her to see if she was all right, and she said she was. It didn't matter that I despised her on general principle, I was raised to be polite. The next morning she didn't show up for the wedding. End of story. Except for your father."

"How very strange, Mrs. Pearson," Jolie said as the maid who'd let them in arrived with a tray holding three glasses and a pitcher of iced tea. "I can't see why Teddy continued to visit you twice a year. What on earth could you tell him that you hadn't already told him? For instance, what did Teddy ask you this last time he approached you?"

The top of the lighter snapped shut after Angela lit her third cigarette. "If it was just me, I wouldn't have cared so much, I suppose. But he kept asking me about Timothy and about David. Wasn't Cathleen a beautiful young woman? he'd say. Was your brother being kind, offering to take her home, or was he perhaps smitten by her? *Smitten!* Who uses that word? Oh, and how did I feel knowing that David had just set up a scholarship at the University of Pennsylvania in Cathleen's name? That's when I demanded that he leave."

"Your husband set up a scholarship in Cathleen's name? Just this year?" Jolie asked, leaning forward to rest her elbows on the tabletop. "Wow, that had to bite. Here you are, the wife, unable to wear the family diamonds—and your husband is still pining for his vanished bride."

"And that's where you'd be wrong. Your father had the gall to suggest that David's guilty conscience forced him into it. He thought David killed Cathleen because he finally realized she didn't fit in our world and she wouldn't go away quietly. Timothy can tell you, he was here when your father showed up with his latest preposterous theory. Timothy threw him out—and good riddance to bad rubbish, as my mother would have said."

"I wonder, Mrs. Pearson—Angela," Jolie said, almost purred, so that Sam considered the implications to his hopefully macho image if he ducked under the table to protect himself. "Here you are, the woman who consoled him, the woman who married him—and I'll just bet Mama Pearson danced a jig at that wedding. At any rate, and this is what I'm wondering—which would bother you most? That your husband might have murdered Cathleen, or that a dozen years later he still loves her?"

"We're through here," Angela said, getting to her feet. "It's enough that I've given you this much of my time. You couldn't understand how people like us live, how we react. You're his daughter and now nothing but one of those horrible, trashy Hollywood liberals. And Samuel? I will never forgive you for this. Never. You're supposed to be one of us."

Sam got to his feet. "I know, Angela. But I think I got traded to the other side when I wasn't looking. Say hello to David for me. Oh, and by the way? That Sir Joshua Reynolds I saw in your hall gallery? It's a reproduction."

Angela's eyes widened to the point that Sam thought they might just pop out of her head and roll into the pool. "How dare you say that!"

"I dare, Angela, because the original hangs in my dining room. I've always been very good at detecting fakes. Come on, Jolie, time to leave."

He had to grab Jolie's arm as he hustled her back into the house and through the hall gallery, because she wanted to stop, see the painting he'd mentioned. "Oh, God, that was great, Sam," she kept saying. "Which one is it, hmm? Did you see her face? Oh, I loved it! And that suit! Sitting there with her nipples showing through the material like that? And she knew it. Count on it, Sam, she knew it. And you're not the only one good at detecting fakes—those 38Ds are about as real as her painting. She looked like she had two dimpled cantaloupes glued to her chest."

Finally they were back on the patterned concrete driveway and Sam could push her into the car. "Sit. Stay. Don't talk. I'll be right there."

He jogged around the front of the car and slid into the bucket seat before he could relax, and then began rhythmically tapping a fist on the steering wheel as he let loose his pent-up laughter. "You know, Jolie," he said once he could control himself enough to start the car and drive back out onto the winding lane, "it may have been only our first effort, but I think we've got a lot of room for improvement if we're going to play at private investigators."

"Oh, I don't know," Jolie said, belatedly buckling her seat belt. "Or aren't you feeling pretty sorry for David Pearson?"

"If he murdered Cathleen so he could marry Angela? Definitely. That woman makes life without possibility of parole seem like a dream vacation."

Jolie was quiet for a few minutes. "She didn't tell us the whole truth, you know. About what

Teddy wanted to talk to her about when he last came to visit her. About him blaming David and not her. I'm betting it was the other way around. I'm betting she did it. Killed Cathleen. I think Teddy thought so, too, and that's why he kept coming back, hitting at her from different angles or something. Otherwise, wouldn't he have been visiting her husband twice a year instead of her?"

"If Teddy did think she killed Cathleen, he didn't have any evidence to take to the cops. And then there's the small matter of no body, usually meaning no way to prove there was a crime at all. So that's another problem. *We ain't got no body...*" he singsonged, earning him a fierce look from Jolie. "Sorry, not funny. Would you think it was funny if I told you I lied about the Reynolds? I don't own the original. I know what I saw back there was a reproduction, but I couldn't resist the rest of it, just to hammer it home."

"Samuel Becket, for shame! Nice move," Jolie said, grinning at him.

"Thank you. I think you're a corrupting influence, you know. Where to now, Sherlock? David Pearson's office? Brother Timothy, wherever he is, which is probably at the Lutton family cement business. Mama Pearson? She may have hired a hit man, you know, to protect her little boy."

"I'm not sure. But we have to do something. Jade's called the first progress meeting for tonight at eight, remember? You know Jade is going to have pulled some rabbit out of a hat, and Jessica, too. I know this is about Teddy, but it's also a competition among the three of us, even if I'm ashamed to admit that. We've never done anything that wasn't a competition. It's the only way we know how to react around each other. So I'd like to have something to make my conclusions seem more reasonable than to only be able to say that Angela Pearson is a card-carrying bitch and I hope she's guilty."

"Fine. Let's go see David Pearson. He works in a brokerage office on Market Street."

"No, I don't think so. I'm feeling way too much in sympathy with him right now to be objective. Let's drive by Thompson's Diner instead. I want to get the lay of the land before I go in there tomorrow. If Smitty comes through for me—and I'm sure she will."

"Smitty again. You want to let me in on who this Smitty person is?"

"A friend. A friend who also happens to be a costume designer. She's sending me a disguise so I can go into the diner without being recognized. I'm hoping we'll see a Help Wanted sign in the window. I might even be able to get a job there for a few days if I can't get answers right away. After all, it's not like I didn't sling some hash myself before I got my first part."

Sam slammed on the turn signal with more force than necessary and pulled out onto the highway. "I had to ask…."

CHAPTER SEVEN

JOLIE PERCHED ON ONE of the stools surrounding the large kitchen bar and gnawed on the side of her thumb until she realized what she was doing and quickly lowered her hand to her lap.

She'd been watching Sam as he set out the trays of cold meats and salads Mrs. Archer had prepared for them before retiring to her rooms with the boxed set of Harry Potter movies Sam had picked up for her at the video store.

Sam was a...funny man. Born to wealth she could barely imagine, he was just a regular guy. Well, a regular guy living in a mansion and with a net worth that probably edged into the Fortune 500. She knew, even with her success, she didn't have a quarter of the money he had. She couldn't trace her family back past the day her great-grandfather had stepped off a boat at Ellis Island. But neither of those things seemed to matter to Sam, who certainly didn't put as much importance on family heritage as did Angela Pearson and her mother-in-law.

What had mattered to him, always had mattered to him, was that Jolie wouldn't take a penny from him. She hadn't had to sling hash, shove size-nine feet into size-eight shoes for women who would rather live in pain than admit they had big feet or any of the other things she'd done in order to feed herself while she'd worked toward her big break. She could have taken the money Sam had offered her and made everything easier on herself.

But then she would have had to agree to Sam's deadline. A year, he had said. A year in California and then, if she hadn't achieved what she'd wanted to achieve, she was to come back and they'd be married.

Sam really shouldn't have given her a time limit, whether she'd taken the money or not. A person doesn't put a time limit on a dream. That was starting out already with a ticket home in your back pocket. But he wouldn't understand that. He'd wanted her, had wanted them to be married.

Jolie absently rubbed at her fourth finger, left hand. She'd only worn the engagement ring for a week five years ago and yet still could feel it on her finger. It had been stupid of her to accept the ring in the first place, knowing she had to leave, had needed to leave. Needed to *know* if she had what it took to make it in Hollywood.

Before settling. Jolie shivered as those two words slapped at her. Would marrying Sam have been settling for less? Is that what she'd thought? Was that what Sam had thought? Oh, God...

What had Teddy told her? Something about the path not taken being the major regret of his life? He'd urged her to go, telling her that Sam, if he truly loved her, would understand, that he would wait for her. Boy, talk about being wrong! Sam had not understood, and Jolie doubted that he understood even now. To him, she had turned her back on his love and their future, end of story.

Most importantly, had *she* taken the wrong path five years ago? She had her career, and she loved it, but she wasn't stupid enough to believe there wasn't still a huge hole in her heart where Sam used to live.

"Sam?" she asked before she could think through her thought. "Teddy once told me that the biggest regret he had was not taking some path he'd wanted to take. Don't you wonder what that might have been?"

"That's a heavy question." He put down the ice bucket he'd just filled and looked at her. "We all do—or don't do—things that we regret. Teddy had you girls. He had his career in the police department. If it makes you feel any better, whatever he gave up, I don't think he could have regretted it too much. I always thought he was a happy man. Hawaiian shirts and all. Maybe he once wanted to move to Hawaii?"

Jolie pulled a face. "Teddy had his moods. You didn't know him right after my mother left. Every night he'd sit in the dark living room and stare out the front window at the street as if she was going to come back any moment. Jessica finally brought Rockne home, and I swear, Sam, that dog was the only reason Teddy began to pull out of his funk. Now Teddy's gone, and Rockne's in a funk. Or he was until you brought home that ground-up filet."

"Yeah," Sam said, patting Rockne's head, as the dog barely left his side. "We're BFFs now, aren't we, old boy?"

Jolie laughed out loud. "BFFs? Best friends forever? Where did you learn that one?"

"I shouldn't admit it, but I watch some of those television entertainment magazines now every so often, looking for you. Paris, Britney, Lindsay, Nicole—I know more about BFFs than any sane person should. I thought about joining your fan club, but then I'd need to go into therapy. Jolie?"

"Hmm?" she asked, reaching for a rolled-up slice of ham.

"I was wondering. Where was Rockne the night... you know."

She put down the piece of ham, any appetite gone. "I asked Jade that question. She had been out on a job until nearly two in the morning. She said Rockne was outside Teddy's office door—his closed door—when she got home. He was just lying there looking sad, as if waiting for Teddy to open the door and let him inside. Teddy went to bed every night right after the eleven o'clock news, and Rockne slept in his room. But she could see light under the office door. That's...Jade said that's when she began to shake. She was sure something was wrong. But she was immediately thinking heart attack or maybe a stroke. The preliminary report was that he'd died around midnight."

"And he'd closed the door on Rockne?"

Jolie nodded. "Just the way he did when Jess first brought him home. Those first few days, Teddy wouldn't look at him, wouldn't interact with him. But Rockne wore him down. Teddy was Irish to his marrow, as he loved to say. And the Irish can be melancholy. And thickheaded," she ended, smiling weakly.

Sam pulled out the stool next to hers and sat down. "All right. Let's figure this out. How did Rockne, the inseparable companion, end up on the wrong side of the door to Teddy's office that night?"

"I don't know," Jolie said, frowning. "Teddy was at Melodie Brainard's house around nine o'clock, and only for about five or ten minutes. We know that. He came home. If he came straight home, he was back there before ten. He broke open a bottle and proceeded to get drunk. We also know that. Rockne was always right next to him when he was home—the way he's doing with you right now—but Teddy did sometimes shoo him out of the office when he had clients come to the house."

"Okay. So maybe a client showed up somewhere between ten and midnight? But that would have had to be a drop-in, not a scheduled appointment. Not at that hour. And if he'd had an appointment, Teddy would have written that in his calendar and Jade would have mentioned it to us because the client would have to be a suspect, right? I wonder why Teddy even let the person in, don't you?"

"I hadn't considered all the implications of Rockne being on the wrong side of the door. So, no, I really hadn't thought about it."

"But we need to think about it. I don't like saying this, sweetheart, but it's an election year, and Joshua Brainard has already picked up the endorsement of the Fraternal Order of Police union or whatever it is. Not that Brainard's a bad guy or is trying to pull something. He's a good candidate and will probably make a good mayor. But now think about it. A former cop snaps and begins stalking and finally strangles the candidate's wife and then commits suicide? Who needs headlines like that? But declare the case closed and after a few days of press it all goes away, leaving nothing but the public's sympathy for Brainard. Nice and tidy and all tied up with a bow so, please, let's all stop thinking about it now and get on with electing the fair-haired boy. Everything's political, Jolie, when you get to the heart of it."

"You're starting to believe us, aren't you? That's so sweet." She leaned in, kissed his cheek. "I really do like you, Sam Becket."

"Gosh, Miss Sunshine, I'm your number one fan," he said. "Will you send me an autographed picture for my collection?"

"Wiseass," she said, picking up the piece of ham again. "But you've made some valid points, Sam, and we all should talk about this instead of our separate cases. Especially since we didn't exactly make any progress today on ours. Where is everybody anyway? Jade said eight o'clock, and it's already five minutes past the hour. It's not like her to be late."

"And Jessica?"

"Oh, she's always late. Nothing new there. I just hope they've both had more success than we've had. Well, kind of, because they'll rub it in if they have. Sam?"

"Uh-oh, I don't think I liked the tone of that *Sam. Jolie?*"

She looked at him levelly. "Do we need to talk?"

"I thought that's what we were doing."

"You know what I mean. Do we need to *talk* talk?"

"We might, but that depends. Do you want to— *talk* talk?"

"No, I don't think so. Rehashing the past seems like such a pointless exercise. We might just argue."

"And we're doing so well now," he teased, stroking his fingers down her cheek. "At least we are as long as we talk about Teddy and the vanishing bride. And even about Rockne. We probably even agree on the weather, politics and the Phillies' chances for the play-offs."

"Their pitching tanks as soon as they have to bring in a reliever," Jolie said, trying to smile.

"Wait. The big Hollywood star still follows the Phillies?"

"And the Eagles. I still subscribe to the *Inquirer* just so I can keep up on them. Not the 76ers—not since they traded Allen Iverson—or the Flyers, because I've never understood ice hockey no matter how many times you tried to educate me. West Coast sports fans are strange, Sam. They eat tofu at the ballpark and don't cheer, let alone boo. I love Philadelphia fans. We boo Santa Claus."

"I keep telling you—he was a *lousy* Santa Claus," Sam said earnestly and then smiled. "Hey, you know what? The Mets are in town this weekend, and I've still got season tickets. Whoa— you haven't even seen the new ballpark. It's fabulous, one of the best in baseball. Everything's brand-new, but they still sell cotton candy, I promise. Only this time you can't jump to your feet and cheer, throwing your arms up and shoving your cotton candy into the face of the guy sitting behind you. Do you remember that? God, the look on that guy's face—and he was a Braves fan. For a minute there, I thought I was going to have to play the big protector and take a swing at him and...and I've missed you, Jolie."

She rested her chin on her hand as she smiled at him, her eyes burning slightly as tears stung at them. "I've missed you, too, Sam. A lot."

Jolie's eyes fluttered shut as he tilted his head and moved toward her, her mouth opening slightly as she waited for his kiss....

"Hey, here you two are! Looks like I was waiting at the bus station while my ship was coming in down at the harbor...or something like that. Meaning, I was waiting for everyone in the living room, and you're out here. Oh, great—food. I'm *starving*."

Jolie looked sheepishly at Sam as she said, "Hi, Jess. Help yourself. And you weren't interrupting anything, honest."

Sam grinned at her and picked up his soda can.

Jessica grabbed a slice of seeded rye bread, slapped two rolled-up slices of ham on it, folded over the bread and took a huge bite. "Hmm, heaven. I don't even miss the mustard. Much. Where's the mustard? Where's Jade?"

Jolie looked across the room at the wall clock. "Good question. It's almost a quarter after eight."

"Yeah, and when I get someplace first…well, it's spooky. Thanks, Sam," Jessica said as he slid a can of soda toward her. "How did you guys do today? I pretty much struck out everywhere. Not only couldn't I finagle a camera out of our sister station, I think I might soon be looking for another job. Guess who just got engaged to my big boss's daughter? Go ahead, guess."

"Willie Cartwright's son," Sam said, grinning at Jolie. "I heard it on the news."

"So did my agent. She's shopping me around as we speak. But it still has to be cable news. There's more leeway there for independent thinkers, you know? Well, at some of them, anyway. Good ham."

Jolie shook her head as she looked at her baby sister. "Your life would make a good sitcom, Jess. So what did you do today—other than get shot down?"

Jessica reached into her pocket and pulled out a small top-spiral notebook. She used to carry an elaborate electronic organizer, but when she lost it, she'd felt as if she'd lost her entire life. So now she carried notebooks. "I visited one Karen Morrison, mother of the deceased Kayla, grandmother to Keely. Don't you hate alliterative names like that?"

"Hmm, let's see," Sam said, winking at Jolie. "Jade, Jolie, Jessica. Like that, Jess?"

"Yes, Sam, pretty much exactly like that," she said as she frowned at the first page of her notebook. "By the time I followed the other two to school, my official name in most classes was Jade-Jolie-I-mean-Jessica. There oughta be a law, that's what I say. Especially when Jade and Jolie were such good students and I was...never mind, ancient history. Anyway, Karen Morrison seemed marginally pleased to see me. But Keely? Foul, foul mouth on that kid, let me tell you! She told me to take a blankety-blank hike, that she'd had enough of hearing about her blankety-blank mother, the blankety-blank *ho*."

"Poor kid. It can't be easy having everyone know that your mother was one of the prostitutes killed by the Fishtown Strangler," Jolie said, sighing.

"Yeah? You should have seen her, Jolie. Fifteen going on thirty. Ring through her eyebrow, diamond stud in her nose. I think I would have had to use both hands to count up the holes in her ears. Clothes I think she must have painted on. And she was as full of cuss words for her grandmother as she was for me. The old woman must feel like she's watching history repeat itself and can't do anything to stop it. And I *highly* doubt that's what Teddy had in mind when he tried to help them."

"So you were shown the door?" Sam asked.

"Darn near kicked down the stairs," Jessica agreed, fishing through a dish of nuts for pecans. "All I could get out of Karen—the grandma—was that Teddy had stopped in a few weeks ago, but she was in the hospital at the time for a knee replacement, so he talked to Keely. And Keely wasn't talking to me. What a tough nut, that kid. She could give Willie Cartwright lessons on how to deflect questions. Tomorrow I'm going to try Tarin White's family, if I can find them. You know, Teddy wrote his notes for himself, not anyone else. I can't find an address anywhere, just the name Tarin White and a date—again, about three weeks ago. He was a busy man that week, but there was nothing else added to the file to show he was still working on it. Just those two names, Kayla and Tarin. So that's it for now. Jade *really* should be here. Oh, hi, Court. Have you chased Jade away entirely?"

"Why? Where is she?" Courtland Becket entered the kitchen, and the air, to Jolie's mind, became instantly charged with tension. Court was an intense man, no question. She didn't really know much about him, as she'd already been in California when he and Jade met through Sam somehow, and there had been no real wedding. Court's home was in Virginia, Jade's was here, and they'd decided the easiest way to handle everything was to just fly to Las Vegas and be married there. Jolie had been in Chicago at the time anyway, filming, so some old lady in a Priscilla Presley bouffant hairdo had stood up for Jade, and Elvis had married them as they'd stood under an arch made up of two huge guitars.

The quick courtship and Vegas wedding had been totally out of character for Jade, and Jolie was pretty sure Courtland Becket was more the traditional type, as well. Jolie had figured that she should have known then that the marriage was doomed. Marry in haste, repent at leisure. Break your engagement, repent at…

"Jade moved back to the house, Court," Jolie said, trying to cut off her wandering mind, which was really beginning to get on her nerves. "You know, you were in the living room, we were in the kitchen? Maybe she figured that our eight-o'clock meetings would now be at the house instead of here." She slid down from the stool. "I'm going to phone the house."

"And I'll call her cell," Jessica said, tossing one more pecan into her mouth.

But Jade didn't answer either call.

"Sam?" Jolie asked, beginning to have that funny feeling in her stomach that warned her something was wrong. "Let's go over there and—"

"Already on our way," Sam said, holding up his car keys. "But don't go thinking wild thoughts, everyone. Bear Man is there, remember?"

Everyone piled into Sam's sedan, and it was a quiet but quick drive to the Ardmore house. He pulled onto the street, and Jolie could see the black

SUV parked about three houses down from Teddy's. "Is that Bear Man?"

"That's him." Sam pulled in behind the SUV and they all got out and walked over to the vehicle, Sam heading for the driver's-side door and Jolie right behind him. "Bear Man?" he said, knocking on the deeply tinted glass. "It's Sam. Open up."

Nothing.

"Sam…" Jolie whispered, already poised to run for the house.

"Hang on." Sam held up his key ring, selected another key and slid it into the lock. When the door opened, Bear Man moaned as he began to slide out of the front seat. "Shit!" Sam spat, bracing himself to catch the unconscious man and push him back onto the seat. "Court! Check the house—now!"

"This is my fault, this all my fault," Jolie said quickly, her heart pounding as she chased Jessica and Court down the sidewalk and across the lawn to the house.

Jessica already had her key out of her pocket and pushed Court aside to insert it in the front door lock. "Jade! Jade, where are you!" she yelled as Court then pushed her to one side and entered the dark house ahead of her.

"I smell smoke," Court called out as he turned into the living room. "Somebody call the fire department! Jade! *Jade!*"

"I'll check upstairs," Jessica said, already

heading for the stairway as Jolie switched on the lights. "You check the kitchen."

"Go, Jolie," Sam said from behind her. "I'm already on with 911."

"Carroll?" Jolie asked quickly, her feet seemingly frozen to the spot as she hoped the man wasn't dead. She'd thought she'd heard a moan, but she could have been wrong. And if Carroll was dead, then…

"…and the fire department," Sam was saying into his cell phone. "My name is Samuel Becket and—he's okay, Jolie—yes, ambulance, police and fire. That's right, the whole nine yards. Yes, I'll stay on the line." He held the phone away from his ear. "Where's Court?"

"*Here!*" Court yelled as he emerged from Teddy's office carrying a limp Jade. "She was behind the door. I didn't see her right away. Fire's out, but I think the smoke got to her."

"Omigod, Jade!" Jolie, the fear that had momentarily paralyzed her now shooting adrenaline into her every muscle, raced after Court as he carried Jade outside and laid her on the grass. "Is she breathing?"

Sam and Jessica were standing beside her now, all of them watching as Court straightened Jade's limbs and then tipped back her head. He inserted a finger into her mouth and moved it around as if checking that her mouth was empty.

"CPR—right," Sam said, dropping to his knees

on the other side of Jade's body. He laid his crossed hands on her chest below her breasts and looked at Court. "I'll take the compressions, you do the mouth-to-mouth. On my count…"

Jolie and Jessica could do nothing but hold on to each other and watch as the two men worked over their sister.

"My fault," Jolie said again. "If I hadn't opened my big mouth and let Gary Tuttle broadcast it everywhere that we were investigating…"

"Shut up, Jolie," Jessica warned her, giving her a squeeze. "We knew what we were doing. We thought we knew what we were doing…."

Jolie could hear the wail of sirens in the distance, and Jessica ran to the curb to flag down the EMS ambulance that was the first official department to arrive on the scene.

"She's not breathing!" Jolie and Jessica both shouted to the uniformed people tumbling out of the ambulance. "Hurry, she's not breathing!"

"She's breathing," Court said as Jade flailed her arms and coughed. He helped her roll onto her side, and she began to vomit onto the grass. "That's the girl, Jade. You're going to be all right."

Then Sam had Jolie held close against his side, and she could only watch as the emergency workers took over. "You heard Court, sweetheart. She's going to be fine."

But Jade didn't look fine. After the longest ten

minutes of her life, Jolie watched her older sister being lifted onto a gurney, an oxygen mask on her face. There were IVs in both of Jade's arms, and her hands were wrapped in gauze. EMS workers held the tubing and bags high as everyone moved in a sort of controlled chaos toward the ambulance.

Jolie and everyone else moved with them, close behind, and Court made to climb into the back of the ambulance.

"Sir, we can't allow you to—"

"I'm her husband, and you damn well can," Court answered tersely before turning to Sam. "I'll phone your cell as soon as I know anything more. She's all right. She's all right." The doors closed with him inside the ambulance. Lights and sirens were next, and then Jade and Court were gone, and everyone turned to look at the house and the fire personnel hauling a huge fan through the doorway.

"Excuse me? You're Jolie Sunshine, aren't you? The movie star?"

Jolie impatiently looked to her left to see a tall, slim sandy-haired man of about forty or maybe more approaching across the lawn. He wore his hair parted on the left and shaggily short, exposing a permanently furrowed brow above piercing gray-blue eyes. His cheeks were defined by the slashes that traveled from the sides of his nose to the corners of his mouth, and his top lip was topped by a near dent just below his nose. He had a small scar that ran across his chin that seemed to complement a rugged, all-man face. He wore a dark blue suit, a white shirt, a really ugly tie and a chain around his neck that ended in a leather square with a gold shield pinned to it.

If she were casting a movie, she'd hire him in a minute to play the jaded, world-weary cop. Even if the badge hadn't been a dead giveaway.

"Yes, I'm Jolie Sunshine. This is my father's house."

"I know, I was here before, a few days ago. Lieutenant Matthew Denby, Homicide," he said, extending his right hand. "How's your sister doing?"

"Homicide?" Jolie looked down the dark, empty street, lit now mostly by flashing red lights. "They say she'll be fine. Can this wait? We really want to go to the—"

"Sam Becket," Sam interrupted, shaking the lieutenant's hand. "I'm a friend of the family. And this is Jessica Sunshine, Jolie's other sister. We haven't seen anything, but we understand there was a fire."

"Yeah, a small one, and Captain Russell tells me it looks like Miss Sunshine managed to put it out before she collapsed. It's still smoky in there, but the damage was pretty much limited to some files that seem to have been piled up on the floor. Any of you know why she'd do that?"

"Oh, for crying out loud." Jessica pushed past

Jolie and went almost toe-to-toe with Lieutenant Denby. "You think Jade started the fire? What, she was going for some Girl Scout badge? Are you *nuts?* And we've got an injur—hey! Sam? Let me go. Where are you taking me? I'm not done with this jerk."

Jolie watched as Sam half dragged her sister to the sidewalk, which is when she noticed that the SUV and Carroll were both gone. She added two and two, made four and wheeled back to smile her best smile at the lieutenant. "My sister's…a little overcome. You didn't really mean that you think Jade decided to have an indoor bonfire of our father's files, do you?"

"I'm sorry, no, that came out wrong. I was trying to ask why she'd risk her life over some old files," Matthew Denby said, rubbing at the back of his neck as he watched Jessica and Sam, heads together, speaking earnestly. "You know, I didn't make the connection. I'm probably the only person in the world who hasn't, but I didn't realize Jessica Sunshine was your sister."

"She's the black sheep. We try to keep her under wraps," Jolie said, dancing as fast as she could as she neatly stepped more fully into the lieutenant's sight line, blocking his view of Sam and Jessica. Sam didn't want the lieutenant to know about Carroll, that much was obvious. But why not? "You said files were burned?"

"Yeah," Matthew said, motioning for her to follow him. "You want to take a look? The fire department's about done. They'll leave the fan with you overnight, to help with the smoke smell, but that never really works. Oh, and please don't touch anything."

"No, of course not. Are you considering this a crime scene?"

"Miss Sunshine, I just happened to be driving nearby when the call went out and radioed in that I'd take it. I'm not in charge of anything. Arson will be out to inspect the place tomorrow morning, I'm sure."

Sam and Jessica had rejoined them by the time they'd entered the house, and Lieutenant Denby stopped to speak with one of the fire personnel for a moment.

"They're going to keep someone here for another hour or so to make sure nothing flares up again and then tape the place off," he told them when the fireman left the room, heading toward the kitchen. "Oh, and they're checking the floor joists from the basement. You could have had a real disaster, with all that old, varnished knotty pine in there, but better for the house to burn to the ground than try to put out a fire by yourself."

"Oh, gosh, officer, sir. Thanks so much for such good advice. When Jade feels better we'll be sure to tell her that you think she's an idiot," Jessica said in that too-sweet tone she used while ripping out someone's jugular.

Matthew Denby grinned, a grin that made his eyes sparkle and turned him somehow younger. "That's *Lieutenant, sir,* Miss Sunshine. I know how you reporters like to make sure you get the facts right."

"Is that supposed to be a jab at my profession in general or at me in particular? You said you were Homicide, right? What's the unsolved rate in Philly for homicides, Lieutenant? Any better this year than last year? Or the year before that or the year before that? Because your solve rate stinks, Lieutenant. It might even be time for a *reporter* to take a closer look at why it stinks."

"Well, now I'm scared. I'll warn the Chief that you're coming," Matthew said, and then he turned his back on her.

"Jess, back off, please, this isn't the time," Jolie whispered as they all headed for Teddy's office, Jessica all but stomping as she went. "Let's just get this over with and head for the hospital."

"Sorry, Jolie. I guess I'm a little upset. He's *Homicide,* for crying out loud. If anything bad had happened to Jade—oh, hells bells, would you look at this mess?"

The electricity had been cut off in this area of the house and Lieutenant Denby had borrowed a large flashlight from the fireman. He turned it on full and aimed it at the floor in the center of the room. "Everything's scattered now, and wet, but you can see that what we're looking at are files, probably from that cabinet over there." He swung the flashlight toward the metal four-drawer file, its drawers hanging open.

"Any ideas, Lieutenant?" Sam asked, taking hold of Jolie's hand and giving it a comforting squeeze. If there had been anything of her father left in this room, it had been destroyed now by fire, smoke and water.

"A couple, but they'd only be preliminary and only guesses. I'd say that someone got in here somehow—there's no tampering on any of the door or window locks—looking for something. Maybe some one thing in particular. And when he couldn't find it fast enough to suit him, he decided to just destroy everything. Miss Sunshine was either in the house, maybe upstairs, and our guy heard her and panicked and wanted to get out fast, or she walked in on the fire before it got a good hold on the place and managed to put it out. There's an empty fire extinguisher over there," he said, shooting the flashlight beam toward a discarded red canister in the far corner. "According to the fire chief, another five minutes or so and the whole house would have gone up. At any rate, unless your sister was having a bonfire, you've got an unlawful entry and arson here, that's pretty evident."

"Did Jade change the alarm code?" Sam asked Jolie quietly.

"I don't know," she answered, feeling slightly sick. "Sam, if Jade was in the house and the guy heard her, she could have been killed. Same thing if she walked in on him. As it was, she nearly died. Oh, God, what have we started here?"

"That's a good question," he answered just as quietly. "Lieutenant? Do you have a minute? There's probably something you should know. Jolie here told a reporter yesterday that she and her sisters were going to investigate their father's death, hoping to prove he didn't kill either Melodie Brainard or himself. You might have seen something about that in this morning's *Inquirer*."

"I did," Matthew said, leading the way out of the office. "Let's go outside, shall we? This isn't going to be my case, but I do have a few questions."

"Here we go," Jessica grumbled, following after Jolie. "Get ready for the big brush-off, sis, just like we've gotten before from the local yokels."

Jolie wasn't so sure, although she did have a question for the lieutenant once they were standing on the sidewalk. "Lieutenant Denby? You said you were here before, a few days ago. You meant the night Teddy died, didn't you?"

Matthew winced and rubbed at the back of his neck again, telling Jolie, who had made a study of body language in one of her acting classes, that the man made that move a lot. Probably when he was thinking, maybe when he was getting ready to tell a big lie. She'd have to wait and see which it was.

"I was at the Brainard location when the call came in about Teddy. Since we'd already done a quick on-site review of the tape on the Brainard security cameras, I came right here, yes. I liked your father. He had a reputation as one of the good guys."

"But you helped ram through that murder suicide baloney, right?" Jessica asked him. "Being the primary badge on the scene? And don't look at me like that. We're a cop's daughters, remember?"

"Then you should know that things aren't always so black and white, that there's a chain of command," he told her, beginning to lose his accommodating demeanor.

"Oh? So you *didn't* agree? But you let them get away with it, didn't you? Ramming through that ridiculous murder suicide stuff?"

Matthew looked to Jolie as if to plead *Can't you do something with her?* "No, Miss Sunshine," he said out loud. "I gather evidence, I investigate, I draw conclusions if I can and pass everything along to my chief. But it's up to the D.A. to decide if a case is, well, a case. This one came down from the top, and I mean the very top. Close the book and file it under Solved."

"You don't sound too happy about that," Sam

said, giving Jolie's hand another quick squeeze, probably to warn her to silence. "Is there a reason?"

"I told you—I liked Teddy. We all did." Matthew smiled a crooked smile. "He used to stop in at the precinct wearing those Hawaiian shirts of his, handing out doughnuts and calling us all a bunch of losers, working stiffs. I pulled his old desk, and he once warned me about how the bottom left drawer was stuck shut, which I already knew, and then showed me a trick on how to open it. He told me I still shouldn't put anything in it, not unless I got canned or retired. Then I should put a tuna fish sandwich in it, close the drawer and just walk away, like he did. I liked Teddy Sunshine. He shouldn't be dead. That's all I've got to say."

CHAPTER EIGHT

SAM WAS WAITING FOR Court when he finally returned from the hospital. He poured his cousin a scotch, neat, and handed it to him as they both sat down on facing couches.

Odd. Such a large house, and he lived mostly in this living room and, maybe even more odd, the kitchen. His office, his bedroom. But mostly he worked. He worked when he didn't have to work, would never have to work again and never feel the financial pinch.

If he didn't need to keep himself busy so that he didn't notice that he was so damn alone and Jolie was so far away.

Five years. It felt like a lifetime. It was only a little over a year for Court. If Court looked this bad, how did he look?

Those Sunshine girls sure could age a man....

"How is she?" Sam asked as Court loosened his tie and undid his top shirt button. "When we left the hospital, you still hadn't spoken to a doctor."

"Lied to a doctor, you mean," Court said, taking a sip of scotch. "Jade's sedated because of the pain in her palms. She couldn't tell them I'm not her husband, so I'm keeping up the charade as long as I can. But at least I got to see her doctors. Lungs look pretty good, but there's always a chance of some kind of pneumonia, inhaling smoke the way she did. Some of the burns on her hands are second-degree, although most aren't, and there's a line just beneath the fingers of her left hand that's third-degree. Painful, but she won't need skin grafts or anything. The guy drew pictures of her hands for me. Scars? She'll have some light scarring, maybe, but no loss of function—or so the burn guy told me. What in Christ was she thinking, Sam?"

Sam had been waiting for that question and the anger that accompanied it. "I guess she was thinking that her father's files and her family home were going up in smoke, Court. What do you think she was thinking?"

Court set down his glass and leaned his head back against the cushions and stared up at the ceiling. "I don't know. The same things, I guess. See the fire, put it out. Don't call 911, don't get yourself the hell out of there. Do it yourself because you do it better than anyone else. That's Jade."

"Oldest-child syndrome?" Sam suggested,

reaching for a coaster for Court's glass. Not only was he a lonely, overworked bachelor, he was also turning into a neat-freak Felix Unger. "And Jolie said something interesting. She thinks Jade felt responsible for Teddy. Tonight, while we were hanging out in the hospital cafeteria, she reminded Jessica that Jade is the picture of their mother. Maybe she just began taking up the slack when her mother left and doesn't know any other way now to behave?"

"Did Claudia show up for the funeral?"

"Claudia? The mother's name is Claudia? I didn't know that. Jolie always just says *my mother*. Her mother who left her father. Do you know that story, Court? Because I don't."

Court nodded, sitting front, his elbows on his knees. "It's a soap-opera story. Claudia ran off with Teddy's brother. John? Jake? Something like that. They live on Maui, I think it is." He nodded. "Yeah, I know it is. Maui. Teddy's Hawaiian shirts. I don't quite get the connection, but I'm figuring there is one."

Sam looked into his own glass. "The road not taken," he said quietly. "I guess sometimes while you're still planning and not acting, someone else starts down that road without you. And maybe takes your brother along for the ride. Damn. No wonder Teddy told Jolie to follow her dream. He knew what could happen if you don't. So were the

Hawaiian shirts something he just liked or were they some twisted form of penance?"

"Enjoying that conversation you're having with yourself, Sam?" Court asked, getting to his feet. "I'm heading up. I want to be back at the hospital by seven and then I need to call in to tell my assistant that I don't know when I'll be back."

"I sort of figured that. How will Becket Hotels run without you?"

"I don't actually give a flying—I have good people."

"It's good being the boss, isn't it?" Sam said, trying for some levity. "I don't know why either of us works as hard as we do. We may be insane."

"I've considered that possibility, at least for myself, but then I tell myself it's the Becket work ethic. Ingrained in the genes or something. You should see Becket Hall, that enormous, ugly but still standing pile in Romney Marsh. We've heard some stories about old Ainsley, but I think we've missed a lot."

"Two hundred or more years are a long time. I'd like to hear about our cousin Morgan and what she had to say to you."

"One puzzle at a time, cousin."

"Meaning?"

"Honest to God, Sam, not now. Maybe tomorrow. Tell the girls I'll phone them the moment I see Jade, to report in, or I can just call your cell, as I already know that number. Thanks for waiting up for me, Sam, and for the scotch."

"You're welcome," Sam said, also getting to his feet. "Jolie and Jessica are planning to head out as soon as the malls open to get Jade some clothes. We don't know when the police or arson team will release the house, and everything Jade owns is going to smell of smoke, anyway."

Court reached into his pocket for his wallet. "Here. Let me give them my credit card."

"And have it thrown back in my face? No, thanks, Court. And, hey, before you go?"

Court shoved his wallet back into his pocket. "What? There's something else?"

"I'd say so, yes. There's somebody out there spooked by what Jolie said in this morning's—yesterday morning's newspaper. Trying to burn Teddy's files? I don't think Jade was the primary target, Court. The target was Teddy's files. The girls can't investigate if there's no files, no paper trail to follow, right?"

"So the fire wasn't a warning to back off?"

"I guess it could have been both. But I don't see it. Deliberately burning the files shows they're on the right track, that there is something, someone, out there, waiting to be discovered. I think the house was empty and dark and the guy just let himself in, already knowing the code, and used the files to start the fire he expected to burn the entire house to the ground."

"An accident. He wanted it to look like an accident? I got enough out of Jade before they sedated her to know that she hadn't as yet changed the code and that she'd been upstairs. She'd lain down to take a nap and somehow overslept and then woke up smelling smoke. She didn't see anybody, though she pushed hard at telling me that someone had set the fire and I needed to tell Jolie and Jessica to be careful. So do that, too, Sam. Tell them to be careful."

"Because somebody else killed Melodie Brainard and then killed Teddy to cover his crime. Because Teddy had been at the Brainard house earlier and was a convenient dupe. Is that it?"

"It's all I've got, but, yes, that's it. Christ! Would you listen to me—to both of us? Here we are, two grown men, reasonably successful men, moderately intelligent men, and yet we've climbed aboard the loony train, haven't we?"

Sam smiled. "I'd like to think we're more than reasonably or moderately successful or intelligent, thanks, cousin. But at least we're not the only two passengers on that train. Lieutenant Denby phoned me a while ago. Unofficial, off the record, all that crap, but he wants to talk to us about Teddy's suicide and the fire."

"Who's Lieutenant Denby?"

"Oh, right, you didn't meet him. He was one of the cops on the scene the night Teddy died. In fact, he was also on the scene at the Brainard house. But he could top that. He's also the guy who took over Teddy's desk, had met Teddy and liked him. I don't think the quick closing of the two cases made him real happy. I told him about Bear Man being there tonight, about him being hit with a stun gun."

"So you like this Denby guy?"

"More than Jessica does," Sam said, smiling slightly. "I think the two of them make a lovely couple. If nothing else, he'll be the one she drives nuts, and not us, because we can't let her out on her own anymore."

"So they're going on with this, even with Jade out of commission? Checking up on Teddy's cold cases?"

"That's a rhetorical question, right? Come on, Court, I'll walk upstairs with you. It's been a long day, one way or another."

Sam passed by Jolie's bedroom, his steps slowing, stopping. He called himself a selfish bastard as he raised his hand to knock on her door and then lowered it again. If she wanted him, she knew where he was, right?

And he knew where she was.

The hallway between their rooms was a two-way street.

And modern technology was a marvel. He could have been in California in only a few hours. She

could have been back in Philly in just as many
hours.

Any time. In five years.

Neither of them had made that move, that first
move. Why?

Teddy's death, Jolie's grief, her fear tonight…
outside influences of any kind could not be what
brought them together. Reasons like that couldn't
last.

Especially if she ever learned what he had done
for purely selfish reasons.

His ancestor, this man Ainsley Becket, this
swashbuckling privateer or pirate or whoever he'd
been, had built his house on the rocky shores of
Romney Marsh, and that house still stood. Until
and unless Sam told Jolie what he'd done, any
house they built together, mansion or hovel, on
any shore, anywhere, would be built on shifting
sands.

"At least the cork coasters would float when we
slipped into the sea," he muttered to himself,
pushing open the door to his bedroom suite even
as he began unbuttoning his shirt. He didn't bother
with the light switch, as the moon was full and gave
him more than enough illumination in the familiar
surroundings.

"Sam, is that you?"

His hands stilled on another shirt button as he
looked toward the bathroom, belatedly realizing

that the door was ajar and some of the light in the room wasn't coming from the moon shining in the windows. "Jolie?"

"No, Julia Roberts," Jolie said as he pushed open the door to see her up to her chin in bubbles in the large freestanding marble bathtub he'd bought with her in mind. With both of them in mind. "I thought maybe we could take a run at the tub scene in *Pretty Woman*. You're no Richard Gere, but we could fake it."

There were no lights on in the large bathroom suite, but every fat ivory candle in the room was lit, throwing fantastic shadows on the marble walls, casting a golden glow on Jolie. She'd set the stage, the scene. She'd been waiting for him.

Damn. So much for good intentions.

She looked beautiful, she sounded brittle. Nervous. Her eyes were too large in her somewhat pinched face. And clearly the agenda for the night was: *Forget what just happened. Help me forget, please, if just for now.*

Sam wasn't about to try to reason her out of her plan. Not for tonight, not for just now anyway.

He kicked the bathroom door shut behind him. "I suppose we could do that. Except I haven't seen the movie."

"Oh, too bad. It was fairly G-rated, the original. But that's all right. I'm an actor, and everybody knows all actors really want to direct. I'll direct you. You can start by taking off your clothes. Slowly. I'll watch."

"A nude scene? Richard Gere did a nude scene?"

"Sort of. Both of them. But I think the remake should strive for the NC-17 rating, don't you? Everyone wants more sex these days."

"Everyone has the right idea," he told her, slipping out of his shirt, tossing it in the general direction of the brocade chaise that was positioned in front of the fireplace. Oh, yes, he'd spent long hours planning this bathroom. All with Jolie in mind.

"Very good, Sam. Now the shoes. You don't want to get your slacks all tangled up in them, do you? That's so not romantic. We're doing Richard Gere here, remember, not Robin Williams."

"Robin Williams does nude scenes? Isn't he a little hairy for nude scenes?"

"Just shut up and take off your shoes," Jolie ordered, her hands disappearing beneath the bubbles.

"Fine. And what are you doing?"

"Never mind what I'm doing. An actress has to prepare for her scene, you know. Good...good. Now the socks."

He had a pretty good idea what she was doing. Hiding beneath the bubbles just made the whole thing more erotic as she kept her gaze tight on him, as her features began to soften, blur with arousal.

"Maybe I'll take a shower first," he said just to watch her reaction. After all, he couldn't let her get too far ahead of him. Not that he was too far behind…

"Not funny, Sam. The socks—now."

"Should I twirl them in the air, like a stripper does with her long gloves, and then toss them to the crowd?"

Her eyes had begun to become unfocussed, and he could see her shoulder muscles moving. She was having a good time under those bubbles, and all at his expense. "Mmm. Uh…when did you see a stripper? Only losers go to see strippers."

"That wasn't what you told me the night you stripped for me."

She opened her eyes wide. "I forgot. I don't think I did it very well. I was so nervous."

"I know. That's what made it all so…interesting. Jolie? Can I take my slacks off now? Not that I'm pushing, you understand. I know you're the director."

"Why don't…why don't you come over here, Sam, and stand next to the tub. Let me do it."

"Are you sure?"

"I told you I owed you one."

"You don't *owe* me anything, Jolie."

"Don't make me beg, Sam. Just come here."

He approached the tub and she reached up her right hand, allowing him to help her open his belt, lower his zipper. Her left hand remained below the bubbles.

"Step out of them," she said, her voice rather breathless now. "And your shorts. Come on, Sam, help me."

He helped her. He'd pretty much decided that he'd be a helpful kind of guy tonight. That was his role. For now. But there was still a lot of night left....

She turned sideways in the tub and rose to her knees, looking up at him, lowering her gaze, looking into his face again. Her long, perfect torso was awash in bubbles; the scent of jasmine drifted up to his nostrils. The rose of her nipples and the thought of his mouth on them nearly drove him over the edge.

"I love how you're so golden, Sam. All over. Like a young lion."

"If you're hoping for a roar, you might just get one," he said, trying to control his breathing, among other things.

Her left hand remained below the thick layer of bubbles. She closed her other warm, wet hand around him. Smiled at his instant reaction.

"You like that, Sam? I like it. I...really like it. Uh-oh," she said—purred—the lioness to his lion. "Looks like we're going for X-rated...."

JOLIE SNUGGLED IN THE circle of Sam's arms, waiting for contentment. Hoping for sleep.

Neither seemed in a hurry to come to her.

Physically, she still tingled from their lovemaking. In the tub, playing with the water jets. And then again in this bed, with Sam taking on the role of aggressor.

Mind-blowing sex. They were good together. They'd always been so good together. Inventive. Uninhibited. Two halves of the same whole…or something like that. Bold, fearless. Even shameless.

But something was missing. There was still this hollow place inside her, and a nagging voice that whispered, *You're trying too hard, Jolie.*

And maybe she was. Maybe they both were.

They really should talk about it—whatever *it* was. Whatever they were doing, trying to do, and failing at. Badly. As they had failed once before.

"Sam?"

"Hmm?"

She couldn't do it. Not now. She closed her eyes. "Nothing. Go to sleep."

"You don't want to make love again, do you?"

"No," she said, snuggling closer. "You?"

"God, no. I'm not as young as I used to be, you know. Even now, I could be flirting with a coronary."

"He came and went, very happily," Jolie teased, remembering an old joke. "How's that for your tombstone?"

"Depressing, unless I died at one hundred and two after making love to you in a hot-air balloon over Italy."

"That's nice, Sam. Probably impossible but very nice." Why was she avoiding the inevitable? No moment was going to be any better or worse than this one. "Sam?"

"Yes? I am waiting, you know. I recognize the tone. What's wrong? Are you worried about Jade?"

Again she faltered and gratefully grabbed at the straw he'd offered. "Yes. I know that she'll be fine, but there's a part of me that's still standing frozen in the doorway, watching Court run past me with her limp body in his arms. I don't think it's a vision that will go way anytime soon."

"I'd rather rip off my right arm than say this, sweetheart, but maybe it's time you went back to California. And took Jade and Jessica with you. Jade can recover and…well, Jess always finds something to do. Let me hire someone to look into this—the old files, the fire, all of it."

"I can't do that, Sam. None of us can. We're Teddy's girls and we're going to clear his name. What happened tonight only made me more determined, and I'm sure Jess and Jade feel the same way. But I am scared. I'm not an idiot."

"You should have said you're not a *complete* idiot, so I could say no, not a complete idiot, but you're getting warmer."

"Oh, Sam," Jolie said on a sigh as she pushed herself up against the pillows. "We've really pulled you into a mess, haven't we?"

"Yeah," he told her, sitting up and pushing her still-damp hair out of her eyes. "But it's got its fringe benefits."

There. He'd given her the perfect opening. Now all she had to do was take it.

"Sam?"

"Again with the *Sam,* the tone. Jolie, is this— whatever's bothering you—really something we have to get into tonight or even tomorrow? Don't we already have enough going on here?"

"Yes, I suppose we do. But—"

"No buts, Jolie. It's after three, and we've got to get moving again early in the morning. You'll want to go see Jade and then go shopping with Jess. And Lieutenant Denby is joining us here for dinner."

"He is? Why?"

Sam averted his eyes for a second and then took a breath, let it out slowly. "I never knew what a big mouth I had. I wasn't going to get into this tonight." He shifted on the mattress to look at her in the light from the candles they'd brought with them from the bathroom. "He called here after you'd gone up to bed. It seems that someone from upstairs—Matt's words—is already floating a pretty bizarre idea about the fire."

"What sort of bizarre idea?"

"That Jade set it."

"What!" Jolie wrapped her fingers together and actually beat her clasped hands against her forehead a couple of times. "Dumb, dumb, *dumb!* I never heard of anything so dumb! What's the matter with the police? Where's the loyalty? Teddy was one of them, for crying out loud!"

"I knew you'd handle it well," Sam said, taking her hands in his, lowering them to her lap. "Now just listen a minute, Jolie, okay, because it does make some sort of sense—not that I believe it, so don't glare at me like that."

"But it's stupid. Why would Jade burn down our own house?"

"Ah, sweetheart, but it didn't burn down, did it? The only really lasting damage was in Teddy's office, which was already a mess. And something the police don't know and we probably shouldn't tell them—because it would only help to cement this theory—is that we have all the important files here."

"Stop, I've got it. So Jade loads some old, unimportant files in the middle of the floor, sets them on fire and then saves the day with her mighty fire extinguisher. She calls the cops, says someone broke in, proving Teddy didn't kill anybody, and now someone is worried about what the three of us might find as we *investigate,* and the whole case is reopened."

"Exactly. Except she didn't count on the amount of smoke when she turned the extinguisher on the fire and was overcome, yes. Matt doesn't buy it, but unless they find some fingerprints on the alarm or the file cabinet or somewhere, it remains a workable theory. Oh, you and Jessica have to go down to the precinct tomorrow to be fingerprinted so they can rule you out. Or in, I suppose. God, what a mess."

Another thought hit Jolie, and not happily. "And you wanted all three of us out of here, all the way to California. Knowing what Matthew Denby told you. Sam, you don't buy into this stupid theory, do you? We're talking about Jade here. Smart, strong, tough, sane, dependable Jade."

"Who has a gun, pepper spray and could own a Taser, for all we know. She knew Bear Man was out there, and he didn't see who zapped him through the open car window before closing it with him unconscious on the front seat. We'd all naturally think the bad guy had taken Bear Man out, adding weight to Jade's story that someone else set the fire. And then there's the closet, Jolie. We both saw what she did with that Belleek collection."

"Yes, but that's different," Jolie argued quickly, hoping she sounded confident, because what they'd found in the bottom of Jade's closet still unnerved her. "She was upset and she only destroyed what was hers. She didn't—omigod."

"Omigod what?"

"Nothing," Jolie said, beginning to pleat the sheet as it covered her lap. "Oh, all right. Late last year? After the divorce became final? You probably know how she refused to take a penny of Court's money? Anyway, Teddy called Jess and me and asked if we minded if he deeded the house and the business over to Jade. We didn't mind. We both have our careers. But Jade was working with Teddy, with the office right there in the house. He wanted to make sure she'd be all right financially if anything happened to —Sam, we have to find out who did this. Jade's injured, maybe in more ways than just the burns, I'll agree to that. Reluctantly. But she didn't do this. I know she didn't."

"I agree, sweetheart. I think Matt's also convinced —or at least he's got enough remaining questions to keep looking."

"So do we stop working the cases we've chosen, do you think, and begin to work on who could have tried to burn Teddy's files?"

"Aren't they pretty much the same thing?"

Jolie sighed. "Yes, I suppose they are. I can't think about any of this anymore tonight, I really can't. I should go back to bed."

"I'm not evicting you," Sam told her.

"Oh, Sam, I know you're not," she told him, touching her hand to his cheek as she moved closer to kiss his mouth. "But this thing we have to talk about that we aren't going to talk about now? It's still there, hanging between us."

"Unfortunately, I understand what that means. As long as you don't mean that tonight was a mistake. That anything we've done since you came home was a mistake."

She looked at him for long moments and then slowly shook her head. "We get along so well when we don't talk. When we don't think."

"I know. Good night, Jolie."

She slipped out of the bed, reaching for his terry-cloth robe that they'd brought with them from the bathroom. "Good night, Sam…"

CHAPTER NINE

JOLIE AWOKE AT PRECISELY eight o'clock. Or at least that's when she opened her eyes. She didn't really come awake until several moments later, when her mind kicked in with one word: *Jade*.

She stumbled from the bed, mentally counting on her fingers and coming up with at least five hours too little for her to consider that she'd slept at all, and made her way to the bathroom to stick her head under the shower. Maybe raise her head, open her mouth and drown herself. Anything rather than face another day like yesterday.

Was that being too dramatic? Probably not. After all, she was an actress.

As she soaped her body with a large soft-net shower puff, her treacherous, traitorous mind recalled the previous evening. As mistakes went, last night's had been a real zinger, just like every move she'd made with Sam ever since he'd rescued her from the cemetery.

They were over. History. Hadn't it taken her

long enough and more than enough tears to figure that out? Why was she opening herself up to the same sort of hurt again?

In less than two weeks she'd be back in California, doing what she did. Doing what she loved. And then she'd be off again to Ireland. And Sam would be here. That was the decision they'd come to, it was the decision they'd both lived with for five long years. No contact, no second thoughts.

She'd offered him back his ring and he'd accepted it. End of story.

It was the way it had to be.

And it had hurt. It had hurt so bad. She didn't want that kind of hurt again.

As she toweled off, Jolie suddenly had a memory of an old song she'd heard for the first time in the movie *Love Actually.* Such a sad song, made even more poignant by the brilliant, nonverbal acting of one of her idols, Emma Thompson. Something about having looked at life from both sides now, only to realize that she really didn't know life at all.

"I know enough of it to know I'm making a mess of mine," Jolie told herself as she automatically smoothed moisturizer on her face before pulling a skirt and a sleeveless top from the in-bathroom closet. She slipped her bare feet into a pair of sandals and turned around, to stop dead when she saw Jessica standing in the doorway. "Don't *do* that, Jess! Can't you knock first?"

"I did knock, twice, and then I hung around, very politely waiting for you to come out of the bathroom. You talk to yourself a lot?"

"Not until recently, no," Jolie said as she brushed past her sister and back into the bedroom. "I overslept, I know."

"You've also got a huge box down in the foyer," Jessica told her. "Looks like a care package from La-La Land. What's the matter? Are your friends worried you'll run out of sushi and pesto? I'm more of a cheesesteak gal myself."

Jolie quickly finished pulling up the covers and piling decorative pillows on the bed. Some lessons learned as a child couldn't be unlearned in adulthood, not when struggling in a studio apartment on Oxnard Street in Van Nuys, not when living in a beachfront property in Malibu. "It's here? Terrific. I had a friend send me some costumes and makeup and a couple of wigs. I'm planning to go to Thompson's Diner to talk to people my bride knew, and I don't want to be recognized."

"Well, damn, aren't you the genius," Jessica said, following her sister into the hallway and down the stairs. "Do you think there will be something for me, too? I'm also famous, you know. Maybe only in the tristate area, but I've got my fans."

"You're well on your way to being a legend," Jolie agreed because it was easiest. "Let's go get a knife and cut this thing open."

"Already done."

Jolie turned on the bottom step. "You opened the box? And then acted as if you didn't know what was in it?"

Jessica shrugged. "What can I tell you. I'm a great liar."

"And a snoop." Jolie halted in front of the box. "Wow, big box. Looks like Smitty outdid herself." She reached inside and pulled out an obvious wig box and then two more and zipped open the lids. "Not the blond for you, right? Which do you want to be, Jess, a redhead or a brunette?"

"I *am* a brunette underneath this fabulous color job. A mousy, washed-out one, remember?" Jessica pointed out. "But I've always wanted to be a fiery, sexy redhead. Hand it over."

"No deal. I'm already a brunette, and the blond doesn't appeal to me. It looks like Smitty only sent the three, so the red wig is mine, at least for today. And the blond wig is short, so your style will be completely different. Now put those cases on the table and let's look at the clothes."

Five minutes later Jessica held up the last pair of slacks and sighed. "We could have just gone to Wal-Mart. Here I thought I was going to see some hotshot designer stuff. A little Armani, a little Versace…"

Jolie packed the remaining few items back into the box and stood up straight, pushing at the small of her back. "I don't think you're quite grasping this, Jessica. I don't want to be recognized. I want to blend in, not stand out. Got that? Now how do we get all of this upstairs? I shouldn't have packed it all up again, huh?"

"Don't ask me to lug it up there. I'm the dumb blonde who doesn't *grasp* anything, remember?"

"Only when you see your colorist every four weeks. Once the roots are showing, you're just obnoxious. Come on, Jess, I want to grab a quick something to eat and get to the hospital."

"Mrs. Archer still has some eggs and bacon and stewed fruit under covers in the dining room," Sam said from behind her, and Jolie felt a shock to her system that nearly knocked her off her feet, as she certainly hadn't been expecting it. *It's Sam, it's just Sam,* she told her quivering nerve endings. *Just the guy you had wild monkey sex with for hours last night. Now stop it, don't let Jess see how you're feeling, or she'll pounce all over you....*

"Thanks, Sam," Jolie said brightly. Probably too brightly. "And do you think you can carry this box up to my room? When you have time."

"No problem. Court called a few minutes ago," Sam said as all three of them headed for the dining room. "Jade's being released early this afternoon. She told him to tell you not to bother coming to see her because Court has volunteered to find her clothes to wear home. There's a small mall only about a mile from the hospital. Home being here, by the way. We're all going to be one big happy family again. I'm thinking about putting in for a hotel license, maybe making this house part of the Becket Hotel chain."

"Cute. But don't count on that happy-family part with Jade and Court under the same roof." Jessica laughed as she lifted one of the silver lids on the long buffet. "But I'd pay down cash money to see Court Becket shopping in a mall. Ah, pancakes. You forgot to mention the pancakes, Sam. And with blueberries in them, no less. Yum. There's only four. Jolie, you want some? Please say no."

"You go ahead, Jess," Jolie told her, as she already had designs on some bacon, and maybe some stewed fruit, as long as it wasn't prunes. "You did tell Court that we planned to go shopping for Jade, Sam."

"I did. So you're not as amazed as I am that Jade is allowing Court to help her?"

"I'm trying not to think about it, to tell you the truth. It can only mean she's feeling really helpless. Rockne, no, this is my plate." The setter looked at her as if she were the worst of traitors and padded over to Jessica, his look turning hopeful. "Jessica. Do *not* give that dog blueberry pancakes."

Sam pulled out a chair for Jolie and she sat down, giving him a second look, as he had an inquiring expression on his face, his eyebrows sort of raised. He nodded his head toward Jessica and mouthed the words *Do we tell her?*

Jolie shot a look at Jessica, who was pouring about a cup of maple syrup on her stack of pancakes. She'd kill for Jessica's metabolism. "Tell her what?" she whispered.

"I *hear* you," Jessica said as she put down the crystal pitcher. "Not only that, but I can *feel* the tension in here. What's going on? Well, what's going on that's worse than what's been going on? Because this isn't going to be good news, is it?"

"You do it," Jolie said to Sam and then she concentrated on her bacon as Jessica reacted to the police theory that Jade may have started the fire on purpose.

"They're nuts, right? To believe crap like that? Jolie? What are we going to do about this?"

"I think we're going to talk to Lieutenant Denby about it at dinner tonight. Right, Sam?"

"Denby?" Jessica put down her fork with unnecessary force. "What do we want with him? He's the enemy, remember?"

"He's also about to become your bodyguard, Jess," Sam said as Jolie ducked her head and prepared for the explosion. "Unless, of course, you agree to stop investigating the Fishtown Strangler until some one of us can go along with you."

"The *hell* I am. The *hell* he is." Jessica pushed

back her chair as she glared at Jolie. "And you like this idea? *Traitor.*"

"That was fun," Sam said in some amusement as they waited for the front door to slam in the distance. "Will she be here for dinner?"

"Count on it. Mrs. Archer is a very good cook," Jolie told him. "We might want to warn the lieutenant, though. May I borrow one of your cars, Sam? I want to head over to the diner and maybe talk to some of the waitresses about Cathleen."

"Didn't we just have this argument with Jessica? Nobody goes out on their own, remember? Just give me an hour or two and I'll go with you, okay? Or maybe you'll come with me. I have to go down to the warehouse and check up on some, er, some possible damage to one of the shipments."

"Somebody broke the nose off an ancient Egyptian sculpture or something? Wouldn't that just add to the value?" Jolie asked him teasingly, grabbing a banana from the fruit tray for her mid-morning snack.

"Hardly," Sam said, his hands on his hips as they once more stood in front of the really large box in the foyer. "You know, the accepted story about the Sphinx—if that's what you're thinking about—is that German gunners took off its nose while practicing mortar rounds during World War II."

"I didn't know that," Jolie said, ecstatic that

they were talking, just talking, and not about last night.

"I'm a fountain of useless information. I'm thinking of trying out for *Jeopardy*. Okay," he said, looking at the box, "the guy who brought this used a dolly. Since you're the only dolly in this house— I'll pause now, wait for the appreciative laughter— I think we'll unload the box down here and just carry everything upstairs that way."

"You *are* in a good mood this morning, Sam," Jolie said as she opened the box and pulled out the wig carriers once more.

"Yeah. It seems I got lucky last night."

Jolie didn't know what to say but quickly realized that Sam had said just the right thing, set just the right tone. They'd had a great night, but he wasn't trying to attach any strings to that night, carry them over into today. The tension in her shoulders eased. "And I suppose you're going to go bragging to all the other boys in the locker room after gym class?"

"Nobody does that anymore. It's the Internet or nothing."

"Sam! That's not funny! You've seen what my life can be like. You were there at the cemetery. And at the house when that awful Gary Tuttle— Sam?"

"Uh-oh. If we were in a cartoon, I think I'd be

seeing a light bulb going on over your head right about now. What?"

"Gary Tuttle, Sam. We used him once, we can use him again."

"Fine. Good," Sam said, his arms full of clothing as he turned for the stairs. "We'll use that Pulitzer prize-winning photo journalist, Garry Tuttle. To do what?"

"I didn't know Pulitzer gave a booby prize. And to make the cops back off about this stupid idea with Jade, of course. Jolie Sunshine's Family Victims of Police Harassment. What Price Celebrity? Sunshine Nears Collapse Over Police Bias. I don't know. I don't write head-lines, I just read them. Oh, and there'd have to be a big push in the story about how Jade and Jess and I are getting closer to the truth about the night of the murders—notice I said murders, plural. I should go call my publicist right now. Getting the press, even the sleazy press, on our side will go a long way toward—stop looking at me like that!"

"There's a whole other world out there on the West Coast, isn't there?" Sam said as he dumped the clothing on Jolie's bed. "And then again, maybe not. Politicians do it, the government does it, Wall Street does it. I guess the only difference is in how much tinsel hangs from the story, huh?"

"Probably," Jolie said, feeling somewhat

deflated. "You don't think I'm considering this just for the publicity I'd get from it, do you?"

"No, Jolie, I don't. I think your intentions are great. But, at the same time, taking what we know—and we don't really know it, remember, as Matt made me promise to keep the information confidential—could only push the D.A. into going forward with charges even if he knew they had no merit. You don't want to push the D.A. into a corner, Jolie, or he'll fight back. I think we need to wait until Matt comes to dinner and see if the Jade-did-it theory has been dismissed."

Jolie nodded. "You're right, of course. I guess I'm just so angry that anyone could think that Jade would do anything so stupid as to pull a stunt like that. And I'm really glad Court is here."

"I doubt Jade shares that feeling."

Jolie sighed as she held up the red wig. "He seems like such a nice guy from the little I've seen him. And I think he really cares about Jade. You saw his face when that ambulance guy tried to keep him from riding to the hospital with her. Court was going to plow straight through the guy to get to her."

"He still loves her, Jolie. He gets madder than hell at her, but I know he still loves her. But they're oil and water—or they're both the same combustible chemical. Either way, my best suggestion is that we all stand clear and let the two of them have at it."

"Relationships are so difficult to understand. Movies are easier. There's either a happy ending or there isn't, but at least you understand *why* the ending is happy or sad. Hell, you pretty much know what you're going to get even before you buy your ticket and your bucket of popcorn. Maybe what we all need is a good screenwriter."

Sam stepped behind her, put his hands on her shoulders and began kneading her tight muscles. "Life isn't a script, sweetheart. Sometimes we just have to take a deep breath and jump off the cliff, hoping we have wings."

She turned in his arms. "Why, Sam, that was lovely. Scary, too. Who are we talking about now?"

He'd put his hands on her shoulders again and had begun rubbing the pads of his thumbs against the base of her neck. "Whom do you want to talk about now?" he asked her, his voice low and faintly husky.

Jolie felt herself melting into him.

"And *another* thing. What makes you think I need a babysitter following me a—oops, sorry. This time I didn't knock."

Jolie and Sam looked toward the doorway to see Jessica standing there, a silly grin on her face.

"Not a good time, huh, Jolie? I came back to yell at you some more," Jessica explained. "I'll go now. Carry on, pretend I was never here."

"No, Jess, wait," Jolie said as Sam dropped his

arms to his sides. "I really don't want you out there alone."

"Oh, that's the other thing I was going to tell you. I won't be alone. Bear Man is going with me, riding shotgun."

"Carroll?" Jolie asked, getting a mental picture of the muscle-bound fireplug. "He was hit with a stun gun or something last night, you know."

"I know. So he called one of his wrestler friends to watch the gate today, but since he's feeling better, he said he'd drive me anywhere I want to go. I guess that isn't riding shotgun, is it, not if he's driving? Yeah, well." Jessica spread her arms and grinned. "See? I don't need Lieutenant Denby. I've got Bear Man!"

"And I'm getting a headache," Sam grumbled quietly as he touched a hand to his face.

"What was that, Sam? Never mind, I probably don't want to know. I'm off to fight crime. See ya!"

Jolie took advantage of Jessica's interruption and, not wanting to continue her conversation with Sam, not the way it was going, she quickly picked up the wig and the makeup carrier and headed for the bathroom. "I'll be ready in ten minutes, all right? Don't leave without me."

In the end, it was more like twenty minutes before Jolie headed downstairs in a denim skirt that looked as if it had hit the washer one too many times and a yellow-and-white-striped tank top with a purple dinosaur on the front of it. Her long light brown hair was hidden beneath the short red wig that relied heavily on bangs and forward-turning side curls to mask the shape of her head. Smitty had even sent along flip-flops that didn't quite fit, and trying to keep her toes curled to keep them on her feet actually changed the way Jolie walked.

"Jolie Sunshine—I'd know you anywhere!" Sam shouted mockingly as she joined him on the front step, his sedan already pulled around into the drive.

"Oh, you would not," Jolie said, pushing on her oversize sunglasses. "I wouldn't know myself in this outfit. What do you think of the makeup?" she asked, lowering the glasses to give him a good look.

"A little heavy with the blue eye shadow, don't you think? What happened to your eyes? Where did that blue go?"

"Contacts, Sam. I'm a brown-eyed redhead now. Smitty thought of everything."

He opened the passenger-side door for her. "I'll bet she didn't think about how turned on I am right now, brown-eyed girl." He gave her bottom a playful slap just before she slid into the front seat.

Jolie smiled as she watched him walk around the front of the car to the driver's side. He wore neatly pressed khakis this morning and a knit golf shirt that was a sort of muted orange that set off his tan and his sun-streaked hair. He looked less like an antiques dealer and more like a movie star than half the men she'd played against—at least before they'd hit the makeup chair for an hour.

In a perfect world, some screenwriter would find a way that they could be together and both be happy, satisfied. But it wasn't a perfect world. He had his life here, his home, his business, and her life was in California, playing at make-believe.

And with each day, with each night spent in Sam's arms, the time was counting down to the day she had to leave.

"I don't think I've ever been to your warehouse, Sam," she said as they turned onto the Blue Route and headed toward I-95. "From the way we're going, I'm guessing it's near the airport?"

He didn't answer her.

"Sam?" She looked at him, but he was looking in the rearview mirror. "What is it?"

"It's that Action News van again, as they say on the commercials," he said through tight lips. "Love the commercial, hate having one of those things following me. They came onto the Blue Route with us—or at least that's when I first noticed them. I wondered how long it would be before somebody who saw my photograph let them know where to find me. Us."

"That's why you haven't been to the shop, right? Because you figured someone would run you down there?"

"It gave us at least a day without the media all over us, yes, especially when I knew Bear Man or one of his pals wouldn't let anyone through the gates. And we lucked out last night on the fire call to Teddy's house. Your call now, though. What do you want to do with these guys, Jolie?"

She turned in her seat and looked back at the large white van with the number six painted on it in blue. "I'm wearing this wig, Sam, remember? If they see me like this, I'd have to explain what I'm doing."

"Right," Sam said, depressing the gas pedal as he slipped the car into the left lane at the split that joined with I-95. "Hold on."

Jolie held on. She also closed her eyes. The I-95 wasn't a California freeway. On the California freeways, everyone crawled along at a snail's pace. By rights, motorists on I-95 should do the same thing. Except that they didn't. Passing on the right was considered a sport, and riding the bumpers of idiots who drove too slowly in the middle lane probably classified as an Olympic event.

She opened her eyes just as Sam cut across all three lanes to shoot off one of the exits leading to a service road to the airport. She looked at him, her eyes wide, and noticed the white news van heading past them, still on the highway. The driver hadn't been able to follow them across the highway. "I think you might have a second career as a stunt driver, Sam. That was impressive."

His grin was wicked. "I've got Steve McQueen's *Bullitt* on DVD. The first and still the best car chase ever filmed. I watch it every year. I never get tired of playing that shot of the top of the hill and then— bam—here comes his car, completely airborne."

"I'm going to have to look at your DVD collection. I didn't know you were a movie buff, Sam."

He pulled up to a gate in a high chain-link fence and waited until a uniformed guard opened the gate. "How little you know me. I can recite lines from Shakespeare, too, but that's not something I want to become public knowledge."

"Yes, I can understand that," Jolie said, keeping a straight face with some difficulty. "A man has his reputation to consider. Still, you're a real Renaissance man, Sam. Sports, antiques, art, movies, Shakespeare. I'm impressed."

"You forgot to mention my prowess as a lover in that list," he reminded her, pulling into a parking spot clearly marked *Samuel Becket*. "Now do you want to stay here or come inside with me? I'll only be a few minutes."

"No," she said, unbuckling her seat belt. "I'll come with you."

Jolie looked around the cavernous warehouse in some amazement as Sam spoke with another uniformed employee. There really wasn't much to see, just wooden crates and plastic-wrapped objects that defied description. An acre of them, row upon row upon row, which was impressive. She knew Sam had family money, but she'd always thought his import antique business was a sort of toy he played with, a rich man's diversion.

How young and self-centered—and stupid— had she been five years ago, that she hadn't even realized he was a *real* businessman?

"Let's get you out of here," Sam said from behind her as she tilted her head, attempting to look through the protective wrapping around what might have been a life-size statue of some Greek goddess. "Larry's going to drive you to Thompson's Diner in his own vehicle and then deliver you back to the house, all right? Just sort of hunker down in the seat until you're clear of the area. Nobody's going to think to follow Larry, so you'll be fine."

"Sam? What's wrong?" she asked as he put his hand under her elbow and all but marched her toward the door. "Something's wrong, isn't it?"

"Nothing that hasn't happened before, but I wanted to see it myself to be sure," he told her as a large blond-haired man walked past them, heading for a red pickup truck that hadn't been new five years ago. "Two crates somehow managed to make it through Customs, which is easier than you think, but we picked it up here."

"Picked what up here?"

"Drugs. I keep my own dogs, just to be doubly careful, and they sniffed it out. We always have to be on the lookout for drugs, especially shipments that come in from South America. I've already got a call in to the authorities, but I don't want you to be here when they get here, all right? You've got enough going on as it is."

She put her hand on his arm. "Will you be all right? Nobody will suspect you of trying to smuggle in those drugs, will they?"

"No, they won't. But I can't go with you now and probably won't be home until dinnertime. Would you consider just letting Larry drive you back to the house and forget about this Thompson's Diner deal until tomorrow?"

Jolie thought about what she'd planned and about how yet another day was ticking away from her time here, her time with Sam. "No, I can't. It probably won't be any help, but I want to try. Besides, I hate these contacts and don't want to have to wear them again. They aren't supposed to change anything, but the whole world looks like there should be a smog alert posted somewhere."

She went up on tiptoe to give him a quick kiss, but Sam wasn't settling for a quick kiss. He pulled her fully into his arms and opened his mouth over hers, sliding his tongue inside and causing her toes to curl into the flip-flops hard enough to leave dents in the rubber. "I won't try to stop you, but be careful, sweetheart," he said as he then put his head next to hers, whispered the words into her ear. "I think we're getting too close to having something good here to make any mistakes now."

She had no answer for him, nothing that would make sense, so she just nodded and allowed Larry to hand her up into the cab of the pickup truck.

An hour later she was sitting at the counter of Thompson's Diner, inhaling the smells of eggs, home fries and bacon, as well as strong coffee, and watching the waitresses work the booths. The morning crowd was thinning out, and Jolie nursed a cup of tea while nibbling at an order of buttered toast, biding her time.

She liked the diner. It was one of those old chrome-sided prefabs from the fifties, she believed, and from the too-large pies in the glass turnaround case to the cracked red fake leather on the counter stools, it was like every other diner she'd ever eaten in with her sisters and Teddy. Their favorite had been Elias's Diner, and she was pretty sure remnants of their Monday-night meat loaf, mashed potatoes and heavy brown gravy could still be found somewhere on her hips.

A gray-haired waitress who looked as though she might also have eaten at Elias's Diner every night plopped down Jolie's check and then leaned one generous hip against the back end of the counter. "I'm getting too old for this," she said as if she said those same words at least a dozen times a day. "I totaled your check without asking if you wanted anything else. Do you want something else? Lemon meringue is fresh this morning."

"I wish I could, but I think a single slice of lemon meringue pie is about twelve hundred calories."

"Not here. Here it's probably fifteen hundred," the woman told her with a wink. "You know, you look familiar. Have you been in here before?"

"Nope, first time," Jolie said and then had to only slightly amend what she'd planned to say, believing the waitress had made her job even easier. "But there are people who tell me I look a little like my aunt Cathleen. Not the hair, of course. She was blond, and I get my red hair from my dad. I really don't remember her, but I've seen photos. I'm taking some classes at Temple—you know, summer stuff? And I figured, heck, I'm here in Philly, so why not go see where Aunt Cathleen worked so many years ago. Mom has a picture of her standing in front of the diner, you know, and that's how I knew the name. Mom keeps that picture right next to the TV in the living room, so I saw it every day. Last picture we ever had of Aunt Cathleen. I was surprised the place was still around, to tell you the truth."

Okay, that was good. Enough but not too much. Jolie picked up the check. "Well, I guess I should be going. Have a nice day."

"Wait, hold on a minute," the waitress said, motioning Jolie back onto the stool. "Cathleen, you said? Cathleen *Hanson?* Last picture, you said. So I was right? She never went home again—wherever that was, 'cause we never knew, you know? Not in these, what, ten, twelve years?"

"Aunt Cathleen disappeared twelve years ago, yes. The night before she was going to get married, supposedly, although my mom wasn't invited to the wedding. They'd had a fight, you understand, before Aunt Cathleen moved to Philly. It was a couple of years before we even knew she'd left here. We don't know where she went or why she never got in contact with my mom again."

The waitress leaned closer to Jolie. "She didn't *go* anywhere. They killed her, that's what happened. They killed her and then they threw that sweet little girl away somewhere like so much trash. I *knew* it. I told that cop, I told him then and I tell him each time he comes back every year since—something's wrong here. Cathleen was a good girl, she wouldn't steal no bunch of stupid diamonds and take off. I know what it was. She wasn't one of them, so they killed her."

CHAPTER TEN

"So that's what I've got, Sam. Cathleen Hanson was a good girl, a shy and very sweet girl, and crazy in love with her David. She left the diner that day all loaded down with presents from the other waitresses and promised to come back with pictures of the honeymoon in two weeks. They were going to go to Paris."

"Jolie, you keep blinking, in case you haven't noticed."

"I know. It was those contacts. I couldn't wait to get them out of my eyes. I feel so much better now."

"I'm happy for you, I really am," Sam told her. "Kind of miss the red wig, though. I actually was beginning to make plans for it, for later tonight. Darn."

"That's insulting on so many levels, Mr. Becket," she told him, pushing at her own long hair.

"I know. Men are all hormones. And, speaking

for the rest of my gender, we're not ashamed to admit it."

"Pig," Jolie said, but she laughed. "Now where was I?"

"They were on their way to Paris."

"Right, except they never got there because there was never any wedding. Cathleen was nervous about the rehearsal party that night because David's mother wouldn't really talk to her and made things uncomfortable. But that was all right because David said it would be all right. Cathleen's David might be a little bit afraid of his mother—Mother Pearson, who I think I hate even though I haven't met her yet—but he loved Cathleen enough to marry her no matter how his mother felt. Et cetera, et cetera. Last time Luann saw her, she was a happy bride-to-be who was anything but a gold digger. She refused to take a cent from David or quit her job until they were married. Which they never were. End of story."

Sam handed Jolie a glass of wine as she settled herself on the couch, figuring she needed it even if it was only three o'clock. "Pretty much of a letdown, I guess, sweetheart? But what else could you hope for?"

"I think I could have hoped that Luann hadn't pulled me aside before I left and told me she's sorry about my dad because he'd always seemed like a good guy to her and that she knew Cathleen had been an orphan, totally without a family," Jolie said, taking a sip of wine. "I should have known better. Nothing gets past a good waitress. But she did like my last movie even though it wasn't a comedy. There is that. How did it go at the warehouse? Oh, and is Jade home yet?"

"First things first. Court called me a while ago. She's been released, but he couldn't talk her out of stopping at the house to inspect the damage. They should be showing up here fairly soon. As for the other? It would seem that Larry and the rest of my warehouse employees are going to have a few days off. Instead of removing the drugs, the crates are going to be sealed again and kept at the warehouse until whoever knows what's in them makes a move to recover them, which will probably be soon. Right now I've got a warehouse full of orders to be processed, new inventory for all of my shops sitting in limbo and a bunch of DEA and Homeland Security agents playing at forklift operators. I don't think I have enough insurance for that. In any case, I'm all yours, sweetheart, at least for the next few days, as I've also been told to stay away."

Jolie seemed to have picked one piece of information out of everything Sam had told her as being most important to her. "Shops? As in plural? I thought you only had the one, on Broad Street."

Sam sat down on the facing couch. "Becket Imports are located in fourteen of the three dozen or so Becket Hotels across the country, Jolie, as well as stores in Toronto and Montreal and one in Acapulco. I'll be opening another store in the high-end shopping promenade that will be part of a new casino in Atlantic City early next year. We've never discussed this?"

She shook her head. "Never. To tell you the truth, Sam, I've always pretty much thought you were born with a silver spoon in your mouth and the antiques were just your hobby. I mean, those months we were together? You seemed to have all the time in the world for me." She winced. "Sorry."

"There wasn't anything or anyone else in the world for me when you and I were together," Sam said quietly. "I think we pretty much spent those four months trying to consume each other. Nothing else mattered."

Jolie nodded. "Physical attraction. We certainly did have that, didn't we?"

"I hadn't noticed that it went anywhere," Sam told her as he heard the front door open and stood up. "It's when I put the ring on your finger and we started talking marriage that everything went to hell. I think that's Court and Jade now."

Jolie hopped to her feet and went running toward the foyer. He wondered if she was running toward her sister or away from their conversation. Again. By the time he joined them, the sisters were holding on to each other while Court deposited several shopping bags on the floor near the staircase.

Jade looked all right, Sam supposed. A little pale, and the gauze covering her hands made her look as if she was about to have a pair of boxing gloves secured over them before she stepped into the ring.

"Court?"

"She'll be fine, Sam. One of these bags is filled with gauze and salves and tape and God only knows what else. They showed me how to dress her burns, and I have to do that twice a day. Jade would rather eat nails, but she needs me right now. I had to button her blouse and slacks."

"I'm getting the idea Jade wasn't very grateful for your help?"

Court smiled, a genuine smile. "Miss Independence? She's hating every moment of this. I'm loving it. Watch." He walked over to Jade and Jolie and said, "Jade? The doctor wants you to rest as much as possible. We made a deal, you and me. I'd take you to the house and then you'd take a nap before dinner."

"I don't need a nap before dinner, Court," Jade told him shortly. "I don't want a nap before dinner. I want to talk to Jolie. And Jessica, whenever she gets here. We've lost too much time already."

"But a deal's a deal," Court said firmly, still smiling. "I kept my end of the bargain, Jade. I know you want to keep yours."

"Fine," Jade said, and for a moment Sam thought he heard a bit of Jessica in her oldest sister. "But Jolie will help me. Jolie? I have to go to the bathroom. And I want to hear what's been going on since last night."

Jolie looked at Court, who nodded.

"Don't look at him for permission," Jade warned her. "He only thinks he's in charge of me. He's not. I'm just compromising because it's easier right now and I really have to go to the bathroom."

Jolie looked at Court again and shrugged her shoulders. "All right. But you have to lie down while I tell you, okay? I think I'm afraid of Court."

Sam watched them go up the stairs, Jolie walking behind Jade with her arms out, as if she could catch her if she fell, as Jade couldn't hold on to the banister, and then grinned at Court. "I don't believe this. What miracle did you pull off?"

"She's not exactly putty in my hands," Court said as they headed for the living room, "but I think she had a real scare last night. Contrary to what she's always believed, she is not a one-man army. Sometimes a person needs some help."

"In Jade's case, like in going to the bathroom. How long must she wear those bandages?"

"I'm not sure. We see the burn guy again tomorrow at some clinic. The bandages are mostly to keep the salve on and because it's difficult to cover just small parts of her skin. Maybe a week?"

"A month—or that's how it'll seem to her," Sam said, shaking his head. "You know, you seem happy, Court. But I don't see a love life in your near future. Or is that over? Is this just you being you, caring for your ex-wife who happens to need help right now?"

"Good question," Court said wryly, accepting a glass of wine. "When I figure out a good answer, I'll be sure to get back to you. I want to hold her, comfort her—and I want to strangle her. It's still a toss-up as to how it's going to end up. Jade mentioned Jessica earlier. She's not here?"

"Not yet, no. But she took Bear Man with her, so she should be fine. Bear Man might have his own problems, though, with her. Did you ever get the feeling we men are the fierce-looking but still fairly helpless wildebeests, surrounded by lionesses? Teddy raised some dangerous daughters."

"That's half their attraction, don't you think?"

"You're probably right, and we probably should give the matter a whole lot of thought one of these days. But not now. While we have some time, maybe you can fill me in on our newly discovered cousin. You said you would at some point."

Court took the seat Jolie had vacated. "All right. It's strange, Sam. We know some of our family history. We all know the name Ainsley Becket, probably because he had such an interesting background. The privateering, before he began his shipping business and became a pillar of the community in Hampton Roads. We knew there was an English branch somewhere, but I, at least, didn't know the half of it. For instance, you and I aren't really related. Not by blood."

Sam blinked. "Well, if that's all. I never really liked you much anyway. What do you mean we're not related? We're both Beckets. Have you just insulted my mother? Or yours?"

"It goes back a lot farther than that." Court stood up, depositing his glass on the tabletop. "Let me go upstairs for a minute. I've got a copy of the family tree in my luggage. Morgan gave it to me. It'll be easier to explain this if I have props."

"All right. And I'll take Rockne out back for a minute. He's beginning to get that certain look in his eyes."

Sam didn't bother with the leash, as Rockne had yet to show a desire to run, but just opened the door for the dog and then stood outside, watching as the animal searched out the perfect spot of manicured lawn to destroy.

To give Rockne some privacy, he turned away, idly checking out the flowers that had been planted in one of the urns next to the French doors, and frowned at the cigarette and lighter he saw hidden behind one of them. Picking up both, he shoved them in his pocket, figuring that one of the gardeners had forgotten them, and then whistled to Rockne and they both reentered the house.

"Wow, that's not a family tree," he said as Court joined him once more, now holding a large cylinder, the sort used by architects to carry their drawings. "You could have an entire forest in there. How can we not be related?"

"We are talking about two hundred years or so of history, Sam," Court reminded him as he pulled the top off the cylinder and dumped out a large rolled-up sheet of paper. Together, they spread it out on the coffee table, holding down the corners with four coasters. Not just a simple chart; someone had drawn an actual tree, with actual branches, the names and dates all listed on them in careful calligraphy. Instantly fascinated, Sam knew he had to have the thing copied and then framed for himself.

"All right, there's Ainsley," Sam said, standing up again and locating the top of the family tree. "And three, four—eight children? Two wives? Busy man. Must have been the lack of television and those long winter nights."

"Right, not to mention no electricity. What else was there to do? Except that seven of those eight he adopted, according to Morgan, who also is not a blood relative, by the way. Let's keep this simple for now, and we can get into the details another time. Suffice it to say you, cousin, are descended from Rian Becket and his wife, Lisette, who first emigrated to New Orleans, while I'm descended from another adopted son, the original Courtland Becket, who ended up in Virginia along with Ainsley. In fact, my branch of the family is the only one that carries Becket blood, because it seems that Courtland married Ainsley's only natural daughter, Cassandra. Confused yet?"

"Getting there," Sam said, now bent over the table, tracing his finger along the branches of the ornately drawn family tree. He found Rian Becket and traced the branches until he came up with his father's name and then his own. "Why didn't I know any of this?"

"Sam, we haven't even scratched the surface of what you and I don't know. Morgan's ancestors— in her case an adopted daughter—stayed in England at the family home. More about that home later, okay?" He pointed to another branch. "Here's Eleanor, who married a Jack Eastwood. So it has been all Eastwoods in Romney Marsh since the early 1800s, not Beckets, although the place is still called Becket Hall."

"Beckets and now Eastwoods. I don't know how much more I can take, Court. It's already getting so you can't tell the players without a scorecard. There's more?"

"Plenty, Sam. Just follow those top branches. Eleanor stayed in England, and so did a son, Chance—who I understand was knighted for services to the Crown at some point—and another daughter, the first Morgan, who married an earl, no less. We have—or I should say *had*—titled cousins. Chance's male line died out in the 1940s, I believe. *Our* Morgan is chasing down the female line now. There was a fourth Becket daughter, Fanny, also married to a title. But the last of that line—two old-maid aunts, Morgan told me—are long gone. And the last of the original Morgan's male descendants was killed in action in Iraq two years ago. That's when Morgan—the current Morgan—decided it was time to look up her American relatives."

"Interesting. You notice something here, Court? We Beckets don't seem to reproduce much, do we? At least not for the last few generations. You and I are only children, and so is Morgan, I think you told me. And see here? The Spencer Becket line also died out."

"No, Morgan doesn't think so, which is why she had the artist who made this up leave room for more names on that branch. She just can't find anything on Spencer yet. Notice that in the late 1800s there were only daughters listed—again, no sons to carry on the name. Five daughters. There could be a lot of relatives out there somewhere. Morgan's trying to chase them down on genealogy sites on the Internet. God knows we wouldn't be able to do it by family resemblance."

"No, I suppose not. So we're not really cousins?"

"Not by blood, no. But we certainly do share the same history, including The Empress."

"We've got an empress in the family? Where?"

"Good question, Sam. *What* is the Empress would be another. You're the antiques expert in the family, as I told Morgan, so maybe you can help us figure it out. Or the whole thing is just a story handed down long enough for it to seem real, when it really isn't."

"Well, that was clear."

"I know, sorry." Court began rolling up the family tree, preparing to slip it back into the tube. "Why don't I wait until we're all together at dinner to tell you the rest. I think we need something to take our minds off Teddy and these cold cases, anyway. And everybody loves stories about buried treasure, right?"

Sam grinned. "No, don't say it. Don't tell me old Ainsley really *was* a pirate and there's a map somewhere with a big X on it that Morgan wants us to go looking for?"

"Something like that," Court said, returning Sam's smile. "But it'll keep until dinner. Is there anything else happening around here that I should know about?"

"Not much," Sam said, still grinning. "Jolie took off the red wig before you and Jade got here, so you missed that, and her undercover operation meant to get information from one of the vanishing bride's old coworkers was pretty much a non-starter. I'm barred from my offices and the warehouse until the DEA releases both, because some enterprising bastard packed a couple of kilos of cocaine into a shipment of fourteenth-century pottery that came in from Colombia. The only good thing about that is that I'm free to watch that Jolie doesn't get into too much trouble. You've got Jade—God help you—and Jessica isn't really happy that Lieutenant Denby has requested to join our little circle of amateur detectives. That's about it."

"That's more than enough. Jade told me that she did manage to locate and talk to Jermayne Johnson yesterday afternoon," Court told him as they settled on the couches again. "He works at a car wash somewhere in North Philadelphia and told her he couldn't take off for Teddy's funeral because the owner would have docked his paycheck. She said he seemed nervous. Upset about something. He wouldn't look her straight in the eye."

"There aren't a lot of people who can look straight in Jade's eyes, not if she wants something from them," Sam pointed out.

"Jade knows that, you know. She knows she can be intimidating. But she swears it's more than that, that Jermayne is hiding something. She pushed at him. She told him that Teddy had made a note in his files indicating there had been a visit to him near the end of May. The kid denied it but then finally agreed that he had seen him—but said they only talked about Teddy wanting him to start taking some classes at a trade school this fall and Jermayne not wanting to do that. Jade says she's going to give Jermayne about a week and then go back at him again."

"Why? Do you really think there's something there?"

"I don't. But Jade said the kid was crying, all broken up about Teddy. More than she thought he would be, I guess. And he kept saying he was sorry, he was very sorry."

"Sorry Teddy's dead?"

"No, just *sorry.* Either that or Jade's reading too much into Jermayne's behavior. He must have been fond of Teddy, if nothing else. The way Teddy moved him and his grandmother out of the city after his brother was shot? The way he kept checking up on them over the years?"

"And his brother wasn't just a fantastic basketball player, Court," Sam said, becoming more interested. "He was a scholar-athlete. One of those bright, shining hopes for the future, you know? A good kid. But you said Jermayne works at a car wash? Teddy was trying to push him into a trade school? Maybe that's what Jermayne is so *sorry* about, Court. That Teddy took such an interest in him, but he couldn't be his brother. He couldn't be another Terrell, even helped by having so many advantages Terrell never had."

"You minored in psychology or something?" Court asked him, shaking his head. "The kid is eighteen, Sam. Jade's just looking too hard, trying to find anything at all that helps make sense of Teddy's death."

"Maybe. The vanishing bride? One of the women who worked with her, one of the last people to see her, is convinced that the Pearsons murdered her because she wasn't one of them. Because Cathleen didn't fit in with their inflated opinions of themselves. The classic rags-to-riches story without the fairy-tale ending, Court. A poor but honest waitress up against the Pearsons' blue blood and high opinions of themselves."

"A modern-day Cinderella meets the homicidal mother-in-law?"

"Something like that. I tried to tell Jolie that the whole thing sounded like a book or movie plot and not real. But she wasn't buying it or any thought that Cathleen really did decide to tote up her losses, pawn the diamonds and take a hike. People can find reasons for anything, if they look hard enough if they want to see trouble badly enough. But that doesn't make any of it real. Teddy was obsessed by these cases. And now his daughters are doing the same thing, sharing his obsession and refusing to look at what's important."

"What do you mean what's important?"

"Melodie Brainard's murder, that's what I mean," Sam said, picking up his wineglass once more. "*That's* what they should be investigating, Court—Melodie Brainard's murder. But they're not."

"Because they might find out something they don't want to know," Court said and blew out his breath as if an unhappy reality had just punched him in the gut. "You're right. They've decided— Jade decided—that Teddy visited Melodie Brainard for some reason, left, came home, got drunk, and then someone killed him."

"Leaving no defense when the cops saw the tapes from the Brainard security cameras. Which," Sam said, holding up one finger for emphasis, "does not mean that the whole night, both tragedies, were one big coincidence. I don't think these cold cases have a damn thing to do with Teddy's death."

"Then it's a good thing you're not in charge here, Sam," Jade said from the hallway before walking into the room, Jolie following after her, holding up her hands in surrender as she rolled her eyes.

"Ever try to stop a runaway train, Sam?" Jolie asked as she plopped herself down beside him, her long legs an immediate distraction beneath a pair of denim shorts he recognized from the box that had been delivered earlier. "Here's a clue— nothing works."

Court got to his feet. "I thought you were going to take a nap."

"No," Jade said, glaring at him, "you thought you'd gotten your own way. You didn't. I'm old enough to know when I need a nap—and I don't need one. I need to explain to Sam here why we're doing what we're doing. *Again.*"

"We're trying to connect one of Teddy's old cases to the reason he was talking to Melodie Brainard," Jolie explained quickly. "She wasn't a client, Sam, at least Jade is sure she wasn't, so it stands to reason that something Teddy found out in his regular rounds of working his old cases led him to her." She looked up at Jade. "I've got that right, don't I?"

"Yes, Jolie," Jade said, at last sitting down beside Court, "you've got that right. And Sam's got it right. We *should* be looking at Melodie Brainard's murder. But *how,* Sam? The police aren't sharing with us, the case is closed and we have no access. The only way to do this is to come at it from the cold cases."

"We've got Lieutenant Denby," Jolie said, putting her hand on Sam's thigh. He doubted she even noticed the easy intimacy, but he did. "Isn't that right, Sam?"

"That's going to be up to him, Jolie. I don't know what he's going to say or how much he's going to offer us, if he offers us anything. And it seems to me that we'd decided that he should team up with Jessica, remember? She's following the Fishtown Strangler case. Again, I don't know how we can draw any parallels there. Or with Terrell Johnson's murder or the vanishing bride."

"Or the baby in the Dumpster," Jade reminded them, rubbing at the tip of her nose with the back of her forearm, "but they're all we've got. Damn it. Why do things only itch when you can't scratch them?"

Sam looked at Jolie as he covered her hand with his own and then leaned in to whisper to her. "Court's probably asking himself that same question. So am I. We've got about two hours before dinner, *Red*."

Jolie slowly shifted her gaze toward Jade and Court, who was rubbing at the tip of her sister's nose as she made a face, and then back at Sam. "Red? Is that going to be some new nickname? Are you saying you've got an itch?"

He squeezed her fingers. "I think it's a possibility, yes. I think it started earlier, with the wig. And those shorts aren't helping, believe me."

"They weren't meant to. I thought you'd like them." She shot another look across the coffee table and then picked up the empty wineglasses and motioned for Sam to join her at the bar. "You make an interesting offer, Mr. Becket. But Jade might need me," she told him quietly as she walked behind the bar and put down the glasses. "Her hands…"

He followed her behind the bar. "Court can help her. It's obvious he wants to. Come on, Jolie, toss the guy a bone. Look at him over there. Look at the two of them. He really cares about her. And he may be just what she needs right now."

"You'd say anything to get me upstairs, wouldn't you?" Jolie told him, moving a little closer to him. "Tell me your troubles, Chester, and maybe we can work them out."

He turned his back to Court and Jade, at least partially shielding Jolie's upper body from their sight if they happened to look their way, and eased his hand up beneath the hem of her shorts.

"Sam, don't, I didn't mean here…."

"Shh, stand still. We're behind the bar. And it's a big room, Jolie. They're at least twenty feet away from us. But you don't want them to know what I'm doing, do you?"

"*I* want to know what you think you're doing," she told him and then closed her eyes as he pushed aside her panties and began gently spreading her, stroking her.

"Does that give you a hint?"

"You're not playing fair."

"I know," he said, smiling at her. "I'm thoroughly ashamed of myself. Really. And I should probably point out that you could step away from me anytime you want to."

She bit her bottom lip and then blew out a breath. "I know…I know that. Two hours? We have two hours to—"

"And I'm telling *you*, Court, that if you won't drive me to Brainard's campaign headquarters tomorrow, I'll find somebody else to do it," Jade said in some heat, her voice carrying all the way to Sam and Jolie.

"Damn it, I said I'd do it, Jade," Court said with just as much heat. "Why in hell can't you accept help in the spirit it's offered? Would it make you less of a *man?*"

"And what is *that* supposed to mean?"

"You know damn well what it's supposed to mean. Just once, Jade, admit that you might need somebody else."

"You know what killed our marriage, Court? You wanted some soft and clinging Virginia buttercup. I'm not her."

"Now tell me something I don't know!"

"Oh, boy," Sam said as Jolie stepped away from him, her eyes wide now with something other than passion. "Time to go, sweetheart?"

She was already halfway around the bar. "I'll race you up the stairs."

CHAPTER ELEVEN

DINNER WAS DELAYED until Matthew Denby could get away from a gang-related drive-by shooting in South Philly, but he arrived in time to be told by Jessica thanks but no thanks to any offer he might want to make concerning her investigation of the Fishtown Strangler case.

"That's too bad," he told her as they all made their way into the dining room, "considering that I've broken every rule by photocopying everything in the Murder Book that was added after Teddy left the force."

"Matthew," Jessica purred, rounding on him with her best on-camera smile as Jolie tried to cover a smile of her own, "don't ever listen to a word I say, really. Of course I want your help. We definitely should put our heads together, right after dinner. Maybe we could go out for a little drive, get something to drink?"

Sam held out a chair for Jolie, bending to whisper in her ear. "Are you as embarrassed as I am?"

"Double it," she told him and then watched as he walked to the head of the table and sat down once Jessica and Jade had been seated. He really was a wonderful man. Polite. Funny. Intelligent. Handsome. Sexy. Living on the wrong coast…

Mrs. Archer entered pushing a two-tiered cart loaded with covered dishes, and within minutes they were handing those dishes around, family-style, so that they could talk without worrying that the housekeeper would be coming in and out and possibly overhearing things best kept more private.

Jolie watched as Court cut Jade's roast beef for her and then helped her find the best way to hold on to her fork. She could almost feel the force of her sister's frustration, but Jade only thanked Court and told him she was fine, she could take it from there.

What had happened after she and Sam had bailed, leaving the two of them to either work out their differences or kill each other? Whatever it was, Jolie was fairly certain theirs was only a temporary truce and that there would be more fireworks to come at some point.

Jolie turned down Matt's offer of the gravy boat, longing to accept it and pour the rich-looking gravy all over her meat and the spoonful of mashed potatoes she'd allowed herself. She was already resigned to filling up on as much salad as she could stand before worrying that her nose might begin to twitch like a rabbit's.

And she blamed Sam for the menu choice. He'd done it on purpose, she was sure, after talking about the way her childhood home always smelled of pot roast. He was tempting her to eat, that's what he was doing, and he wasn't being subtle. She wished she could remember where she'd left her lighter and her last cigarette. Smoking it would have helped cut her appetite.

"Rolls?" Matt asked her.

The rolls smelled fresh. They were most probably still warm. She imagined one topped with melted butter, another dipped in gravy. Then she imagined the look on Smitty's face if she had to let out the gown Jolie was going to wear to the premiere.

"I'm not really that hungry, thanks," she said, smiling at Matt. A smile that faded as she then looked toward the head of the table to see Sam frowning at her. He didn't understand, he just didn't. He sat here in his huge house, surrounded by all these lovely antiques, prosperous, settled, secure. She was as secure as the box-office statistics of that first weekend of her next movie. If she'd thought breaking into the movies had been hard, it was nothing compared to what it took to *stay* in the business.

"I told Sam a little of what I learned about our family tree while I was in England," Court said conversationally, which was when Jolie realized that nobody had been saying much of anything for several minutes. "I won't bore you with details, but I did learn something interesting. According to our English cousin, Morgan, our earliest known ancestor left behind a fairly intriguing mystery when he sailed to America shortly after Waterloo. Something called the Empress."

"Ainsley Becket made his original fortune as a privateer in the late 1700s," Sam told them. "But we're thinking there might have been some outright piracy there, too. Right, Court?"

"Many of the best families began their fortunes in sometimes less than laudatory ways," Court told them, grinning. "The Astors, the Rockefellers, the Duponts. Or at least I hope so. But ours is a little bit different. It seems the Empress comes with a curse—or something like that."

"A curse? You're making that up," Jessica said, but her eyes were twinkling. "Tell us more."

"Morgan only knows what her grandfather told her when she was young. He'd take her on treasure hunts around the house—and it's an enormous and very strange house, by the way. Ainsley had two special concealed floors built into the place and armed them with cannon and hidden portholes, just like a ship. It seems the man had a few enemies back in the bad old days, and the house was very isolated. Those floors are used strictly for storage now, but they're still really something to see. At any rate, there's some legend attached to the Empress, a trail of bad luck, greed, murder and mayhem, you name it. So much so that Ainsley decided to hide the Empress away until its bad luck wore off."

"And? Has it?" Jessica asked him. "I'm sensing an Al-Capone's-vault-Geraldo-Rivera-type fiasco here."

"Has it worn off?" Court repeated. "Nobody knows, because nobody knows where the Empress is, where Ainsley hid it. Morgan's grandfather used to tell her that Ainsley was certain the Empress would resurface when it was time, when its bad luck was gone. A romantic man, Ainsley Becket, the product of a romantic and dangerous age, I suppose. The grandfather also tried to weave the story around that Morgan was the chosen one, the one who would finally find it. You know, like King Arthur being the only one to be able to pull Excalibur from the stone?"

Jolie absentmindedly selected a roll from the covered basket, broke off a piece and began buttering it. "Imagine growing up listening to such a fantastic fairy-tale and even starring in it, thanks to her grandfather."

"Fairy-tale," Court said, nodding. "That's all it probably is, too, Jolie. But the grandfather was convinced Ainsley hid this Empress somewhere in the house, although Morgan believes he also might have brought it with him to America, to Virginia. Meaning," he added with a smile, "I might be living in the same house with the Empress and not know it."

Jolie had been watching Sam's face while Court told his story, but she couldn't read his expression. "Sam? You aren't saying anything. Isn't this exciting?"

"I'm not sure yet. It is only a story told from grandfather to grandchild and passed down for generations before that. I can't tell you the times a family member has come to me to tell me all about this ceremonial sword that was given to their ancestor by George Washington or a Fabergé egg that was presented to their great-uncle Fred by the last czar. And always with some long, convoluted family history to go with it. And always dead wrong. So let's get this much out of the way, Court. What is this Empress supposed to be?"

"An uncut emerald the size of a woman's fist," Court told them all and then watched everyone's faces for their reactions. "Ainsley and his partner had a falling out over it, supposedly. Ainsley's first wife was killed and he was forced to flee from some island near Haiti, all the way to England and Romney Marsh. Years later, the partner surfaced again, and this time Ainsley killed him before half the family emigrated to America. A good story, if we can believe it."

"The Caribbean?" Sam sat forward in his chair, resting his elbows on the table. "All right, now that's interesting. There was a lot of piracy in those waters at one time, and some privateering, which was really not much more than state-sanctioned piracy. It is possible, I suppose, that Ainsley and his partner could have raided a ship carrying uncut emeralds from mines in South America. Some of the premier-quality emeralds have been found there, as well as near the Red Sea. The larger stones were actually worshipped as holy stones at one time or believed to be good luck or even to ensure their owner's eternal life. The Mogul emerald, for instance—"

"That's all terrific, Sam, you're a real expert, aren't you?" Jessica interrupted hastily. "But if we're only talking one emerald, so what? I was thinking more of a buried treasure chest filled with all sorts of precious stones and gold bars and maybe even some Spanish doubloons or whatever they're called. A couple of skeletons of old pirates killed and buried with the treasure to protect it would have been cool, too. Great television— Geraldo, eat your heart out. But one measly emerald? Big deal."

"It is a big deal, Jessica, whether you're thinking of it in monetary terms or for the pure beauty and history of such a rare stone. The largest emeralds are actually, carat for carat, worth more than diamonds. An emerald as large as a woman's fist, uncut? That would mean we're talking upwards of five hundred carats, possibly a lot more. Depending on the size of this unknown woman's fist, I guess you'd say. The Mogul emerald, for instance, as I was trying to tell you, is just over *two* hundred carats and it sold at Christie's a few years ago for more than two million dollars. In today's market or two hundred years ago, an emerald as large as this Empress stone is supposed to be, uncut, could only be considered priceless. And an emerald is much more portable than an entire treasure chest. If Morgan's grandfather's story is true, it doesn't surprise me in the slightest that people died for the Empress."

"And a single stone is also easier to hide," Jolie said, watching out of the corners of her eyes to see if Jade appeared to be interested. Anything to take her sister's mind off her current determined course, at least for a few hours. "Do you think your ancestor brought it with him to Virginia, Court? I don't think I would, not with having to carry all that bad luck with me across the ocean in one of those small ships. I would have left it in England, hidden away until the bad luck wore off or something."

"Oh, I'm loving this," Jessica said, rubbing her hands together. "This has prime-time special written all over it. When do we start looking?"

Jade's fork fell from her clumsy grasp to clang against the plate. "Haven't you forgotten something, Jessica? Forgotten *somebody?*"

"Here we go," Jolie heard Court mutter beneath his breath. "Jade, it's only dinner-table conversation. It's theory. It's something other than Teddy and these damn cold cases for just five minutes."

"Yeah, Jade," Jessica teased, "lighten up. Matt and I are on the job. Right, Matt? What new information to do you have for me, anyway? Because I'm pretty much striking out here on Kayla Morrison. I still can't locate any of Tarin White's family or even anyone who vaguely remembers her. And Tarin and Kayla are the only two names in Teddy's most recent notes, out of the six victims."

"I think I have an address on somebody named White, but it's a few years old," Matt said, putting down his fork. "You want to go look at the photocopies I brought?"

"Does Paris Hilton like to drive? Of course I do."

"All right," Matt said, putting down his napkin. "But it's *look,* not *touch.* I'm still a cop and you're still the media."

"The enemy, you mean."

"Close enough," Matt said, getting to his feet and holding back Jessica's chair.

"Now, Matt, you know you can trust me."

The lieutenant frowned down at Jessica as she

smiled up at him. "Do I? I saw the Willie Cart-wright interview. You'd throw your own sisters under the bus if it got you a good story."

"Don't exaggerate. Not *all* the way under the bus," Jessica said, winking at Jolie and Jade before following Matt out of the dining room.

"Two gone," Sam said from the head of the table a moment later. "More dessert for the rest of us."

"Jade?" Jolie asked, looking past Court as her sister raised the back of one bandaged hand to her face to wipe away a tear. "What's wrong, honey? Are you in pain? Jessica didn't mean anything. She's just being Jessica."

"I know, Jolie. It's not that. I was just thinking. The Empress? Teddy would have loved that story. And then he would have told us a story all about leprechaun gold, or something, making it all up as he went along. Oh, God, I miss him."

"Come on, time for the pain pill you wouldn't take earlier," Court said, getting to his feet and sliding back Jade's chair. "Excuse us, please."

"No, Court. I want to hear what everyone is planning for tomorrow and—oh, all right. I give up. Let's go."

"Mark that one down in your calendars, ladies and gentlemen. Jade, giving up," Sam said from his end of the table once Jade and Court had left the dining room. "How's the weather down there at that end, Jolie?"

Jolie suddenly noticed that she was holding what seemed to be the last of a heavily buttered roll. She considered putting it down but then decided the hell with it and popped it into her mouth. "I thought it was going to get pretty hot there for a minute after being really cold, but it's not so bad now. Why don't you come slumming at the bottom of the table and find out for yourself."

"I would, but I think I have a better idea. While you were in the shower, I phoned a friend who has a friend who has Joshua Brainard's private cell number. Candidate Brainard would be happy to meet privately with that marvelous actress, Jolie Sunshine, at his campaign headquarters at eight o'clock tonight. Interested?"

"It's *actor,* not *actress.* And, yes, I most certainly am interested. Plus, it would probably be better if I saw him instead of Jade. She's too intense right now," Jolie said, getting to her feet. "Why didn't you tell me this sooner?"

He joined her and they headed for the foyer. "I was worried you might want to thank me, and there is this getting-older business, you know. I might not have been ready to accept your thanks."

Jolie slipped her arm through his. "Sam? About sex…"

"We were talking about sex? Really?"

"Shut up. I've been thinking about this and I want to say it now, while you're still feeling old, I hope."

"Nobody's that old, sweetheart, not with you in sight. But go ahead. Just wait until we're in the car."

She waited until they were outside the gates and then told him what was on her mind. "I don't want us to have sex anymore. Sam? Did you hear me?"

"I heard you. I'm just deciding which of these telephone poles I want to steer into to end it all."

"That won't work, Sam," she teased back at him. "I think this car must have a gazillion air bags."

"True. Why don't you want us to have sex any-more, Jolie? And I prefer to refer to what we do as making love, sentimental sap that I am."

"I'm saying it because I think we…well, I think we depend too much on sex. On our strong physical attraction to each other, we'll say."

"I'll say," he said, winking at her. "Sorry. I'm trying to be serious here as I listen to the woman who not forty-eight hours ago seduced me in my own bathtub."

"But that's just it, Sam. I came to your room to *talk* to you. About us. About what happened five years ago. About what didn't happen five years ago. And I chickened out. More than once, because I've had more than one opportunity. It's just easier to fall into bed with you and pretend everything is all hunky-dory between us."

"Hunky-dory. No, everything isn't all hunky-dory between us," Sam agreed. "If Teddy hadn't died, we wouldn't even be having this conversation, because you'd be in California. All right, Jolie, tell me what you want."

"That's the problem, Sam," she told him honestly. "I don't know what I want. It would be really easy to say I just want what we have."

"Great sex."

"It's not just great sex, Sam, don't say that. Don't cheapen it. We like each other. We may even love each other, I guess."

"You guess." His tone had gone flat, and Jolie felt butterflies taking wing in her stomach.

"I loved you once," she told him, reaching over to cover his hand on the steering wheel. "You loved me. You asked me to marry you."

"I did. The asking the father first, the romantic candlelight dinner, the ring, the down-on-one-knee bit, all of it. Biggest mistake in my life. You were packed and gone within the week, leaving so fast you left skid marks. As a matter of fact, I think there's a country song in there somewhere." His voice turned twangy and singsong. "She laid rubber on my heart and now she's gone. I blinked twice and found that she's no longer—what rhymes with *gone?*"

"Nothing, and you don't rhyme the second line with the first. I think you need to rhyme the second and third lines," Jolie told him, facing forward, refusing to look at him. "How's this?" She imitated his ridiculous twang. "She laid rubber on my heart and now she's gone. I blinked twice and found that she's no longer *here*...."

"So won't somebody please buy me a *beer*...." Sam continued.

Jolie could no longer keep a straight face. "It's not funny," she told him, laughing. "I mean it, Sam, it's really not funny. Stop laughing!"

"I will when you do," he told her. "I mean, consider the alternative."

Jolie sobered immediately. "It wasn't all my fault, you know. You weren't very understanding."

"Agreed. I was a bastard. I wanted a wife, not a would-be starlet. I thought I was saving you a lot of heartache and disappointment. I thought you loved me enough to see me, being with me, as being more important than some one-in-a-million shot at making it in the movies. I doubted that you had the luck or the talent, I guess. I was wrong on all counts, dead wrong, and I apologize."

"Thank you," Jolie said, blinking back sudden tears, because now that Sam had said the words, she realized that those words didn't change anything. What had happened happened, and nothing could change a moment of any of it, from their wonderful beginning to their explosive and almost nasty ending. "Now what, Sam?"

"Now? Now we're here." He pulled into a

parking space behind a small building at the end of a strip mall. "Can't keep the candidate waiting, can we?"

"Sam, kiss me," Jolie said, putting a hand on his arm to keep him from getting out of the car. "Please?"

"I thought you said we weren't going to do that anymore," he reminded her quietly.

"Just once more? And just a kiss, Sam."

"Jolie, with you, a kiss will never be enough."

"All right. Never mind, pretend I didn't say anything. I'm just so confused and—"

He cupped her chin with his hand and covered her mouth with his own, a closemouthed kiss that was soft and nonthreatening, that was anything but sexual. Caring. Yes, that's what it was. A caring kiss.

He looked at her for a long moment and then got out of the car, and Jolie pressed a hand to her mouth to hold back a sob. What was she doing? What had she done?

Before Sam could open the door for her, Jolie quickly pulled down the sun visor and pretended to inspect her physical appearance. Makeup fine. Hair fine. Eyes? She refused to meet her own eyes in the small mirror.

But she was an actress. She put on and took off roles, emotions, actions and reactions as required. So she took a deep breath, squared her shoulders and began to turn in the seat, ready to exit the car.

"Don't," Sam warned just as she was about to swing her feet out and onto the ground. "We've got company."

Jolie looked past Sam as another car pulled into the small lot. "Gary Tuttle. How did he—"

Sam leaned in, physically protecting her from view. "Do we care how? I should have been paying more attention, damn it. What do you want to do?"

"I don't know. How do you think Joshua Brainard would react, seeing him?"

"Brainard? Are you kidding? Rumor has it that if you want to find the guy, even in the middle of a desert, just pull out a camera and he'll show up in five minutes, tops. He'd probably agree to pose for pictures."

Jolie considered this. "All right. Then that's what we do. We promise Tuttle some pictures if he waits for us out here and then let Brainard decide what he wants to do."

"The whole world is going to know you went to Brainard's office. The whole world is going to want to know why. Are you ready for a headline on how Jolie Sunshine secretly visited the grieving widower to apologize because her daddy offed his wife?"

"That's not why we're here. We're here to—no, you're right, Sam. What do the facts ever have to do with a juicy story, right? Still, he is here and he is going to snap photos. He's probably already taking a million pictures of you shielding me from the lens. I think I'd rather have at least half a chance of something he writes being marginally true. What surprises me most, truthfully, is that Tuttle is still the only one following me."

"You're complaining?"

"No," Jolie said, smiling. "Philadelphia is blessedly off the beaten track when it comes to the usual Hollywood paparazzi, especially since I'm their only local action right now. I don't even want to think of what it would be like outside my house in Malibu if this were all taking place out there." She slipped her sunglasses out of her purse and put them on even though it was nearly dark. "All right, here we go. Back up, Sam, and let me out."

"Jolie! Look here, sweetheart!" Gary Tuttle called out loudly as he immediately hopped out of his car and trotted toward her, this time armed with more than his cell phone camera. He was snapping one picture after another, using a flash that made it obvious why celebrities wore sunglasses after dark. It was either that or walk around seeing spots all the time. "What's up, Jolie? What's going on? I helped you, now you help me. What's happening, Jolie? Why are you here?"

Sam sighed rather theatrically. "Why is there never a fly swatter around when you need one?"

"Shh, Sam, we're playing nice, now." Jolie stepped back as she shifted the majority of her weight to her left foot, turned her body slightly to the side. She consciously relaxed her shoulders, dipped her chin to tighten her neck muscles and raised it again and then looked directly into the camera lens. She'd considered a smile but had quickly rethought that option, composing her wide, full mouth into the sexy semipout that reproduced so well in the magazines. Sunglasses. Cheek bones. Lips and hips. Always a good *sell*.

She had been amazed when the studio had told her to take lessons in how to pose for the cameras. Now, if she ever saw a celebrity, male or female, who had been photographed facing the camera straight on, without the body angle and figure-slimming weight shift, she knew the photographer had caught the person unawares. Tuttle knew the drill and had waited for her to "assume the position."

"There's my girl. There's America's new sweet-heart." Gary Tuttle quickly snapped another half dozen shots. "What are you up to this time, Jolie?"

"We're here on a personal call, Mr. Tuttle," she told him, obligingly removing her sunglasses for a few more shots. "Give us ten minutes inside, un-interrupted, and we'll talk, all right?"

"For you, Jolie? Sure. But those last pictures only got my little Susie through one semester at that damn private school my ex has me stuck for. I need more. I'll just catch a smoke while I'm waiting." He reached into his shirt pocket and pulled out a pack, held it out to Jolie. "Want one?"

Jolie thought she might swallow her own tongue, but she recovered quickly—she hoped. "Uh, no. No, thanks. You have one for me, all right?" She would have said *No, thanks, I don't smoke,* but then Tuttle would sell some photo he had of her somewhere, lighting up, and it would all hit the fan. Most especially, she was pretty sure, with Sam, who disliked her constant dieting already without knowing she sometimes used nicotine as a diet aid.

"I guess I have to hand it to Tuttle. At least the guy knows he's a leech," Sam muttered as he escorted Jolie toward the typical strip mall plate-glass storefront of the Brainard campaign head-quarters.

"As my publicist reminds me, we all have to make a living."

"Even leeches, right. We're to buzz twice and he'll let us in. Ah, and here he comes. Look at that, Jolie, he's got the monogrammed dress shirt but with the cuffs turned up to show he's hard at work for all us little people. The tie on but loosened, the hair a little too carefully mussed up—I'd vote for him. What are issues when the guy looks like he sees his dentist twice a year and flosses after every meal?"

"Shut…up," Jolie warned tightly as she watched

Joshua Brainard make his way from the back of the rather long building, down a center aisle flanked by desks, now empty. She smiled as the man opened the door and stepped inside ahead of Sam. "Mr. Brainard," she said, extending her right hand, "how kind of you to see me. I promise not to take up too much of your valuable time." Wasn't that the line as she'd heard it in a million movies?

Joshua Brainard took her hand in both of his and held on. Just a beat too long, Jolie thought, unless that was the politician-touch and expected of him. "Miss Sunshine, a pleasure. I was delighted when Sam phoned and said that you wanted to see me. Hi, Sam. I don't think I've seen you since the club championship last year." He never took his gaze off Jolie as he added, "Actually, all I saw was his back, as he ran away with the First Flight. This year we bumped him up to the Championship Flight just so someone else gets a chance to win, right, Sam?"

"That's what I hear," Sam said, looking around the room. "Damn, Josh, one more poster with your smiling face on it and I'll begin to believe that rock-star rap your opposition is putting out there."

Brainard turned around slowly, looking at the walls. "My staff. They're enthusiastic. Although I think they missed a great opportunity in leaving the ceiling bare, don't you? Now, come on back to my office, away from all those shiny teeth. What can I do for you, Miss Sunshine?"

That was a good question, and Jolie wished she'd prepared more of an answer. She highly doubted that Joshua Brainard was going to volunteer that he strangled his wife and threw her into the family pool in order to jump a few points in the polls, grabbing the pity vote. She would have asked Jade why she had wanted to see Brainard, but then Jade would be here and any chance of a semipleasant interview would already be gone.

"Well, first of all, Mr. Brainard—"

"Josh. First of all, please, call me Josh. My father is Mr. Brainard."

Behind her, as he held out a chair for her, Sam quietly cleared his throat. Jolie was pretty sure it was to cover a laugh at what he most probably saw as Joshua Brainard's carefully rehearsed self-depreciating act.

"Very well, *Josh.* Please let me begin by offering my most sincere condolences on the loss of your wife."

"Thank you. And let me please say that, regardless of the circumstances, you have my sympathy on the loss of your father. It had to have taken some real courage for you to come here tonight, Jolie."

Jolie smiled. She wasn't surprised he had so easily slipped into addressing her by her first name, as if he'd just bypass asking permission he was sure she would give him. They were all just pals now, the three of them. Very cozy.

And smooth. The man was really smooth. She was almost ready to ask for one of his campaign buttons. "It wasn't easy, no. What's even more difficult is that I would like to ask you about your relationship with my father. Yours and your wife's."

"Relationship?" Brainard sat down behind his impressively cluttered desk and tipped back his desk chair. "I don't think I'd glorify that by calling it a relationship. Sunshine—your father, that is— he tried to make an appointment with me a few times but never got past my staff. Unfortunately. Maybe if he could have gotten to me, he wouldn't have found it necessary to contact my wife."

"So Teddy came to you first and then to your wife only when he couldn't get to you?"

"Exactly, Jolie. And not once but four or five times, until Melodie was nearly frantic, begging him to stop bothering her, although I never knew that until after her death. She'd gone to my father for his help, his guidance. She knew my campaign didn't need to be muddied by word of some ex-cop P.I. stalker bothering my wife. He told her, to his great distress now, to ignore the man and he'd go away. We all know how that ended. Dad will never forgive himself. This whole thing has aged him badly."

"So you don't know why Teddy wanted to speak to you?" Sam asked from his casual perch on the corner of Brainard's large desk. "Your wife never told you?"

Brainard audibly sighed, rubbing at his mouth as he looked from Sam to Jolie and back again. "You know how it is, Sam. Melodie and me? We couldn't have kids, you know, and that hit Melodie hard. Me, too, for that matter. She refused to adopt and…well, ancient history. What's important, I guess, is that Melodie and I had no real shared interests for years…we'd drifted pretty far apart. She had her rather large circle of acquaintances if few close friends, the club, some fairly extensive charity work. And she was quite the swimmer, nearly Olympic-caliber. That's why it's so ironic that she should be found in the pool that way. She loved that pool, swam laps every morning and evening, even in the winter. We had it heated, you understand. Oh, I'm sorry. I'm veering a little off track, aren't I?"

"Please. There's no need to apologize. Or to explain."

"I'm not telling you anything my own friends wouldn't tell you, Jolie. Melodie and I had a good relationship if no longer a loving one, in the usual way of married couples, that is. She was delighted that I was running and saw herself as First Lady. And she would have been a damn good one, too, Sam. But that was about it for us, for too many years. We suited each other, but we…we weren't close. I don't like admitting that, but we're being confidential here, right?"

"Definitely," Jolie said, impressed again despite the fact that she was probably being manipulated by the man's aw-shucks, I-wish-I-was-perfect-but-I'm-not routine that, again, sounded just a little overrehearsed to her attuned ear. And she knew it would be so nice and neat if Joshua Brainard had killed his wife. "My sisters and myself, we're looking into a few of our father's old unsolved cases from his years on the police force. Jade, my older sister, noticed that he'd been working on four cases in particular in the weeks before his death. I guess I want to ask you if you know anything about any of those cases."

"Me? You think that's why your father wanted to talk to me?" Brainard hitched himself forward a bit, holding on to the arms of the chair. Mr. Cooperative. The guy could give acting classes in Smooth. "I doubt it, Jolie. But go ahead, try me."

"Well, let's see. We could start, I suppose, with the one they call 'the baby in the Dumpster.'"

"Ouch, you are talking old cases, aren't you? That one hurt everybody, didn't it? For me, a man who longed for children and was denied them, I guess maybe the impact is even more pronounced. You know, that someone could throw a child away? But, no, other than to say that, like everyone else, I'd love to see the bastard who did it strapped down for a lethal injection? No, can't help you. What else? This is interesting…in a macabre sort of way."

"Uh...the case of the disappearing Pearson bride? About a dozen years ago?"

He pointed one manicured finger at her. "That one I do know. We were guests at the wedding that never happened. Although I will say we ate well, as Althea Pearson insisted we still make a party of it, all three hundred or more of us. Awkward, awkward day. Poor David. I think he genuinely loved that little gold digger. But I don't get it. Where's the crime? She ran away, taking some of the family jewels with her—but they got those back, right?"

"I think my father believed someone made her disappear," Jolie said and again watched as Brainard looked up at Sam. Birds of a feather, she imagined, all members of that same "club" of the rich and accepted. Her entry was her celebrity, but she knew that people like the as-yet-unmet Mother Pearson would consider her very much below their social strata and good only for her entertainment value.

"You mean David? You think *he* killed her?" Brainard laughed out loud. "Sam, tell her. *David?*"

"Jolie hasn't met him yet," Sam said, smiling man-to-man, which frustrated Jolie, who wasn't in on the joke. "But she did meet Angela."

"Okay, now there's a suspect, Jolie, if you're looking for suspects. She and David were pretty hot and heavy there for a while, until the little blonde showed up. Cathy? Kate?"

"Cathleen," Jolie said, unreasonably upset that the girl was most probably dead, and nobody even remembered her name.

"Yes, that's it. She was the only time David ever overruled his mother, I'll bet. She wanted Angela, definitely. And, come to think of it, she got her. Hmm…" he said, swinging his chair from side to side. "But there's no proof, right? Otherwise we wouldn't be talking about any of this, would we? And I can tell you, Melodie never liked Althea Pearson—or Angela. We did not socialize. Oh, the wedding, certainly. That was different. But as a regular thing? No."

Jolie nodded her understanding. It would seem there were levels and levels, even inside the cream of society. But she was running out of cases. "Sam? You know more about the scholar-athlete case than I do."

"Terrell Johnson, Josh," Sam said, pantomiming a two-handed set shot at an imaginary basket. "Found shot dead on a playground. High school basketball phenom."

Brainard nodded that he understood and only said, "Nothing I can add to that one, either. And Melodie wouldn't have known anything even remotely sports-related, other than aquatic sports. She used to complain that baseball had too many *quarters* and we'd be late for dinner or some party. I guess I'm not being very much help, am I?"

"Not much help with what, son? You're always helpful. That's why you're going to make a great mayor."

Brainard got to his feet. "And there you go, ladies and gentlemen, my biggest supporter. Cliff Brainard, meet Jolie Sunshine. And you probably remember Sam Becket? Dad, take a bow."

Jolie turned in her chair to see an older, slightly faded version of Joshua Brainard standing in the doorway.

"Miss Sunshine," the older Brainard said with a slight inclination of his head. "I've enjoyed your performances. Sam, how are you? I don't think we've seen you since that last charity affair at the park."

"Fine, sir, and I think you're right. Good to see you."

Jolie was becoming uncomfortable, definitely the odd man out in this reunion of acquaintances, if not friends. She looked pointedly at Sam, who quickly got the hint—thank God—and explained why they'd come to see Joshua.

The elder Brainard seemed unimpressed.

"There's one more case Teddy was investigating," Jolie told him, not feeling very hopeful. "The Fishtown Strangler."

Brainard the younger and Brainard the elder exchanged what Jolie thought a scriptwriter would call *telling looks* in a note scribbled on the relevant script page.

"Again, Jolie," Joshua Brainard said, "I don't think I can help you. Melodie certainly would have known nothing about anything so...well, sordid."

"I would have," Cliff Brainard said rather coldly as he walked past Jolie to stand behind the desk, next to his son. "Don't frown, Josh, I don't mind talking about it. I was asked to be on the mayor's task force. Horrible thing, horrible crimes. Those poor women. No matter their, well, their choice of profession. But I don't remember your father. I don't see how I can help you, Miss Sunshine."

"If I knew what questions to ask, maybe you could," Jolie said, smiling weakly as she and Sam also stood up. She guessed he also felt the tension, saw the body language. It was time to go, the Brainard men standing together, a united front if she'd ever seen one. "I only know my father was still actively working the case when he died."

"When he cravenly committed suicide, you mean, after cold-bloodedly murdering my dearest daughter-in-law," Cliff Brainard said, and although he and his son bore a striking resemblance, suddenly the older man was demonstrating none of his son's charm. "Why did you really come here, Miss Sunshine? I saw the photographer outside, you know, as I was coming in. Is there nothing you people won't stoop to? You're not going to use my son for some cheap publicity."

"Now wait a minute, Cliff," Sam said, stepping

in front of Jolie. "What's this *you people* thing about?"

Cliff Brainard laughed shortly and without real mirth. "It means just what you think it means, Sam. Go, have fun. I saw the pictures in the newspaper. Go for it if she's handing it out." His eyes narrowed. "Just don't involve my family. We've been hurt enough by trash like her loser father. We've got wounds to heal and a campaign to win."

"Sam, don't," Jolie warned quickly, grabbing onto his arm as he moved forward. "It's time to go. Really."

"Dad, that was uncalled for, damn it," Joshua Brainard said, following Sam and Jolie back down the path between the desks and out onto the pavement. "Sam, wait. Jolie, I'm so very sorry. He's…he's getting old, you know? What clsc can I say?"

Jolie decided she'd had enough. "What else can you say? I'd say you could tell me why you and your father exchanged such intense looks when I said *Fishtown Strangler.* That's what you can say. Explain that to me, Mr. Toothy Grin."

"Okay, time out—on both sides," Sam said. "Josh, thanks for seeing us, but we're leaving now."

"No, don't do that. Jolie asked a question and I'll answer it. Not happily, but I'll answer it. Dad told you he was one of the civilians asked to participate in the special task force set up when that serial killer was operating in Fishtown. What he didn't tell you was the price he paid for offering his help. He took flak from police who thought the task force meant nobody believed they could solve the crimes on their own and then more flak from the community who felt the commission was just a whitewash and no one was really working to solve the murders of a bunch of black and Hispanic prostitutes—their words, Sam, not mine. When the murders stopped with no arrests, Dad couldn't take it. He felt like a failure. He had his first heart attack only a few months later."

"And that's why you looked at him the way you did," Jolie said, embarrassed. "You were worried about him. I'm so sorry."

"No harm, no foul, Jolie," Brainard said, slipping his arm around Jolie's waist—and the smile and the candidate were both back. "Now, where's that photographer? Sam shouldn't be the only one to have his picture taken with a beautiful woman, should he?"

CHAPTER TWELVE

NEITHER SAM NOR JOLIE spoke a word on their way back to Villanova. Because one word wouldn't be enough, and any more than one could have started a war.

Sam pulled through the gates without more than a terse smile to Bear Man's stand-in—who probably could have also played as stand-in for a small mountain—and pulled the car to a stop at the front door.

"Out," he commanded. Yes, commanded.

"Sam, I know you're upset, but—"

"*Out.* Now."

"I did apologize. At least half a dozen times. You're being an ass, you know," Jolie told him, opening the door. "The unmitigated kind. An unmitigated *ass.*"

"Right," Sam said, putting the car in gear once more, with Jolie standing on the drive, hands on hips, glaring at him. "I also have to live here, damn it," he muttered as he drove around to the bank of garages, hit the remote built in to the car, and drove into the first bay. He cut the engine and sat there. Staring at the blank wall in front of him. Took several deep breaths. They didn't help.

Leaving the keys in the ignition, he headed for the terrace and one of the French doors that led into the living room. He needed a drink. He deserved a drink.

Jolie was standing in front of the bar, waiting for him.

"I made a mistake, Sam," she told him as he brushed past her to walk around the bar and open one of the doors to the Chinese cases.

"Pardon my vulgarity, Miss Sunshine, but, no shit, Sherlock." He wanted a shot of whiskey. A double shot. Neat. He took out the bottle, looked at it, and then slammed it back on the shelf and turned around. "What in *hell* did you think you were doing?"

"Oh, come on, Sam, it wasn't *that* bad. You're overreacting."

Okay. The double shot was still a viable option, and he grabbed the bottle again, and a shot glass, putting both down carefully on top of the bar.

"Not that bad? Let's review, shall we?" he said, pouring the liquid until it reached the brim, then throwing it toward the back of his throat. His eyes immediately stung, but he didn't care. "We go outside, we pose for a few pictures, and then, instead of thanking Brainard, you slit his throat. Sabotage his campaign. Turn him into a suspect in his wife's death, for Christ's sake. And maybe not just her murder. That's not too bad?"

Jolie held up her hand, began ticking off points on her fingers. "One, I never accused him of anything. I merely said that we're—"

"Hold it right there. First problem. *We.* You meant you and Jade and Jessica. I know that. But your sisters aren't going to be in any of the photographs in tomorrow morning's paper, are they? No. The *we* looks to be you and me. That *we.* I do business in this town, remember? The kind that needs building permits and zoning variances, both of which I'm in the process of asking for right now, to expand my Broad Street store. For God's sake, Jolie, I'll probably be fielding calls from the opposition party tomorrow, too, asking me to do commercials endorsing their candidate. Did you think of any of that? I'll answer my own question. *No,* you didn't think of any of that. Now ask me how happy I am about all of this."

"I don't have to ask. But all I said was that *we* were speaking to anyone who is remotely involved in the deaths of Melodie Brainard and Teddy Sunshine."

"Right. *Involved.* Not a great choice of word, Jolie. And then you had to go and add that line about how Joshua Brainard, while helpful at first, cut short your *interview* when one of your questions seemed to hit too close to home."

She winced. "*Interview* was the wrong word. I've already agreed with you on that one. And the *too close to home* thing? I don't know, Sam, Brainard's father did have that heart attack, so it was sort of *too close to home*. The words just came out wrong. I should apologize to the Brainards, and then call Garry Tuttle and elaborate on what I meant."

"Unfortunately, apologies aren't going to help, and if you say anything else to the press things will only get worse," Sam said, deserting the bar to pace one of the large Aubusson carpets laid on the cherrywood floors. "So now we have Josh trying to explain about his father's position on the special commission set up for the Fishtown murders, and by tomorrow morning some jackass reporter is going to try to link the two somehow."

Jolie walked over to the conversation area and sat down on one of the couches. "Hmm, you're right. Wow, I hadn't thought of that. Those women were all strangled. Melodie Brainard was strangled. Wow, I hadn't thought about that. I hadn't made the connection, Sam, but you're right. Wow."

"Three wows. I give up," Sam said, sitting down on the facing couch. "Now you're actually pleased with yourself, aren't you? The guy did me a favor, Jolie. He graciously agreed to meet with the daughter of the man who he believes killed his wife, and you stabbed him in the back. The guy who is so far ahead in the polls it would take a major scandal to lose him the race—and now you've given the press a step up, if that's what they want to do. The guy who will be mayor for the next four or maybe eight years, while I have to see him socially, and do business in this town, not to belabor the point."

Jolie dropped her head forward into her hands. "For the last time, Sam, I apologize. But the man is no saint, you know. He was standing there for those photos, his hand on my ass, saying how he'd been happy to welcome me back to my hometown, even in such tragic circumstances…"

"His hand on your ass?"

She looked up at him. "Yes, Sam, his hand on my ass. Cupping it, *squeezing* it. With you standing right there, on my other side. The whole time Gary Tuttle was snapping shots and asking questions. I know he said he and his wife weren't close, and all of that self-depreciating baloney, but she's only in the ground a couple of days, for crying out loud. A little soon to be copping a feel, don't you think? So I like him, sort of, because he met with us, but I don't like him, because he's as phony as a three-dollar bill. I was *so* angry, Sam. So maybe what I said wasn't all an innocent mistake. I really can't be sure, can I?"

"Never mind."

"Because I shouldn't have let my emotions overcome my—never mind?"

"Right. Never mind. And you know what, Jolie? I overreacted. Big-time. Let the press go digging back into the Fishtown Strangler case, why not? Those women *were* strangled. Melodie Brainard *was* strangled. Josh's father was on the commission, and the Fishtown case was never solved. The whole thing is going to make for some interesting questions for the next few days on the campaign trail. Maybe old Josh won't have time to floss."

Jolie shook her head. "So you're not going to blame me if you can't get that zoning change or whatever it is? We're okay? You and me?"

"Yeah, I suppose so. Just warn me next time someone makes a pass at you like that, damn it. Not that Tuttle's daughter wouldn't like to be put through Harvard on the pictures he sells of me breaking somebody's neck if they touch you."

"Oh, Sam, that's so, so *caveman* of you. I'm flattered." She shifted on the couch as the sound of the front door slamming brought their attention to someone's arrival in the foyer. "Hi, Jessica," she said as her sister stormed into the living room ahead of Matthew Denby. "Lieutenant Denby."

Jessica stopped, one arm pointing back toward Matt. "*He* is out. O-U-T. Out. You got that? *Out.* I will not work with this idiot. Oh, hell, I need a drink."

"Whiskey bottle is open and on the bar," Sam said, grinning. "Help yourself. You, too, Matt. You look like you might need one. And let me add—I know the feeling."

"She's impossible," Matt said, shoving his fingers through his hair. "Like a steamroller, just rolling over people, me included. And the law? To her, it's like some handy guidebook on making sure she does everything she isn't supposed to do. Reporters. I've seen barracudas with more ethics. And larger brains."

While Matt complained, Sam watched Jessica approaching from the bar, a can of diet soda in her hand. He hadn't noticed at first—God only knew how he hadn't—but the girl was dressed like a, well, like a hooker. Not a call girl; they dressed better. Four-inch heels, bright yellow skirt up to her crotch, belly-exposing red tank top that let her black bra straps show. Blond hair teased into a rat's nest, her makeup laid on with a trowel. "Cripes, Jess. How did I miss Halloween?"

"Funny, Sam," Jessica said, plopping herself down beside Jolie, who immediately grabbed the cashmere afghan on the back of the couch and flung it over her sister's lap. "When it comes to pimps, I should have hired Sister Mary Claire from junior year English. At least she had a sense of humor and wasn't half as prudy."

"Prudy?" Jolie asked, adjusting the afghan after Jessica crossed her legs.

"Yes, *prudy*. All I did was go up to one car. Just one! You know, to stay in character? And—bam— here comes my knight on his white charger, pulling me away, flashing his damn badge and completely blowing my cover."

"For the record," Matt said, carrying a can of beer with him as he joined them, "she was half in the damn car window, her arms folded on the door, half of her hanging out the front end of that outfit, the rest hanging out the back end, and all with her ass in the air—wiggling in the air. And the gum. Jesus, the wad of gum she was chomping on? There's only so much a man can take."

"Oh, like I was *wiggling* at you? I don't *think* so, buddy boy," Jessica said before leaning over to unstrap her shoes. "He made me throw away my gum, too, and it hadn't lost its flavor yet. Straw- berry. Not to mention that I was getting some- where with the ladies on the corner. I think they liked me."

"While you were just standing there, talking to them, sure, then they liked you. You were bringing in business," Matt said, cupping the beer can between his palms. "You didn't see their faces when you walked over to that car. You were about two seconds from learning one of the basic rules of street-corner hooking—you want your own square of turf on the corner, you fight for it."

Jessica looked at Jolie. "He's just saying that. I

was fine, really. And one of the girls remembered Kayla Morrison and two of the others. I told them who I was and what I was doing. And they were all happy to hear that I was looking into the Fishtown Strangler case again. These women are born victims, you know that? Worse—nobody cares. No matter how this all ends, I'm going to do a piece of those women. Do you know what police call it when one of them is cut up or murdered? They call the crime NHIs. No humans involved. That's disgusting."

Matt crushed his empty beer can. "Only the jackasses do that."

"I'm not talking to you," Jessica said, pointing a finger at him. "You're just lucky I was able to give Flo my card before you pulled me away. Not that she'll talk to me now, with you waving that badge of yours around like that. God, I was so embarrassed."

"Did you hear that, Sam? The woman was *embarrassed.* Not by that outfit. Not by the way she was acting. But by my badge. I won't work with her again. I'm not a babysitter and I'm damn well not a masochist."

"No, you're a tease. You tell me you've got information you photocopied from the Murder Book and you won't even let me touch it. Look, Jessica, but don't touch—that's what you said, like I was going to *steal* your precious photocopies and go running through the streets yelling how I got them from you, the big, bad cop. I know how to protect a source, Matthew Denby. And if you think you're going with me tomorrow to that address for Tarin White, you are *so* wrong."

"You're damn well not going alone. Sam?"

Sam held up his hands. "Oh, no, don't look at me, either of you. I've got more than enough going on controlling Jolie, believe me. And don't even think about asking Court."

"Controlling Jolie, Sam?" Jolie asked, and he tried not to wince.

"Bad choice of words. But Jolie did sort of stumble over something tonight. The Fishtown murders were by strangulation, and Joshua Brainard's wife also was strangled. There can't be a connection, too many years separate the crimes. But Jolie connected the two cases, along with the others, in front of a reporter, so you can count on something about it hitting the newspapers. Whether that helps or hurts what you two are doing, I don't know."

"I'm not seeing a police pension in my future," Matt said, rubbing at the back of his neck. "Remind me how I got mixed up in this?"

"And there he goes," Jessica said, glaring at Matt. "Did I ask him in? I don't think so. He invited himself in. Naturally, at the first speed bump, he decides to turn it all around, blame it on me.

Typical man. I'm going upstairs. My head's beginning to itch from all the hairspray. You coming, Jolie?"

Sam looked at Jolie, who was looking at him. He raised one eyebrow, as if not understanding the question in her eyes. She was the one who'd said no sex, not him. But what the hell; they'd argued—for the very first time, he believed—so maybe it was time to see if makeup sex was all it was cracked up to be.

He gave it a shot. "I've got to call the number the DEA agent gave me to find out whether or not it's safe to let my employees go back to work in the morning. And I've got some paperwork to catch up on while I'm at it, before I might go for a swim. One way or another, it's been a hot night."

Jolie looked at him for another long moment, and then nodded her head before saying good-night to Matt and following Jessica out of the room.

"Can we trust them?"

Sam looked at Matt. "Excuse me?"

"It's only nine-thirty. Can we trust them to stay upstairs—that's what I'm asking, I suppose. I'm telling you, Sam, another five minutes with that woman, trying to control her, and I was going to pull out my handcuffs. Then I got this sort of wild image in my head and—yeah, well, forget that. She could drive a man crazy, and I don't think she's even trying. And if she calls me *Grandpa* one more time, I won't be responsible."

Sam laughed and suggested the two of them get another beer from the minifridge. He stood behind the bar as Matt leaned against one of the stools and slid a can toward him. "Teddy didn't raise any of them to be shy and retiring types, that's for sure. What I can't figure out is why the three of us—I'm including Court in this—are following them around like they're in charge."

"That's because we aren't entirely stupid. We're smart enough to know that they *are* in charge," Matt said and took a long swallow from the can. "I could back off, I know that. But after seeing Jess tonight? It would be like letting a kitten out in the middle of lion country. She talks big, but she doesn't have a clue what goes on in the real world on those street corners. Tonight was a game to her."

"Not really, Matt."

"Oh, I know. They're dead serious about Teddy. I think maybe it's easier, at least for Jessica, if she approaches the whole thing like what she's doing is some television special or something. She's detaching herself from the fact that Teddy may have killed himself—and Melodie Brainard—and concentrating on building a good story. She makes a pretty convincing prostitute, though, I'll give her that. When she first hit the light from the streetlamp on the corner, I thought there was going to be a three-car pileup of johns trying to pull over to the curb. It was all I could do to stay in my car, out of sight."

Sam smiled. "Joshua Brainard posed for pictures tonight with Jolie and copped a feel. She didn't tell me until we got back here. Otherwise, I would have decked him. Careful, Matt. There's something about all three Sunshine girls that brings out the testosterone. You've just entered dangerous territory."

"And I plan to get out of it as quickly as possible," Matt said as he put down the empty beer can. "I'm on duty tomorrow at seven, so I'd better make it an early night and get going. I put in for two weeks of vacation the department owes me, but it will be a couple of days until I know if I've got it. In the meantime, watch her, okay? She won't have any luck going back to the street corners until after dark, but God only knows what trouble she can get into in the daylight."

"I'll do my best," Sam promised. And then an idea hit him. "You know what, Matt, I think I know just how to keep Jessica out of trouble tomorrow."

"I don't think her sisters will let you lock her in the basement."

"Damn. Well, that was my second choice, anyway," Sam said as he accompanied Matt to the front door. "If I haven't said it yet, thank you. I don't want to consider what might have happened if Jessica had been on that corner without backup. But now tell me something. Is this all about Teddy—or about Jessica?"

"You're forgetting something else, Sam," Matt said, his expression dead serious. "You're forgetting that I was primary on the Brainard murder and got it yanked right out from under me when the brass caught wind of the who the victim was. I don't like how fast everything moved, how convenient it was that Teddy committed suicide, none of it. I was already quietly doing some investigating of my own. Why else do you think I was so close to Teddy's house when that emergency call came in about the fire? I'd been on my way to talk to the daughters after I read what Jolie said in the newspapers about investigating the deaths on their own."

"There are no coincidences," Sam said, shaking his head. "I should have known."

"Then know this, Sam—if it hadn't been for that fire, I don't know if I'd be here now. That," he said and then grinned, "and taking one look at Jessica. I think I like the way she doesn't like me. If she begins to hate me, things might really get interesting."

Sam laughed, clapped Matt on the shoulder and sent him out into the night.

He headed for his office, already pulling his wallet out of his pocket to locate the card from

George Wallitsch, the DEA agent he'd met that morning. Or was that yesterday morning? His days had begun to blur, merge. Or was he trying not to let the days pass too quickly, knowing Jolie would soon be leaving Philadelphia, leaving him yet again?

The message light was blinking on the answering machine in his office, and he hit it as he sat down at his desk, even while his mind calculated how late it would have to be before Jessica, Jade and Court were all in bed, asleep.

"Sam? Josh Brainard. What the f—what the hell did you get me into tonight? That was dishonest, Sam, trading on our friendship like that. Now I'll be fielding calls for days, distracting me from the real issues of the campaign, dragging up poor Melodie like she's some new victim of the Fishtown Strangler or something. And my father. Do you know what this could do to him? I thought you said ours was going to be a friendly visit, to help you convince Jolie and her sisters that they were making a mistake with this insane investigation they're carrying on. A favor, to keep them from dragging Melodie and me into any more press on the whole ugly story. Do me a favor, Sam—don't do me any more favors."

"Got, it, Josh. I guess I don't see any more foursomes in our future," Sam said, deleting the message.

There had been two messages, and Sam waited for the second one.

"Mr. Becket, Agent Wallitsch here. Change of plans, sir, if you'll agree. We want to release the two cases from the warehouse and deliver them as you would normally do. Your warehouse is very well protected and we've concluded that the pickup won't be here. I see here that both cases are to be transferred to your store downtown—a piece of luck for us, sir, logistically—and that's what we want to do. We'd like to deliver them tomorrow evening at your regular closing time and then have our men in place, inside and outside the building. We'll do everything as usual, sir, stay within your normal routine for deliveries, and then wait for someone to attempt to retrieve the drugs. I see that it is your practice to be on-site for all major deliveries, but we'll work on that. I'll be in touch with you tomorrow morning to make arrangements. Thank you again, Mr. Becket, for being so cooperative."

Sam hit the delete button a second time. *Cooperative?* As if Wallitsch had left him a choice? And what was that business about how they'd *work on that?* If the DEA thought someone had already planned to break in to his store, he damn well was going to be there. It was his store, and this was the second time someone had tried to use his imported merchandise as a conduit for drugs. There wasn't going to be a third time.

"Unless there already was a third time, unless there were a lot more times and we only got lucky twice," Sam said quietly.

He woke up his computer and went into the personnel files for Becket Imports and then narrowed the list of employees to those at the flagship store, the Becket Hotel on Broad Street. He had thirty-two employees at the warehouse, including the security staff, and three full-time employees and five part-time sales personnel in the store. Add three guards, the custodial service that came in every evening, for a total of forty-five people who, to at least a degree, were familiar with policies and procedures. Store hours, when deliveries were allowed, when the Dumpsters were cleared out, all of it.

Sam also kept files on past employees, those who had resigned and those that had been terminated for cause. That added, counting only the past five years, another eight names to his list.

He printed out three separate lists of names.

Next, he went about eliminating names. He began with Larry, at the warehouse, who'd been with him from the beginning. And then Jimmy, who worked the dogs and who had discovered the drugs in the first place.

One by one over the course of the next three hours Sam crossed out names on all three lists, oblivious to anything except what he was doing:

hunting for a criminal, a smuggler, inside his own company.

It was well after midnight when he finally sat back in his chair, a new list of ten names on his desk. Part of him was disgusted with himself for questioning the honesty of these ten employees, while another part of him was mad as hell. If he was right. If they'd just been lucky finding the drugs that had made it through Customs inspection twice. But that they could have just as easily not been lucky other times.

DEA and Homeland Security, his ass. Grandma had to take off her orthopedic shoes at the airport checkpoints, but hard drugs were still flooding the country. Sure, he'd do his part, gladly, keeping his own expensive drug-sniffing dogs. But if the ports, the borders, were any tighter than they were a few years ago, he didn't see it.

"Damn," he muttered, pushing back his chair as he did see one thing—the clock above his desk. "Jolie."

He ripped the bottom off the page he'd printed out, folded the list and tucked it into his wallet before heading for the French doors that opened onto the terrace.

The grounds were strategically lit at night, "up-lights" placed beneath specific pieces of shrubbery, including all of the tall, slim evergreens flanking the length of the wide corridor of stone leading up to and around the pool. His father, when he'd had the pool built and the surrounding grounds landscaped twenty years earlier, had jokingly called the area "the Italian country villa portion of our program." Whatever it was, it still worked. If he didn't live here himself, Sam knew, he'd be damned impressed.

He stepped off the terrace to see the blue-green water of the pool illuminated by underwater lights and closed his eyes for a moment in relief when he saw Jolie sitting at the edge, her bare legs dangling into the water. She was wearing his white terry-cloth robe, her hair hanging wet and loose, so that he knew she'd already been in the water.

She looked his way as he approached. "I thought we got our signals crossed," she said, getting to her feet. "You're still dressed. Where's your suit?"

"I usually don't wear one when I swim at night," he told her.

"Really," she said, her eyes wide and innocent. "I never knew that."

"Then you don't know where the dimmers are—to turn down some of these lights so nobody can see us from the house."

He watched as her gaze shifted to the small decorative bench that concealed the switches below the hinged seat.

She tried to cover what she'd done by lifting her

wet hair up onto her head and then letting it fall past her shoulders once more, but it didn't work. Sam knew that, once again, they were in tune with each other. At least on one level.

"No, I can't say that I do, Sam. Sorry. Although I do seem to remember a supply of swimsuits in the pool house on the other side of those trees behind you."

All right. Maybe he was wrong. "So you meant it?"

Again she avoided his eyes. "Meant what, Sam?"

"You know what. No...lovemaking?"

"I meant it at the time," she said, and he noticed that her breathing had become a bit shallow. "I'll probably mean it again tomorrow. We're only... complicating things, Sam. It's just that...it's just that I ate that roll at dinner, you know? With butter. And...and somebody told me that having sex burns a lot of...calories."

The entire time she'd been talking Sam had been slipping out of his shoes and socks, easing his shirt up and over his head. By the time she'd lapsed into silence once more he was lifting the bench seat and had turned off the pool lights, leaving them in the faint light of the up-lights and the starry sky above their heads.

"Do you remember the last time we went for a midnight swim, Jolie?"

"I remember that I nearly drowned," she told him, reaching for the sash of her robe. "Some underwater...activities should only be attempted by professionals."

"Never underestimate the enthusiasm of a motivated amateur," Sam told her, and then drew in his breath as she allowed the robe to slide from her shoulders, revealing her long, perfect, naked body. "Okay," he said as she turned and neatly dived into the water. "Definitely motivated."

CHAPTER THIRTEEN

JOLIE SAT AT THE breakfast table, holding up her chin with her hand as she leaned her elbow on the wood, automatically chewing on a piece of whole-wheat toast, her eyes closed, remembering the night just past.

They'd swum a few laps, even raced. And then they'd playfully argued about the proper usage of *swim, swam, swum.* Their argument had consisted of shouting out the words as they splashed each other and ended with them ducking each other like children.

But that had all been prelude, their own unique manner of foreplay, she supposed. Because when she'd finally cried uncle and turned onto her back to float in the heated water, and he'd taken hold of her heels and scissored her legs apart and then pulled her close to him…

"Jolie? *Jolie.*"

"Hmm?" she asked, opening her eyes and then blinking away the lovely images behind her eyelids.

"What, Jessica? I already told you—Sam had to go to the shop this morning and he said we're not allowed to go anywhere without him. He'll be back by noon."

"I agree with Sam," Jade said from the other side of the table. "Neither of you two should be allowed out alone. Ever. Thank you, Court," she ended as Court laid a plate in front of her, the ham on it already sliced into bite-size pieces. "Don't let us keep you. Didn't you say you had some calls to make?"

"I did, yes," Court said as he picked up his own plate. "And I can take a hint, too. I'll eat this in Sam's study while I use his computer. Seems my laptop has been commandeered by someone who likes its wireless qualities. Excuse me."

"You copped his laptop?" Jessica asked. "What's wrong with yours? You've got to be wireless."

"I am," Jade said, concentrating on spearing a piece of ham with the fork held precariously in her bandaged hand. "I don't want him spying on me, that's all, and he insists on sitting with me while I'm online. So I told him my battery was dead and the charger is back at the house."

"Trusting sort, our big sister," Jolie said, buttering a second piece of toast. With last night's exercise as a cushion, she figured the second slice was a safe bet. She could probably go back to

Thompson's Diner for a slice of lemon meringue pie and still fit into her gown for the premiere.

"Yeah, and stuck here, just like us," Jessica complained. "Can someone please tell me how those men got to be in charge of us? Denby most especially. Man, can he set my teeth on edge."

"I think he's cute," Jolie said if only to upset her sister, "in a rumpled, Harrison Ford in *Air Force One* sort of way. You know—'Jessica, I said no,'" she said, lowering her voice. "Almost just like 'Get off my plane.' I love Harrison Ford. I've met him several times. I'd kill to work with him."

"Oh, puh-leez. I'd say Dudley Denby is more Clint Eastwood as *Dirty Harry.* Waving his phallic symbol around and whispering menacingly, 'Well, punk, do you feel *lucky?*'"

"Waving around his *what?*" Jade asked, this time while trying to grasp the handle of her coffee cup.

"His gun, Jade, his gun," Jessica said, rolling her eyes. "What else do you call a .357 Magnum? 'The most powerful handgun in the world'—quoting Harry again. I asked to see Matt's."

"Jess, please tell me you didn't. You asked to see Matt's *phallic symbol?*"

"No, Jolie, and stop laughing. Besides, he only has this ugly little snub-nosed thing anyway. I wasn't at all impressed."

Jade's coffee cup tipped, spilling its contents on

the white linen tablecloth, and Jolie quickly grabbed some napkins to blot the spill. "Thanks, I think I'm awake now. Embarrassed by my baby sister but awake. Okay, change of subject."

"God, yes, please," Jolie said, retaking her seat.

"This is about Teddy. I've been going over and over that night in my head and I finally asked Court to take me back to the house to look at the personal property bag I got back from the coroner. I'll admit it, I've been avoiding looking at anything in that bag. His keys were in there, house key and car key."

"And?" Jolie asked, confused.

"*And* he never leaves his keys in his pocket. You know Teddy, a real creature of habit. He uses the house key to get in and then tosses the key ring on the hall table along with his wallet. It drove me nuts that he did that. That night, he obviously kept them with him. His wallet was also in with his personal belongings."

Know, not knew. Uses, not used. Drove, not drives. Jolie lowered her eyes, wondering if Jade realized she was alternately referring to Teddy in the present and the past tense. They were all still struggling with the finality of their father's death. When this was over, whether they succeeded or failed, they were all going to have to come to terms with the one fact they couldn't change—Teddy was gone.

"His wallet and keys weren't where they were supposed to be. What a breakthrough. She's a private detective, you know," Jessica said, rolling her eyes at Jolie. "And a deep thinker. That's why they pay her the big bucks. Nobody always does the same things, Jade. Not *always*."

"Teddy did. You didn't live with him these last years. I did. More and more, he became a creature of habit, of routine. Almost obsessive, just like he was with his cold cases. Listen to me," Jade said as Jolie bit her bottom lip to keep from laughing; Jade was back to giving orders. "And ask yourselves this one—why not put the keys and wallet where he always put them? I think it meant one of two things. One, he was planning to go right back out again. Or, two, he had something really, really heavy on his mind. Or, three, maybe he was distracted? Maybe someone had shown up just as he was opening the front door?"

"A visitor?" Jolie asked, becoming more interested. "A client? And he got home sometime around nine-thirty, right? But the…the time of death wasn't until midnight. That's a lot of time for one appointment, isn't it?"

"And you have to add in time for Teddy to get drunk as a skunk," Jessica said, pushing her plate away, her pancakes only half-eaten. "So let me see if I understand this, Jade. You're thinking he let his killer in? That he knew him? Her?"

"I do. Unless he had *two* visitors that night. One just as he was coming back from seeing Melodie Brainard, and then some time in there for him to get drunk, and then a second—and last—visitor. And nobody took any damn fingerprints, crime-scene photos, nothing," she said hotly. "An obvious suicide, no real investigation needed. He killed the woman, killed himself. There's the bottle of booze, there's the gun, there's the back of his head blown to hell, his brains all over the wall. A good cop gone bad, let's bury him and the mess he made and hope it all goes away. Nobody listened! *God.* You don't know how *insane* that made me."

Yes, I do, Jolie thought, remembering the shattered Belleek. "I'm sorry we couldn't get home quicker, Jade."

Jade blinked several times. "You both got here as quickly as you could," she said tightly. "I was fine. Let's just think about this."

"No, you tell us what you've been thinking," Jessica said kindly. "We're listening, hon, we really are."

Jade bit her lips between her teeth as she nodded, clearly in a effort to control her emotions. "Okay," she said a moment later—whether talking to them or reassuring herself that she could do this, Jolie didn't know. "This is my theory. Teddy came home from Melodie Brainard's house after striking out with her again. He wasn't with her for more than ten minutes—we know that because the security video was time-stamped. I think someone was waiting at home for him."

"A client. A friend. Someone he knew," Jolie said, leaning her elbows on the table. "Go on."

"Step two," Jade said, her voice growing more confident, "the bottle of fine Irish whiskey. I think he was upset, either by his failure at the Brainard house or by something that happened with that visitor, client, whoever. Because it matters that he didn't follow his usual habits. The keys, the wallet, the eleven-o'clock news. Something—or someone— had completely thrown off his routines. Time passes, getting close to midnight."

"He's got his gun case out on the desk," Jolie interrupted. "At some point, he got his gun out, Jade. Why?"

She shook her head. "I don't know, Jolie. He rarely carried anymore. We don't do that sort of work, the kind that gets you shot. Not since last year."

Jolie knew that. Teddy had revamped the focus of the Sunshine Detective Agency immediately after Jade had been shot at, right after Jade and Court had argued and then divorced. The occasional divorce case, sure, but ninety percent of their business was now strictly background checks.

"You don't think he would have been cleaning his gun, do you, Jade?" Jessica asked her. "I mean, he was drunk. He wouldn't do that, not drunk."

"No, he wouldn't. And the gun was loaded, remember? He never kept it loaded. He didn't even keep his ammunition in the same box with the gun. I think Teddy believed he was in some kind of danger."

"So he got himself drunk? That makes no sense."

"I agree, Jolie," Jade said, pushing back her chair and getting to her feet. She began to pace, as if unable to be still. "This is only conjecture, supposition, whatever you want to call it, but I think Teddy came home already spooked, but then something happened. Something else. Some*one* else. Something unexpected that just blew him out of the water."

"And sent him diving into a bottle," Jessica said, looking at Jolie. "It couldn't have been Mom, could it? After all these years? She couldn't have shown up, could she? No, that's impossible."

"You called her, Jade, didn't you?" Jolie hadn't spoken to her mother since the woman left, but Jade had been in contact with her a few times. It was a very one-sided communication, though. When Claudia Sunshine had deserted them, she'd never looked back, not even to check up on her own daughters.

"I left a phone message. I'm afraid it was pretty much a hi-Teddy's-dead-not-that-you-care kind of message," Jade said quietly. "I left my cell number. Nobody's returned my call. Not Mom, not Teddy's own brother. I don't know where they are. Maui, here, the moon. I don't know."

"Well, maybe we should know. If Mom came back? Talk about something happening that would have made Teddy forget anything else that was going on."

Jolie looked at her sisters, the three of them bonded by blood, by their love for Teddy, and by their deep disappointment in their mother. "She tried to hit me up for money a while ago. About the time my third movie came out. She went through my fan club online, if you can believe that. My publicist told me about it, but I never made contact. If I give her money, she'll never stop asking, and if I don't, she might go to the tabloids with some sob story. I really don't care what she does. Unless she finds a way to go back in time, be there for us, for our high school graduations, for our prom nights, for all the times a girl needs her mother, I have nothing to say to her."

"We all belong on a couch," Jessica said, sighing. "I've been, you know. My therapist says we try so hard to succeed because we think Mom left because she didn't love us, we weren't good enough for her. So now we try to be better than anyone else. I think that's a bunch of happy horse poop, but what do I know?"

"I know we're getting off track," Jade said, her cheeks unnaturally pale. "I'm just saying we should probably try to reconstruct Teddy's last movements. We know who he went to see, but now we have to figure out who saw him that night *after* he came home."

"Two different visitors. One tells him something that makes him break out the bottle, and the second may have been the one he was loading his gun about, right?" Jolie said, nodding her head. "Well, good luck with that, because I don't have a clue as to how we're going to do it. What I do have is Sam's idea for something we can do today, and I think I like it, a lot. If you'll help, Jess."

Jessica leaned back in her chair and spread her hands. "If it gets me out of this house before Snub Nose shows up, it works for me. What's your idea?"

"Sam promised to make an appointment with David Pearson for one o'clock today. He's the groom in my vanishing-bride case. I want him to see you."

"See me? Why would you—oh, wait, I get it. The photograph. I don't look that much like your vanishing bride, do I?"

"Not all that much, but enough," Jolie told her. "And if you wear that shorter wig Smitty sent me, and we did a little work with your makeup, I think you could look pretty much like a ghost returning to haunt him. You're about the same age now that Cathleen was back then. We just want to see how he reacts. Are you game for a little playacting?"

"Yeah," Jessica said, an unholy grin spreading across her face. "Yeah, I like this. And you know what, ladies? I think I have another idea, thanks to Jolie. What about Rockne?"

"What about Rockne?" Jade asked, sitting down once more.

"He was there, wasn't he? He saw whoever came into the house that night," Jessica pointed out. "I know he's an Irish setter, not a bloodhound or a pointer, but maybe he'd see the murderer again and, you know, growl or something?"

"Rockne?" Jade smiled. "You've got to be kidding. The only trick that dog knows is how to look pathetic to get a treat."

"But it's worth a shot," Jolie said, looking down at Rockne, who was sound asleep on his back, one hind leg twitching in some doggy dream. "Let's do it. Let's take Rockne with us whenever we're going to see anybody at all involved with the cold cases. This is good, guys. We might finally be getting somewhere."

They spoke for a while longer, pretty much covering ground already covered, and then Court came to get Jade, to take her for her visit to the burn clinic at the hospital.

"She went quietly enough," Jessica commented as they watched the two of them leave. "I think he's slipping tranquilizers into her drinks. It's the only explanation that works. Leaving, of course, the question—why is he being so nice to her? Those two fought like cats and dogs, present dog excepted."

Jolie thought about telling her sister what she and Sam had found in Jade's closet, but to do so felt like a betrayal of her sister's most vulnerable moment. "Sam says Court still loves her. That's probably why he's still here."

"I like him, you know," Jessica said, getting to her feet as Mrs. Archer came into the room to begin clearing away the breakfast plates. "Who does he remind you of?"

Jolie followed her sister outside, onto the terrace beyond the French doors. "What do you mean who does he remind me of? He reminds me of Court."

"No, no. You compared Matt to Harrison Ford. And you do that a lot—compare people to movie stars, physically. Who do I look like, for instance?"

"Nemo," Jolie said, grinning. "Or maybe Dora. You know, the scatterbrained blue fish voiced-over by Ellen DeGeneres?"

"And aren't you the funny one. Come on, Jolie. Who do I remind you of? *Really.*"

"Don't make me say it," Jolie protested. "I'll never hear the end of it."

"Good, huh?" Jessica asked, fluffing her hair.

"It's probably just the name coincidence," Jolie said reluctantly. "All right—Jessica Simpson. Happy now?"

Jessica frowned. "She once posed for *Playboy*, didn't she? *Penthouse?* One of those? I'd never do that."

"You asked, I answered. Let it go," Jolie said, suddenly remembering where she'd left her last cigarette and her lighter. She continued walking along the terrace until she came to the correct French door and then looked behind the urn. Disappointed, she moved to the next set of doors, the next pair of urns. Nothing. Yeah, well, the morning dew would probably have destroyed the cigarette anyway....

"What are you looking for?"

Jolie wondered who had found her cigarette and lighter. She hoped it hadn't been Sam. "Nothing. I think Court looks a little like Ben Affleck," she said, grabbing the name of the first tall, dark-haired actor she could think of. And Mrs. Archer reminds me of Jean Stapleton."

"Who?"

"You probably wouldn't remember her. I don't know why I'm always doing that, but I guess I do compare people to celebrities. Almost like I'm putting them in categories. My agent resembles Holland Taylor a little, especially when she's negotiating, and my publicist, in a good light, looks a little like Russell Crowe."

"Really? Making a mental note here—ask to meet Jolie's publicist."

"Don't bother, he's very happily gay. Even you aren't that good."

"Once more—funny girl. Who does Sam remind you of?"

"Sam?" Jolie turned to look at her sister. "Sam doesn't remind me of anybody. He's just Sam."

Jessica's smile bordered on the smug. "I thought so. Sam's like nobody else in the world to you. One of a kind. Unique, even. He's *just Sam*. Oh, you've got it bad, Jolie. And now the big question—what are you going to do about it?"

"I don't know," Jolie said quietly. "I honest-to-God don't know. How do I...how do I leave him again? I thought I loved him five years ago—and I did. I really did. But now? He's everything I remember about him and yet so much more."

"It has been five years," Jessica pointed out. "You've both changed. Grown?"

Jolie look out toward the pool, its surface a blinding white in the sunshine. "You know when you think something is good, that it's so good that it would be impossible for it to be even better? Not just...enjoyable. Mind-blowing. Deeper, somehow. Meaning...meaning more."

"Just so we're both on the same page here, we're talking about sex now?" Jessica asked her.

"No, little sister," Jolie said, sighing. "I think we're talking about making love. Come on," she said, shaking her head, "let's go upstairs and turn you into a naive little waitress about to marry the man of her dreams."

It took over an hour, with Jessica scrubbing her face clean after their first effort at softening the line of her higher cheekbones, but Jolie was fairly well pleased with the Jessica who followed her downstairs after Sam had called her room to say that he was ready to leave for David Pearson's office.

When Sam looked up at her, Jolie met his gaze straight on, and when he smiled at her, she felt herself blushing. Like a teenager. Like an idiot. It felt wonderful.

"Hi, Sam," she said, descending the last step.

"Hi, yourself. Wow, and who is this lovely young thing you've got with you?" he asked, winking at Jolie.

"I just want it put on the record," Jessica said mulishly, "that Jessica Sunshine does *not* wear Peter Pan collars. Not on a bet, not on a dare, not on your life. I'm acting now, Sam. You will never see this blouse again."

"I'll make a note," Sam promised and then frowned as Jolie attached a leash to Rockne's collar. "We're taking him for a walk before we leave?"

"No, we're taking him with us to see how he reacts around possible suspects."

"A good idea, I suppose, if Rockne has somehow morphed into Lassie. But dogs aren't allowed in downtown business offices."

"He's my hearing dog," Jessica told Sam smugly. "Working dogs are allowed, right?"

"It'll never work," Sam said as they went outside and climbed into his black SUV.

"What? Did you say something, Sam?" Jessica teased. "I can't hear you."

"Shut up, Jess. And we're talking about Jessica, Sam," Jolie reminded him as she buckled her seat belt. "Peter Pan collar buttoned to the neck or not, Jessica can get away with things the rest of the world could never get away with. She'll tip her head and smile, she'll push out the girls, and the next thing you know the guard will be melting. Trust me."

"True. What was I thinking? Oh, and I had an interesting morning, thank you."

Jolie looked at him inquiringly. "You sound angry all of a sudden."

"Pissed off, Jolie. I sound pissed off. Don't pretty it up. It would seem that Agent Wallitsch doesn't think much of my sleuthing capabilities or my ability to be on the premises tonight when, as he said it, he hopes everything *goes down*."

Jessica leaned forward in the backseat, resting her forearms next to Jolie's head. "When what goes down? This sounds like something interesting."

"I'll keep it short and sweet," Sam said as they headed for the Schuylkill Expressway in the light early-afternoon traffic—meaning he could pretty much sustain a steady forty miles per hour if he changed lanes often enough. "We found drugs in two crates that made it through Customs and now we're going to deliver them to my downtown store after-hours tonight and then wait for whoever knows the drugs are there to come and get them. I gave Wallitsch a list of possibles for an inside job—which he blew off—and told him that if he wants this to all look natural, I should be there."

"He said no, didn't he?" Jolie asked, her stomach doing a sudden flip.

"Right up to the moment I told him to take his plans and his drugs and shove them," Sam said, smiling at her. "Bottom line, as of nine o'clock tonight, Underdog rides again."

"Oh, Sam, no. Drugs? Drugs mean guns. You can't be serious."

He eased the SUV toward the exit ramp and slowed for mid-town traffic. "Don't worry, Jolie. The action—if that's what it's called—will all be in the storeroom, and I'll be out front, visible, only because I'm always there for deliveries and everyone knows that."

"Because you think it's an inside job," Jessica said, and her tone told Jolie that her sister wasn't going to be on her side if this came to an argument. "Cool. Who are your suspects?"

"Jess, don't encourage him. He's an amateur. He

has no business interfering in an official investiga—oh, hell, listen to me. Listen to what I'm saying. What are we doing? What are we *all* doing?"

"We're pulling into this parking garage and heading up to David Pearson's office, with your sister dressed like his missing fiancée so you can watch his reaction, and then pumping him about his whereabouts the night Teddy was killed. And we're bringing Rockne the Wonder Mutt with us to see if he bites the guy on the leg," Sam supplied unhelpfully. "Now, you want to give me another lecture?"

"Oh, shut up," Jolie said, knowing she was beaten. She hopped from the SUV as soon as Sam parked it and walked ahead of both of them toward the elevator to the street, her huge, concealing sunglasses in place.

Five minutes later David Pearson's receptionist was escorting them to a set of large double glass doors and handing them off to David Pearson's secretary, who handed them off to David Pearson's personal assistant...who finally ushered them into the man's presence.

The trip through the halls, the receptionist, the secretary and the personal assistant were all as impressive as hell.

David Pearson was about as impressive as a short man, just ten pounds shy of dumpy, balding, wearing glasses and a deer-in-headlights expression that seemed permanently etched into his face, could be. Jolie immediately remembered Joshua Brainard's laughing shock when she'd hinted that David Pearson might have killed his fiancée: *David?* David?

Jolie mentally conceded that the mayoral candidate had a point. David Pearson looked as threatening, as capable of murder, as the meerkat in *Lion King*. He looked a little like the meerkat, too, come to think of it....

"David, thanks for seeing us," Sam said as Jolie tried to stop her mind from running along dead-end tracks, and then he went on to introduce Jolie and Jessica—who had stood behind Jolie and as out of sight as she could.

"Hello, Mr. Pearson," Jessica said in her best little girl voice, stepping out from cover, and Jolie watched as the man looked, looked harder and then seemed to sway where he stood.

"Uh…yes, hello. Ms. Sunshine? Excuse me. For a moment there I—please, please sit down. Tell me how I can help you."

He never looked at Sam, never looked at movie star Jolie Sunshine. All his attention, his melting brown eyes behind rimless glasses, were concentrated on Jessica.

Jolie thought the man might cry and she wanted to kick Sam and herself for coming up with this bad, bad idea.

David didn't question Rockne's presence, and Rockne ignored his, which either meant Rockne had never seen David Pearson or Rockne was lovable but dumb as a stump. Considering that the dog had once eaten an entire Brillo pad, Jolie was pretty sure which was the correct conclusion. Again, what the hell were they doing? Amateurs pretending to be experts. Pitiful! And now Sam was inserting himself into a government operation, probably only because he thought he should, since his girlfriend was already playing at private eye. If anything happened to him tonight, it would be all her fault....

"...so if there's anything you recall about any conversations you may have had with our father in the weeks before his death, Mr. Pearson, any little itty-bitty thing, we'd be *so* appreciative of your help."

Jolie shook herself back to attention as Jessica finished her explanation as to why they were here. "Yes, Mr. Pearson. Anything at all you can remember."

David Pearson shook his head. "But that's just it—I can't help you. I remember your father, yes, from those first terrible weeks after Cathleen disappeared, but then I never saw him again. He was injured on duty or something like that and forced to retire? No, I never saw him or heard from him again. Which is why I asked my wife if she'd had any contact with him."

"And what did she tell you?" Jolie asked just as a door in the corner of the large office opened and Angela Pearson entered behind a tall, thin woman with gunmetal-gray hair and a chin that looked bulletproof.

"I can answer that," the older woman said as David seemed to physically shrink. "My daughter-in-law told him just what I told him. She told him that Theodore Sunshine was a horrible, intrusive, low-bred man of lower character who insisted upon twice yearly dredging up a memory best forgotten. If he had dared to accost my son, I would have had a restraining order drawn up on him, but I was more than capable of sending him on his way. Angela, as well. And now, I see, we have to contend with you, Miss Sunshine. After seeing what you did to poor Joshua Brainard, can we only hope that this time you've arrived without cameras?"

Angela Pearson perched on the edge of her husband's desk and lit a cigarette.

"Angela, please," David said. "We're a smoke-free building."

"Good for your building, I'm sure it's very healthy," Angela told him and then inhaled deeply before blowing out a cloud of blue-gray smoke. "Sam? Is there nothing you won't do for a little Hollywood tail, hmm?"

"Angela!" David Pearson sat down in his desk chair as if his legs could no longer support him.

Jessica stepped forward. Jolie fought the urge to duck under the desk.

"If I looked up *whipped* in the dictionary, would I see your husband's picture?" Jessica asked sweetly. "Bet I would. So you were the maid of honor, right? Was one of your duties disposing of the body?"

"I GUESS THERE'S A FIRST time for everything," Sam said as they walked back to the parking garage. "First time riding a two-wheeler bike. First French kiss. First million made all on your own. First time escorted out of a building by security."

"Oh, come on, it was fun," Jessica told them, opening the top three buttons of her blouse, much to the delight of a stockbroker type coming at them, cell phone to his ear, and nearly backing into a street sign as he watched her walk past him. Jessica was oblivious. "Man, that David Pearson has all my sympathy with those two women in charge of him."

"Wimpy, wimpy, wimpy," Jolie said, using the line from some garbage bag commercial.

"Wrong. Whipped, whipped, whipped," Jessica corrected. "Just like I said. And who's Timothy? That's the name Angela said, right, when she was threatening to have us all sued or beaten up or whatever the hell she was threatening? Timothy? Not Tim? He sounds whipped, too. You must be feeling so proud of your fellow man about now, huh, Sam?"

"I'm feeling something, that's certain." Sam pushed the button for the elevator that would take them up to their parking level. "And it's Timothy Lutton, Angela's brother. I think I want to take a harder look at him."

"Why?" Jessica asked him.

"Because Angela told us that Timothy offered to take Cathleen home that night, after the mess at the rehearsal party," Jolie said. "Right, Sam? Because if Angela did want Cathleen gone, who else would she go to for help but her own brother?"

"Right. The Lutton family owns a large concrete company, but I've remembered that there was some talk years ago that the company was in Chapter 11 for a while. Bankruptcy. Timothy was probably happy when Angela and David were dating and not so happy to watch David marry someone else. It's a stretch, I know, but Cathleen Hanson wouldn't be the first person to become a permanent part of a new building foundation in this city."

Jolie stopped dead, closed her eyes. "Oh, Sam, don't say something like that."

"No, no, Jolie, let him go," Jessica said, her eyes shining. "I like the way you think, Samuel Becket. Do you think we should ask Jade to work her magic on the Internet? You know—finances, then and now? Before his sister married David and after. I'll bet she can even figure a way to find out what jobs Timothy's company was working—pouring?—during the time Cathleen disappeared. Oh, I'm loving this!"

Jolie was quiet all the way home, with Sam reaching across the front seat to squeeze her hand from time to time. Because he knew. She was getting too involved in the disappearance of Cathleen Hanson. In Cathleen Hanson, period.

Making it all personal. She was her father's daughter, making the same mistake that had possibly, probably—almost definitely—gotten her father killed....

CHAPTER FOURTEEN

SAM CONCENTRATED ON tying a neat Windsor knot and then noticed Jolie's reflection in the mirror. "Practicing your sneaking-up-on-people skills?" he asked her as he reached for his suit jacket.

"You're still going?" she asked, standing almost awkwardly in his bedroom, one foot turned in at the ankle, her hands behind her back. Looking painfully young and almost gawky. Nervous. The most beautiful woman in the world. Nervous.

"I'm still going, yes," he told her. "I'll be fine, Jolie, I promise. Even Agent Wallitsch finally agreed that everything should look as natural, as routine, as possible. The store closes at nine, the delivery from the warehouse is scheduled for nine-thirty. Larry always drives the truck, and I'm always on-site to oversee the unpacking of the crates."

"Only you won't be in the back room. You promised."

"Things change, Jolie. I'll show my smiling

face an hour before closing and then *retire* to my office. When the truck arrives, I'll stay inside, watch the unloading from there, and then we'll open the crates as if for the first time, catalogue the contents, carefully overlooking the fact that several of the pieces are hollowed out and packed with drugs. We've never been robbed, Jolie, at least not to my knowledge, so whatever is going to happen—if anything happens—will happen after I leave."

"And you *are* leaving. That hasn't changed?"

He rested his hands on her shoulders. "I will leave. I promise. To stay would also mean a break in my normal routine. It's a hell of thing, Jolie, to be so predictable. I'm beginning to think I lead a very boring life."

"Teddy had a routine," Jolie said quietly.

"Jolie, stop. I'm not an idiot and I'm not a hero. I'm doing what I believe to be the responsible thing to do. This is my company, my store and my name. And—God, I hope not—my employees. People I trusted. The more I consider everything, the more I believe someone in my employ is involved."

"If it's someone at the warehouse, then that person already knows that you know about the drugs."

"Correct. I think I hear wheels turning somewhere," Sam said, smiling. "What are you thinking?"

"I'm thinking that if it is someone at the warehouse, and the drugs are usually removed there and not at the store, then nothing will happen at the store tonight because that person already knows something is supposed to happen at the store tonight. In fact, it might already have happened. Right? Sam? Am I right? Sam? What's wrong?"

"Damn, the woman is a genius!" He kissed her on the lips, quick and hard, and headed for the bedside telephone, already pulling the card with Agent Wallitsch's number on it from his pocket. He punched in the number.

"Agent Wallitsch, Sam Becket here. Look, there could be something else. Yes…yes, I know. Eight o'clock. No, this can't wait. Yes, but…Agent Wallitsch…*hey! Listen to me!* I think there's a good chance my truck and driver are in danger. In danger or the driver's a part of it. So answer me—are your people tailing the truck between the warehouse and the store? What do you mean you're—*yes*. The *entire* route. All right. Okay. Keep me posted."

He slammed down the phone and looked at Jolie, who was now sitting cross-legged on the bed.

"Someone is following the truck, aren't they, Sam?"

"They are now. It's a straight shot from the warehouse to the I-95 exit. They'd planned to pick up the truck once it cut off the highway and follow it in. Staff shortages, Wallitsch said, but I wasn't about to listen to him moan about his tight budget.

It may already be too late if—God, please don't let it be Larry. I have to go."

"Wait, Sam," Jolie pleaded, hopping down from the bed. "Let me go with you."

"No," he said. "No way, no how. Just hope I'm wrong."

"I would if I knew what you were thinking. I still don't know what I said that turned you into Bruce Willis."

"Jolie, not now."

"Yes, now. You know, the guy he plays in his *Die Hard* movies? One man, one angry man against both the idiots and the bad guys. Except in real life he would have been dead six ways from Sunday in the very first movie. Please remember that. Now tell me what you're so worried about. Larry? He seems like a very nice man."

"He is. I hope he is," Sam said, glancing at his wristwatch. "All right, come on. If I'm right, nothing's going to happen. I don't have time to explain and still at least get to the store on time."

They started being tailed by Gary Tuttle and his rental car a block from the house, but Sam didn't bother trying to lose the guy. He had more important things on his mind. Like Larry, who'd been with him from the beginning. Larry, who always drove the truck from the warehouse to the store.

"So that's it," Sam said as he turned onto I-95. "The last time we found drugs, about three years ago, we turned them right over to the authorities. But that doesn't mean this has only happened twice. You don't want to know how few cargo containers are actually inspected as they come through the ports. That's why I have the dogs."

"I understand, Sam," Jolie said quietly, watching the traffic as Sam did his Indy-car-driver impersonation yet again at the Blue Route split that led onto I-95 and a whole bunch more of Philadelphia's amateur Indy-car drivers. "You think either the crates come to the store and the drugs are removed there or they're removed somewhere between the warehouse and the store. And Larry drives the truck. Except he knows the DEA is watching, so why would he take a chance tonight? Omigosh, isn't that Larry's truck?"

Sam was busy changing lanes again, as he'd somehow gotten stuck behind a camper with bicycles strapped to the back. "Where?"

Jolie pointed ahead and to his right as they neared the exit that split to go either toward the city or across the Walt Whitman Bridge into New Jersey. "There, the red one. See the bumper sticker. *I heart deer hunting.* Sam, watch out!"

But Sam had already cut across the middle lane, into the right lane and then onto the exit ramp, narrowly missing the collapsible barriers that were scarred with scrapes and dents from other vehicles that had cut the exit too short.

"Well," Jolie said, hanging on to the grab

handle above the side window, "that was fun. What are we doing?"

"I don't have the damnedest idea. Are you sure that's Larry's truck?"

"He took me to Thompson's Diner, remember? It's his truck. But Larry's driving your truck, isn't he?"

"That was the plan, yes. Hold on, here we go."

The red truck had peeled off to the right, onto the tightly curving ramp that led to the bridge. Sam hung back, but as he was one of dozens of SUVs, and half of those were black, he wasn't too worried about being seen and recognized.

"You shouldn't be with me," he said as he dug in his pocket and came out with his cell phone before he remembered he'd left the agent's card on his bedside table. "But as long as you are, page through my outgoing calls until you find one that looks like it might be to Wallitsch and then call it. He needs to know what we're doing."

"Got it," Jolie said, pushing a key. "What are we doing?"

"Tell him we're on the Walt Whitman and heading straight for Route 42—no, scratch that, we're heading off the first exit. Tell him the first exit just as he leaves the bridge. Tell him to get someone after us and to keep the line open."

He took a quick look into his rearview mirror, hoping that his erratic driving had managed to get some official attention, but no luck. They were on their own, at least for now. "Except for our good friend Gary Tuttle," he grumbled as he kept two cars between the red truck and his SUV.

"What? Tuttle's back there?" Jolie exclaimed, turning in her seat. "Great, and I'm not wearing any makeup," she said, sitting forward once more. "Just what I need—being a part of one of those Web sites where they *expose* us all, comparing us to our professional photos. I know this sounds shallow, but if I look like some of those actresses do without makeup, I may retire."

"You're beautiful, with or without makeup. Now slide down on the seat so nobody sees you. Wait. Don't. Look at the truck again, Jolie. Was there a tarp on the bed when Larry took you to the diner?"

"No, I don't think so. No, there wasn't. I'm sure of it. You think there's something beneath that tarp now?"

Sam didn't answer her because the truck turned right and then right again, into a large gas station plaza. He followed. Gary Tuttle followed. A second black SUV, coming fast, followed. Soon they'd have a damn parade.

He slammed the gearshift into Park just as Gary Tuttle pulled up beside them, blocking his view of the gas station pumps. "Stay here."

"I don't know how Jade does things like this for

a living. I wouldn't move for the world," Jolie said, her head now ducked low. "Don't do anything stupid. Please."

"I'll give it my best shot." Sam exited the car just as two men who couldn't look more like government men if they'd had neon signs over their heads blinking *DEA, DEA* got out of their SUV and joined him. The truck was now parked about fifty feet away, at the row of pumps closest to the minimarket attached to the station, and Sam couldn't see the face of the driver as he headed into the store.

"Your man?" one of them asked Sam.

He shook his head. "I couldn't tell. But my man's truck. This whole thing could be a coincidence. I could be all wrong and——"

"Your man bailed, said he was sick. The loaded delivery truck is still at the warehouse, with the wrong crates in it. Nobody's figured out yet how he managed the switch. He might even have done it right after our first check, before our agents were in place. Oh, yeah, and Wallitsch said to remind you that you're the genius who insisted this guy drive the truck, which is the only reason he was allowed on the premises tonight. Nine gets you ten, the real crates are under that tarp. A total screwup, beginning to end. We'll take it from here, sir. Please remain where you are."

"Yeah. I already got that order," Sam said as the

two men walked away, one heading for the truck, the other into the minimarket.

For a long minute nothing happened. One agent stood at the truck, watching while the second entered the minimarket. As if anyone would think the agent was Joe Average, stopping in for a pack of smokes.

Then two shots were fired in quick succession from inside the minimarket.

"Down! DEA! DEA! *Everybody down!*" the agent at the truck shouted to the other customers at the pumps as he drew his gun. But he didn't fire, which Sam thought was a good idea considering the agent was hunkered down behind a gas pump.

"Sam!"

He ran past Tuttle's car and back to the SUV, rounded the rear of it to open the driver's-side door and reach across to grab Jolie's arm. "Lie down on the seat, Jolie—now!"

Again she obeyed him without question, without protest, and he slammed the door once more and hit the lock button on his keys. Bent nearly in half, he ran to Gary Tuttle's car, still parked between his SUV and the minimarket, to see the man sitting behind the wheel, his eyes wide, his mouth dropped open. He held a camera in his hands but wasn't snapping any photographs. "Tuttle!" Sam banged hard on the window. "Come on, pay attention. You're right in line with the exit. You've got to move your car, get out of here. Tuttle!"

Sam heard a scream and the door to the mini-market opened. At the same time Tuttle put his car in gear and drove off, leaving Sam completely exposed as the gunman exited, holding a young woman in front of him as a shield.

"Larry, no," Sam said, coming out of his crouch to stand up straight. "Aw, damn it to hell."

"DEA! Drop the gun! Drop it now!"

"Larry!" Sam shouted as his employee gripped the sobbing woman tightly about the neck and waved the gun left to right. "Larry, it's Sam! Don't do this, Larry."

He didn't say anything else, because what else could he say? *We can work this out, Larry. Don't make it worse, Larry. Trust me, Larry. Nothing's worth dying for, Larry.* All the dumb, trite things he'd read or heard in movies a thousand times. There had been shots fired inside the minimarket. The DEA agent inside might be shot, might already be dead. Larry wasn't getting out of this one and he had to know that. The absolute terror in the man's eyes showed that he knew that.

Sam heard sirens and moments later the screech of brakes as police cars and more black SUVs skidded into the gas station.

Larry lifted the gun to his own head, the short barrel shoved beneath his own chin. Pulled the trigger even as Sam screamed, *"No!"*

Sam turned away, too late to have not seen what

a bullet tearing through a man's skull could do, the red mist of the explosion, to see Jolie sitting up in the front of the SUV, her palms flattened against the glass, her hauntingly beautiful blue eyes wide and staring....

"I'M GLAD THE AGENT'S going to be all right, Sam. What a night. Your man probably knew it was only a matter of time before the DEA figured out it was him," Jade said, nodding. "And he really thought he could just take the drugs and drive away into the sunset without anyone finding him? The famous one last bank robbery before going straight that always gets the person caught?"

"I don't know, Jade," Sam said, looking toward the foyer to see Jessica coming down the stairs. "I suppose so. The people he usually handed off the drugs to might have been pushing at him to deliver, and people like that don't want to hear about problems. Larry was caught between the proverbial rock and a hard place, and once he'd shot the agent he knew his own life was as good as over. That's what Agent Wallitsch said, at any rate. He also said we overestimate the intelligence of thieves, although I don't think you can prove that by the way we all screwed up tonight. But that's not the worst. Larry worked for me from the beginning. I trusted him with my business. I trusted him with Jolie. I'm going up there."

"I wouldn't," Jessica said as she entered the room. "She's out cold thanks to whatever shot those paramedics gave her. She really went apeshit?"

"Jess, don't," Jade warned her sister. "Can't you see Sam's upset?"

"I'm a damn sight more than upset, Jade. I involved her when I knew I shouldn't have let her come with me. For days we've all been playing at this detective crap, playing at heroes, acting like we know what the hell we're doing. Were we nuts? Something like this was bound to happen sooner or later. But this is it. It's over. No more investigating, no more dressing up and playing stupid games."

Jessica jammed her fists on her hips. "Hey, hold on a minute, Sam. Tonight had nothing to do with what we're doing. We're doing just fine. Quit if you want to, but you don't decide for Jolie."

Sam felt like punching something. "Don't you get it, Jess? Don't you understand what happened tonight? Larry blew his damn head off, and Jolie saw him do it. What do you think she thought seeing that?"

"Teddy. She thought about Teddy," Jade said quietly. "Nobody should see what she saw tonight. All right, Sam, I agree with you. Jolie's out. Jessica?"

Jessica nodded. "Sorry, Sam. You're right."

"Thank you," Sam said and headed upstairs.

He didn't bother knocking before entering Jolie's

bedroom. Someone had left the light on in the bathroom and the door partially open. He could see her in the bed, curled into a fetal position, her right hand resting palm-up on the pillow beside her head.

The beautiful, glamorous movie star. The too-tall, gawky, nervous girl hiding beneath the polished veneer. And now the wounded spirit, vulnerable, hurting. Jolie was all these things. She was every-thing.

He loved her so much his heart hurt.

Sam eased off his shoes even as he slipped out of his suit jacket and pulled his tie from around his neck. He stood at the side of the bed for a long time, his mind racing, watching Jolie's even breathing, the slight rise and fall of her chest and shoulder. At last he lay down beside her, fitting his body against hers. Carefully he pushed back the hair that had fallen across her cheek and then slid one arm around her waist, needing to hold her. Wanting to be there when she woke up, no matter the time, no matter whether she woke weeping or angry or to be as vio-lently, physically ill as she'd been on the scene.

He wouldn't let her wake alone. Not now, not ever again.

RED. EVERYWHERE. LIKE some macabre fireworks explosion. One moment a man, wild-eyed with fright, and the next—

"No…please, no…"

"Jolie? Jolie, it's all right. Don't struggle, it's just me. I'm here."

"Sam," she said, relaxing her body against his in the dark bedroom as she realized where she was. "Oh, Sam…" She turned in his arms and laid her head against his chest. "Oh, Sam…"

He kissed he hair, rubbed at her bare arm. "I know, sweetheart. I'm sorry. I'm so sorry."

"In…in the movies you see it all the time. But you know it's not real. You know when someone yells 'Cut' that everyone gets up, wipes off the fake blood and walks away again. In that first awful movie I made? I had lunch one day with a stuntman who had an ax sticking out of his back. Another guy had a…had one eyeball hanging halfway down his cheek. He'd move his head and it would swing side to side. He kept doing it. We thought it was funny. All that fake blood and gore. I…I can't believe…I never thought I'd ever see…"

"Try not to think about it, Jolie. It's over now."

She sighed. "I know. That poor man. He was so scared. But maybe more frightened of living than he was of dying. Teddy…"

"Teddy did *not* commit suicide, remember? We've decided that. Even Matt is on our side in this one."

Jolie pushed herself up into a sitting position. "It doesn't matter, Sam. He knew he was going to die. Whether he killed himself or someone else murdered him, Teddy knew he was going to die. I can't get that thought out of my head. I saw the look in Larry's eyes. He died terrified. My father…"

Sam had sat up with her and now pulled her close against him once more. "You can't do this, Jolie. You can't dwell on Teddy's last moments. He wouldn't want you to do that. That's not how he wanted to be remembered."

She nodded her agreement. "He wanted a huge wake. Everyone telling stories and laughing. Drinking toasts to him. I told you that?"

"You told me that," Sam said, stroking her hair. "And we're going to do exactly that, sweetheart, I promise. When this is all over we're going to rent a damn hall and have a party for Teddy."

"When we clear his name," Jolie pointed out, pushing away from him to wipe at her moist eyes. "We can't bring him back, I know that. But we can change the ending of the story of his life." She looked at Sam and tried hard to smile. "Because the original ending didn't play well to the focus groups, you know? We're going to film an alternate ending."

"Come here," Sam said, holding out his arms to her, and Jolie went to him, longing to be held safe in his arms. He kissed her cheeks, her hair and then, at last, her mouth. Softly. Sweetly. He kissed her, held her as if she was fragile and might shatter in his arms.

"Yes, Sam," she breathed quietly as he ran his fingertips down the sides of her neck, lightly cupped her breasts in his hands. "Please, yes…make love with me."

"Always…" He continued to kiss her as he gently laid her back against the pillows. Long, drugging kisses that told her he was in no hurry, that they had all night if they wanted it, if she needed that from him.

He kissed away her cotton tank top and sleep pants, taking his time with every part of her body.

He kissed the crook of her elbow, the back of her knee. He moved her onto her stomach and massaged her tense muscles, following his hands with his mouth, pressing kisses into the small of her back, licking at the sensitive skin just at her waist.

Then he turned her over and began again. Kneeling over her, straddling her, he smoothed the skin of her shoulders, his thumbs drawing small circles at the base of her throat as she closed her eyes and let the sensations relax her, soothe her, chase all the demons away.

He skimmed her breasts with his fingertips and she felt her response, the tightening of her nipples, the tendrils of desire that began to run from her breasts to the pit of her stomach and beyond.

Her eyes opened when he closed his mouth around one nipple, the warmth of him, of his breath as he blew lightly on her sensitized skin. First one nipple and then the other, leaving them both moist so that he could draw easy circles on them and then lightly pinch them between his fingers.

He licked at her. Worshiped at her. Held her taut as he moved his tongue faster, faster, until she lifted her hips to him. She imagined herself as a flower. The seed planted by Sam's lovemaking, she felt herself begin to bud. Hard, tight. All sensation centering there, a glorious ache to blossom consuming her.

Still with his hands on her breasts, Sam pressed his mouth to her stomach, lightly kissing her as he drew down her body. His tongue investigating her navel, tying another knot in the silken threads that carried sweet arousal from one part of her body to another.

There was nothing but Sam, nothing but this moment. This glorious garden of delights he was building for her, for the two of them.

His hands were on her hips now, and now pressing against her lower belly, the pressure filling her, tightening something inside her throat, feeding a hunger that grew and grew.

She bent her knees, braced her feet against the mattress. Let her knees drop open. Surrender. Total surrender. Her will was his will. Whatever he wanted. However he wanted it. As long as he took her with him…

With his thumbs he opened her. With his mouth he took possession of her. With his tongue he coaxed the tight bud until it burst into flower and made the whole world beautiful again.

And then his arms were around her, his cheek pressed close against hers as he entered her, joined with her, as the two of them became one. Moving together, soaring together, leaving the earth and all its troubles behind them. There was no world outside their tight embrace. There was no life outside of this sweet union.

Jolie sobbed against his neck, sad, happy, searching, finding. Triumphant. Whole once more.

"I love you, Sam," she breathed against him as his shudders slowed, as the weight of his body filled her with an emotion she had no name for but one that squeezed hard at her heart.

"I love you, Jolie," he whispered in return as he rolled them over so she could once more lay her head in that special hollow just beneath his shoulder blade, where she would willingly remain for the rest of her life and beyond. "You can't begin to know how much I love you...."

CHAPTER FIFTEEN

"ABOUT TIME YOU CAME downstairs," Court said as Sam walked into the dining room at nine the next morning, on the hunt for a cup of strong coffee. "We've got a circus out there now."

"A circus out where now?" Sam asked, his mind occupied with personal problems. One huge personal problem he had to confront soon or it would only get worse.

"Right outside your gates, Sam," Jade told him as she nibbled on a sweet roll. Only one hand was now bandaged, which probably meant that Court was pretty much out of a job. "News vans, satellite dishes, portable lights, wall-to-wall reporters. And it's a good thing I grabbed Jolie's cell phone last night. It hasn't stopped ringing. Well, it has. I turned it off. Her agent, her publicist, somebody named Smitty. Even a call from Australia. Everything hit the fan last night, Sam. You and Jolie are national news again. My sister the movie star, caught in the middle of a drug bust gone bad. I'm so proud—not."

"Damn. Is Bear Man on the gates?"

"Bear Man and three of his posse or whatever he called them. A lot of skin, a lot of flabby muscles. They were posing for pictures from inside the gates the last I saw them. One of them is wearing an Indian headdress. I hope you don't mind, but I didn't ask why," Court said, at last smiling. "I know celebrities can't sneeze without making headlines, but you didn't have to go out of your way to prove the point."

"Why not?" Jessica said, walking into the room, her step light. "I'm loving this. They're all out there and I'm in here. On the scene. My boss called me at six this morning *begging* me to get Jolie in an exclusive on-air interview. Live, from right here in the house. Fire me? Nope. I'm getting a bonus. Life is sweet."

"Jessica, shut up," Jade told her flatly. "You're the only person seeing a rainbow here, you know. Sam? I pulled Timothy Lutton's financials last night. You were right. Chapter 11, but he's out of it now and has been since a month after his sister married David Pearson. Coincidence? I don't think so. And, searching old newspaper stories online, Lutton Concrete poured the foundation for a new parking garage on Chestnut Street the week after the botched wedding. I think you're on the right track. Not that you and Jolie are involved any-more."

"Yes, we are," Sam said, looking at Court, who only shook his head. "Jolie's taking it easy this morning in her room, but she has informed me that she's not a quitter. *Emphatically* informed me. So we compromised. We work on the vanishing bride until she has to go back to the coast, and then it's over for her. No more involvement except to hear updates from you two. Since she'll soon be on location in Ireland anyway, I agreed."

"Wimpy, wimpy, wimpy," Jessica trilled, grinning at him. "Okay, next question. How do you and Jolie do anything without dragging all that media with you every time you leave the house?"

"I don't know," Sam said as he took a seat at the table. "I didn't know about the media when we talked about our plans for the day. Hey, Matt, hi."

Matthew Denby walked into the dining room, followed by a priest. "Great headlines this morning, Sam, although I'm betting you aren't all choked up about them. Vacation time is all arranged, so I'm all yours for the next two weeks. Oh, and I met Father Muskie at the front gate and brought him in with me," he said as Jessica hopped to her feet and went running straight into the priest's arms. "I guess you all know him?" Matt added as Jade also got to her feet and went to hug the old man.

Five minutes later, as Jessica wiped at her wet

eyes and Jade had introduced Court and Sam, the priest was seated at the dining room table, a cup of tea and a prune Danish in front of him.

"My dear girls. I didn't hear until I got back to the rectory last night. I still can't believe any of this," he said sadly. "I stopped first at the cemetery to say a little prayer and have myself a small talk with my good friend Teddy. Now I'm here to see you girls and to assist in any way I can. I did read in the morning paper about how you are out to clear Teddy's good name by solving some old cases." He looked to Sam, Matt and Court. "Tell me how I can help."

"Thank you, Father," Sam said. "I suppose we'd want to know if Teddy ever discussed any of his old cases with you. And any of his new ones."

"Not the ongoing ones, no. Professional ethics, you understand. And perhaps he was a wee bit ashamed to not be chasing down the *real* bad guys anymore and just shuffling papers and playing up to rich ladies who wanted him to spy on their husbands. But the old cases? Oh, yes, we spoke of them. Often. Haunted Teddy, they did, all the time. Most especially near the holidays and every summer. June. He called June his 'summer-school month,' to catch up on what he'd missed that winter."

He looked to Jade and Jessica. "That was his worst month, I believe, after Christmas. The same time your mother left."

"Yes, she left right before Christmas. Their wedding anniversary was in June," Jade said quietly.

"Oh, dear, I didn't know that. Teddy shared, but also he had his secret sorrows," Father Muskie said, shaking his head. "Well, hello there, Rockne. Ah, and don't you look sad. You miss him, too?"

The setter laid his head in Father Muskie's lap and raised his soulful brown eyes to him. The priest gave him his prune Danish, which elicited a long-suffering sigh from Jade.

"Not prunes, Father Muskie, remember?"

"Ah, yes, I do. Too late now, I fear. Well, even grounds as pretty as these need a bit of fertilizer from time to time."

Matt, grinning, leaned forward in his chair. "Can you be more specific about your discussions with Teddy, Father? Your most recent conversations?"

"Yes, well, yes, of course," the priest said, shooing Rockne away. "Let's see. Ah, the boy. Jermayne?"

Now Jade leaned closer, for Jermayne Johnson was her case.

"Broke Teddy's heart how that boy couldn't be reached. A troubled soul, I told Teddy time and again. His brother murdered like that, and now his grandmother gone, as well? Only a boy, only just turned eighteen, I believe, and alone in the world. Teddy has…had been pushing him rather hard lately, trying to get him to further his education after high school. Why, I think he even paid the first semester's tuition at some trade school for him. Auto mechanics? Yes, I think that's it. But Jermayne? He just kept saying Teddy shouldn't help him, that it wasn't right. He wasn't *worth it* the way his brother had been, that's what the boy said. So, so sad. I keep the boy in my prayers."

There was no new information there except that Teddy had once more opened his pockets to help someone else. Jade's shoulders slumped slightly. "Thank you, Father. I'll try to convince Jermayne to go to school. It's the least I can do. Other than that, I've already pretty much decided that Jermayne is a dead end."

Jessica passed the plate of pastries to the priest. "I'm working on the Fishtown Strangler case, Father. Do you remember that one?"

Father Muskie nodded, as his mouth was full of cherry Danish. "Excuse me," he said, dabbing at his lips with a napkin. "Yes, I remember the case— more senseless deaths Teddy grieved over. He mentioned a name last time we spoke. One of the young ladies. Let me think a moment. Carol? No. Karen? That's closer. Yes, perhaps Karen? No, wait a moment. Karen is the name of the mother of one of the other girls, a Kayla Morrison, yes? I confess, sometimes Teddy's conversations upset me and I tried not to listen too closely."

"I think you might mean Tarin," Jessica said, looking at Matthew. "Tarin White, one of the victims. Teddy had both names written in his most recent notes. I spoke with Kayla's mother and daughter, but I can't find anything at all on Tarin except an address that she'd left a good year before she was murdered. That's the only address in the police report, too. It was as if the last year of her life she lived nowhere at all. I'm figuring she bunked around with friends, and they're not talking. What did Teddy say about Tarin?"

"He was very troubled when I visited him before leaving for Canada. So troubled that I tried to convince him to go with me. Nothing like dropping a line in crisp, cold Canadian waters to free the mind and ease the spirit. But he wouldn't go. He was worried that he might be putting someone in danger, but then insisted—to himself as much to me—that he had no choice but to keep digging in order to keep that person out of even worse danger. You know Teddy. He could be cryptic. Although he did promise he was going to take a small vacation very soon. And to Canada. Toronto. Not that he would get his hopes too high—he said that—but I could see he was excited about something. He showed me the ticket."

Father Muskie smiled at Sam as Jade abruptly

got up and left the room. "Does that help? Does any of that help?"

Court's cell phone rang and he pulled it out of his pocket, looked at the number and then also excused himself. It wasn't until Matt had left with Father Muskie, to drive the priest back to his car, that Court returned to the dining room.

"Did Father Muskie have anything else to add?"

"No, not really," Sam told him. "Other than that, of all the cases Teddy still worked on, the baby in the Dumpster haunted him the most. Four cases, no answers. Just more questions. Whom did Teddy think he might have put in danger? Why the ticket to Toronto? More and more, Court, I think the girls are right. Teddy was on to something, but what? Which case?"

"I think Jade is about done with the scholar-athlete case. The consensus then was that it was a gang-related shooting, but Terrell's grandmother was insistent that he was a good boy and not involved with gangs. And, short of trolling the streets to talk to gang members, there's not a lot we can do. She told me this morning she's going to switch to the baby-in-the-Dumpster case. I'm not looking forward to it."

"I don't blame you. Are you able to stay in town?"

Court nodded. "At least for another week or two. I can pretty much troubleshoot from anywhere as long as I have my laptop and cell phone. I have to round up Jade pretty soon to take her back to the clinic. That area of her palm that suffered the third-degree burn has to be debrided every few days. They come at her with scissors to cut off the dead skin, and she just sits there, not flinching. I'm a real hero—I have to look away. That was Morgan on the phone, by the way. She found more Becket relatives somewhere in Ohio."

"Our small family is beginning to grow. But she hasn't found the Empress?"

Court smiled. "Afraid not. But Jade did find some information on emeralds on the Internet, and I have to say, I'm beginning to get very interested. Are you sure you don't want to fly to England with me next month?"

"I might do that. Jolie will be in Ireland."

"You're planning on becoming a groupie?"

"I'm planning on becoming a husband," Sam said, rubbing at his chin. "If she doesn't kill me first."

"I'm back," Matt said, striding in the room. "You should have seen Father Muskie with those reporters as I escorted him to his car. A tough old nut. He's got the 'No comment' response down pat, except he follows it with 'God bless you.' Who's going to kill you, Sam?"

"It's nothing. We've all got enough going on."

"Jolie," Matthew said as if he understood. "My

sympathies, whatever the reason. I've got my hands full with Jessica as my partner, I can tell you that. She's the kind of woman who says things that the man with her finds himself having to punch somebody in the nose for, if you understand what I'm saying here."

Sam laughed and got to his feet. "Jolie promised she'd be ready to leave at eleven-thirty, so I've got to figure out how the hell we're going to do this without dragging a bunch of reporters along with us. You, too, Court, with Jade."

"Make that three of us," Matt told him. "Jessica wants to take another crack at Kayla Morrison's daughter. How she figures taking a badge along is going to help, I don't know, but she isn't going alone. We don't have to go now, there's no rush. Maybe if all three of us left at the same time?"

"That makes it a one in three chance that they're following the right car," Court said, looking at Sam. "It's worth a try. Besides, Sam, the way you drive, you could probably lose anybody."

"I'm a defensive driver," Sam told him, grinning. "I drive as if everyone else on the road is certifiable."

"Right. You know what they say about people who think it's only the rest of the world that's crazy. And where are you driving to today?"

"Believe it or not, Court, David Pearson called me early this morning. To apologize for throwing us out of his office the other day, he said. He wants us to meet him at his home for lunch and to discuss his fiancée's disappearance. *Home,* to me, means his wife is going to be there, and probably his mother, as well. Jolie thinks they want to cooperate so that she doesn't say terrible things about them to reporters at some point. Me? I'm thinking there's going to be an ambush."

"I think you're right," Court said as all three men left the dining room and headed for the living room, where Jade was working on the laptop computer.

"I looked it up on our online account for our credit card," she said without a pause in her one-handed typing. "Teddy charged a round-trip ticket to Toronto. He was supposed to leave yesterday, with his return for tomorrow. Not a long vacation." She looked at Court, who had sat down beside her and put a hand on her back. "He never said a word to me about this. Why on earth would he go to Toronto?"

Sam smiled at Jolie as she walked into the room and stood next to him, her hand sliding into his. She looked...well-loved. He'd take a bow, except that they still had a long way to go before there was any talk of a happily ever after. He kissed her cheek as she asked Jade who was going to Toronto.

"Teddy, Jolie. Father Muskie was here," Jade explained, "and he told us Teddy was planning a trip to Toronto. A vacation, Father Muskie said. When was the last time you can remember Teddy taking a vacation?"

"I can remember the last time I ate calves' liver," Jolie said, making a face. "Halloween. I was twelve and Mom insisted or I couldn't go trick-or-treating. I ended up throwing up and not able to go, and neither you nor Jess would share your candy with me. But the last time Teddy took a vacation? I have no idea. I'd have to say *never*."

"Exactly," Jade agreed. "This has something to do with one of the cold cases, I'd bet on it. But which one? God, I hate this! I always thought he told me everything. At least everything important. I miss him so much—and I get so *mad* at him."

Court continued rubbing her back. "Remember, Jade, that Father Muskie also said Teddy was afraid he might have put someone in danger. Maybe he was worried that if he told you, then you'd also be in danger. Matt? Any ideas?"

Matthew shook his head. "Not a single one, Court, no. We don't even know if the person-in-danger business and the airline ticket are even connected. Teddy was working all four cases, remember. Although I agree with Jade. I think we can rule out the scholar-athlete case. That's just one more unsolved murder that remains unsolved, because there's no motive, no reason. Death by living in the city, period."

"Leaving us with the prostitute murders, the vanishing bride and the baby in the Dumpster," Jolie said and sighed. "One of them has to be the right one or nobody would have tried to burn down the house and destroy Teddy's files. But which one? I feel like we're all just treading water here. I can't believe Teddy carried this feeling with him for years."

"Come on, Jolie," Sam said, sensing her unhappiness. "Let's take Rockne outside for a while. He had prune Danish for breakfast."

Sam called for Rockne and let him run outside before he and Jolie followed. Jolie looked to her right just as she stepped onto the terrace, only for a second, as if looking for something behind the decorative urn. *Damn.* "Jolie?" he asked her as she continued walking away from the house. "Did you lose something?"

"Hmm? What? Oh…oh, no. I was…I was just admiring the flowers. I love Pennsylvania. No palm trees," she said, smiling at him.

"Not in the pots next to the doors, no," Sam agreed, following her as she struck out on the main path that led down to the pool area. "Did you eat enough this morning, Jolie? Did you eat *anything* this morning?"

"I'm fine, Sam. I rarely eat breakfast."

"A good breakfast makes a sound foundation for the remainder of the day—or so I've heard."

"Sam! Stop it! I eat, okay? And I'm as healthy as a horse. I have to be or the studio can't get insurance on me for my films. I just had a physical two months ago for this shoot in Ireland. I'm *fine*."

"But I'll bet the doctor told you to stop smoking," Sam said, mentally kicking himself for going after her when she already had enough going on in her life.

"I don't—" She shut her mouth and turned her back on him. "All right, all right, so I smoke. Occasionally. Maybe three or four a day. But not since I'm here, at your house. And I only do it to curb my appetite. Everybody does. Or they take drugs." She turned back to him. "You want me to take drugs instead, Sam?"

"I want you to *eat*, damn it," he told her and then watched as she walked away from him again. She was beautiful. Gorgeous. But he had traced her ribs and the rise of her hip bones last night, with his eyes as well as his fingertips. Five years ago he hadn't been able to do that. "Jolie, wait. I'm sorry."

She stopped walking and waited for him to catch up to her, standing on the last step, her arms wrapped around her waist. "Do we have to do this now?"

"No, I suppose not. I understand that the camera adds weight—"

"At least ten pounds, maybe more. It's not fun having your hips on a forty-foot-wide screen in the Cineplex, Sam."

"Right. And as long as you're healthy and you don't smoke, I guess dieting is just part of your job description, isn't it?"

She nodded, biting her bottom lip between her teeth.

"So we live with it. Hell, you're twenty-eight. In another five years they'll have you playing somebody's grandmother, and no one will care what you weigh."

Jolie laughed, the sparkle coming back into her eyes. "You don't know how close to the truth you are, Sam. And I've already decided to go the route Annette Bening has gone and refuse cosmetic surgery. So much of Hollywood is artificial, but I don't want to be artificial. I mean, who are you if you're not true to yourself? Besides, then I can eat."

"And have babies," Sam said, putting his hands on her shoulders. "We want babies, don't we, Jolie?"

She nodded, keeping her eyes on him. "Very much. But I don't want to wait five years to have them. I've already lost five years. We've lost five years. My agent will want to kill me, but then she'll start hunting up photo shoots in pregnancy magazines or something, and everything will be fine. It's all a matter of scheduling."

Sam took hold of her hand. "Come over here and sit down, Jolie. I've got this out of order and I don't want go any farther without clearing up something you need to know."

She shot him a look of feigned shock. "You've had a vasectomy?"

He laughed, shaking his head. "Not yet, although I'm not sure about the next five minutes. Jolie, I did something I shouldn't have done."

She put her fingertips against his lips. "Don't tell me. I don't want to know who she is."

That stopped him for a moment, but then he shook his head. "There's never been anyone else, Jolie, not anyone who ever mattered. This is about us. I wanted you back. I was willing to listen to Teddy and give you a year to figure out that you didn't belong in Hollywood, that you belonged here, with me. But when that one year stretched into two, I knew I had to do something. And I did."

"I don't understand. What did you do?"

He said it all, as quickly as possible. "I had a friend of a friend arrange for me to pour some money into the worst movie project ever set to be filmed on the condition that you were hired to play a secondary speaking role. I thought that if you—"

"You—you *what!*" Jolie got to her feet and glared down at him. "You *bought* me that part?" She turned in a full circle, her hands drawn up into fists, and glared down at him again. "Jesus!"

Sam talked fast again, figuring he was fighting for his life now. "I wanted to show you that you didn't belong out in Hollywood, that you wouldn't be happy there, that a single part in one lousy movie was the most you could hope for."

"Well, thank you, Mr. Becket. I'm so happy to hear how confident you were in my lack of talent."

"But that's it, Jolie. You have talent. I don't need to tell you that. You know, you always knew. The world knows. I got an advance DVD and spent the next month waiting for the movie to be released so everyone would know what I already knew after watching the film. What they didn't know—what you didn't know—was that I also knew I had just cut my own throat. I wanted you home and I'd given you a sure ticket to remain where you were. Where you belonged. Where you still belong."

She just stared at him.

"I couldn't go after you once I'd seen you in that film. I couldn't ask you to give up what you were so obviously born to do. Like that old saying, Jolie, I was hoist on my own petard."

"I was coming home," she said quietly. "The struggling, the horrible jobs. All those auditions that went nowhere. I'd had enough. I was coming home, Sam, to crawl back to you on my hands and knees if I had to. And then I got the call to audition for that movie, that horrible movie. Do you understand what I'm saying? Do you realize what you did? I was coming *home!*"

Sam watched as Jolie ran back toward the house, Rockne bounding along behind her.

He didn't follow her. Whatever she decided would be her decision alone. Either she forgave him or she didn't. Either she loved him or she didn't. He was through meddling in her life.

CHAPTER SIXTEEN

"NOPE. SORRY, SISTER mine, I still don't get it," Jessica said as she and Jade sat in Jolie's bedroom. "Where's the big problem?"

"What's not to understand, Jess? He got me the part," Jolie told her, dabbing at her eyes with yet another tissue. "I didn't earn the part. Sam *bought* it for me."

"Yeah? So? As Teddy used to say, the door to success might be marked *push,* but on the other side of that door it says *pull.* Everybody needs a little help at some point, but after that help you're on your own. You made it on your own. And at least you didn't have to sleep with anybody to get the part." Jessica winced and smiled at the same time. "Well, not a producer, anyway. You did sleep with Sam. Why, Jolie Sunshine, you little slut, sleeping your way to the top. For shame."

"You're not helping, Jessica Marie," Jade pointed out, not looking up from her laptop computer.

"She's right, you're not helping," Jolie said, at

the same time deciding that tears weren't helping, either. "You don't understand, Jess. I thought I got that part on my own merits."

"Does it matter?" Jessica pushed. "Who cares how you got the part? You got the *next* part because of how you handled the first part. My God, Jolie, that movie was a disaster. Other than the popcorn, you were the only good thing in the theater that night. Even Teddy said so, and he liked those slasher movies."

"*I* care how I got that part," Jolie said, beginning to weaken under Jessica's logic, which was scary in itself. "I'm a serious actress."

"You're a serious something," Jessica said, tossing her sister an apple from the bowl on the desk. "Here, eat. You're too skinny, both of you."

"Says Miss Baby Fat 2008," Jade muttered, closing the laptop.

"Hey, these are called *curves*. Something you two aren't familiar with, obviously. Now look, are we going anywhere today or not? It's nearly noon. Court sent me up here to get the two of you moving, which I was trying to do before Miss Drama Queen 2008 invited me to her pity party."

"You've always been such a caring sort. But I love you, I guess," Jolie said, shaking her head. "All right, all right. Let me go wash my face and try to look human again. Which wig am I supposed to wear? I forget."

"And what about Sam, Jolie?" Jade called after her as Jessica went wig hunting. "Are you going to forgive him?"

Jolie stopped at the door to the bathroom and turned to face her sisters. "One, Jessica makes a lot of sense, much as it kills me to say that, and it could be my ego that's bruised and that's all. Two, Sam may have been selfish to do what he did, but he thought he had my best interests at heart, his and mine anyway. And three...well, I don't know what three is. Would I have been happier if I had come home three years ago or not? I have to think about this some more. Toss it to me, Jess—thanks."

As she was adjusting the short blond wig over her tied-up hair, Jolie asked herself that last question again. *Would I have been happier if I had called it quits and come home to Sam three years ago?* She lowered her eyes from her reflection, not liking the answer that came to her mind, but then lifted her head and looked herself straight in the eye. "You would have been miserable. You would have made him miserable. You would have made both of you miserable. You love what you do. You do it well. So just knock it off, thank him and move on. So there!"

"And a round of applause for the woman with the belated common sense," Jessica said from the doorway to the bathroom. "You don't make a very good blonde, though, Jolie. Blondes should be voluptuous, not skinny. Men don't expect skinny in their blondes. Trust me on this one."

Jolie leaned closer to the mirror. "It's the makeup. I'm made up for a brunette, not a blonde. And Nicole Kidman is a blonde—most of the time. She's not exactly overweight."

"An exception to the rule," Jessica said, shrugging. "Now move over and help me put this thing on. Here I go, from voluptuous blonde to baby-fat brunette. Thank God it's only Matt who will see me."

Jolie helped pin up her sister's hair and then stood behind her to eyeball how she'd position the wig on her head. "How are you two getting along?"

"Matt and me? We don't *get along,* Jolie. We're working together, and the arrangement wasn't my idea. Although it is sort of fun driving him crazy. Ouch! Are you using hairpins or straight pins?"

Next up was Jade, and the red wig couldn't have been a worse choice for her. The bright color drained all the color out of her already-pale face. Once again Jolie got a quick flash of the smashed Belleek. "Jade, are you all right? I know the burns were on your hands, but you also inhaled a bunch of smoke. Maybe you should stop trying so hard and just let the two of us carry the ball for a while without you."

"I hear that enough from Court, thank you," Jade said, not even bothering to check her appearance in any of the mirrors in the room. "I'll have plenty of time to rest when this is over. And when the house is back in shape. Court wants me to go to Virginia with him while the contractor is working there. I'm considering it. I love walking on the beach near our…near his house. But not until we've cleared Teddy's name."

"Then we'd better hurry up and solve all these cases," Jessica whispered to Jolie as they made their way downstairs. "If she gets any paler, she'll look like a cadaver. Some Virginia sunshine is just what she needs."

Matt, Sam and Court met them in the foyer, Court looking at his wristwatch even as he took her laptop from her. Jade went nowhere without that laptop. "We have a half hour to get to the hospital, Jade, park the car and walk up to the clinic."

"You look really nice, Jade. Love the red hair. It gets me all hot and bothered, so everybody excuse us for a while, because I'm going to jump her bones—and I mean that bones part literally," Jessica whispered quietly to Jolie. "God. They were married? Does the man even *see* her?"

"Don't start, Jess," Jolie whispered back as they all walked outside to the three cars parked in front of the house.

Sam came up to her, his expression inquiring but not pressing at her, as if she might either yell at him again or even hit him. "You ready to do this?"

"I am. Which car?"

"We're taking Matt's Jeep. Jade and Court will take the SUV, and Matt and Jess are taking the sedan. Trade sunglasses with Jess, as she's supposed to be you."

"And I'm Jessica? Excuse me while I go back inside and find a pair of balloons to shove up under my shirt."

Sam laughed as he opened the door to Matt's ragtop Jeep and she slid onto the seat. He had already slipped on aviator-style reflector sunglasses and a golf cap pulled low over his head. "Jess will get most of the followers if the quick glimpse we give the reporters makes them think she's you. But we can't count on that, so buckle up. This could be a fun ride."

"No more than usual with you at the wheel," she told him as he slammed the door.

They headed for the gates together, the SUV first, the Jeep and the sedan following close behind. Matt had already arranged for some of his fellow officers to clear the roadway so they could make their escape without having to run anyone over. Sam seemed a little disappointed in that, especially when Jolie pointed out Gary Tuttle standing just to the left as they turned that way out of the gate.

At the first turn, Matt went left as Sam turned right and Court continued straight across the intersection. Jolie turned in her seat to watch what happened behind them. Three-quarters of the following cars and vans also turned left. Three followed Court, and only one continued on after the Jeep.

"Tuttle's behind us," she told him as she faced front once more.

"It wouldn't be a race down the Blue Route without him," Sam said, shifting into third gear.

"I'm guessing nobody else believes Jolie Sunshine would ride in a ragtop that looks as if it was last washed during the Clinton administration—the first one." She looked down at the floor, which was littered with empty, balled-up fast-food bags. "If Jess ever stops resenting how he's glued to her and starts to like Matt, all she'll have to do is cook him dinner and he'll be her slave for life."

"I think it would take a lot more than a home-cooked meal," Sam said, one eye on the road, the other on the rearview mirror. "Much as this guy is growing on me, I don't want anyone knowing where we're headed. Hang on."'

Sam made a fishtailing-tight turn onto a side road so narrow that the trees on either side of it had grown into a sort of living canopy above their heads. Jolie saw flashes of houses through the trees, all set back from the twisting road, all of them bordering on mansions. She didn't remember ever coming this way, but it was home turf for Sam, and he made blind turn after blind turn as if he knew what awaited them on the other end, until Jolie couldn't see Tuttle's rental car anymore.

But she sure was glad she'd taken time to go to the bathroom before they'd left the house!

Then Sam pulled into one of the driveways and stopped the Jeep a quarter of a mile father along the private entrance. "This is Fred Jacobs's place, and he's in Switzerland. Still hate me?" he asked her as she looked at the unfamiliar house at the top of the hill, wondering what he was doing.

"I take it we're hiding out here until Tuttle goes past? And that depends. Are we going to slow down now?"

Sam put the Jeep in Reverse and turned around, heading back to the road and taking a right out of the drive, heading back the way they'd come. "I think we've lost him, yes. Would it help or hurt my chances to say I don't think I like you as a blonde?"

"Do I remind you too much of Jessica?"

He gave a quick bark of laughter that told her that he was more nervous than he wanted her to know. "That's always a possibility. But you definitely make a great redhead. Know where we are?"

"Not a clue, no," she said, looking out the side windows. "Do we have time to talk?"

He eased up on the gas pedal. "That depends. Am I going to like what you have to say?"

"You interfered in my life, Sam. My life and my career."

He shot her a quick look and then eased back onto a road with more traffic. "I know. We'd said goodbye. You'd given me back my ring. We'd agreed…hell, I don't know what we'd agreed. I guess we'd agreed to be totally pissed off with each other because neither of us was willing to see the other person's side of the argument."

"That about sums it up, yes," Jolie said, keeping her head turned away from him. If he saw her smile now, he wouldn't keep apologizing. She rather liked the way he apologized. As if he was angry. "If Teddy hadn't warned you off, would you have come after me? Would you have come to California? Because I always wondered why you allowed the break to be so final."

Sam pulled over into the parking lot of a doughnut shop and cut the engine. "I don't know what I would have done that first year. Part of me missed you like hell, while the rest of me figured if you missed me, you'd give up your stupid— I'm sorry. That you'd decide I was more important than some pie in the—I can't do this. No matter how I say it, it comes out that I was so damn mad at you."

"Because you were," Jolie said, pulling at the pins that held the blond wig in place. She removed the wig and a few remaining pins and shook her head, her hair falling straight and smooth past her shoulders. "Ah, that's better. I think that wig was about a half size too small. I was selfish, Sam. I wanted you, you know that. But I wanted the dream, too. I enjoyed acting in small theaters around the Delaware Valley, but they weren't enough. I had to know."

"And you had to do it your way," Sam said, pushing an errant strand of hair behind her ear. "Now you're the big movie star, and we've got a whole other set of problems, don't we?"

Jolie bit her lip as she nodded her agreement. "Do you think we're mature enough now to work them out without losing another five years?"

"God, I hope so. I'd like to think so. I do love you, Jolie. What I felt for you five years ago was also love, I know that, too. But not like this. I can't let you go again."

"Oh, Sam…" Jolie leaned toward him as he did the same, their mouths almost touching, when his cell phone began to ring. "Ignore that."

"Exactly my idea," he said and pulled her as close as their seat belts would allow, kissing her mouth with this new tenderness she would never tire of experiencing.

The phone stopped ringing and then began again. They ignored it again, as Sam worked to open Jolie's seat belt. "It's the middle of the day, Sam, and we're in a public parking lot," she reminded him, laughing as she pushed him away. "And you'd better check your phone."

"See? This is what happens when I kiss you," he said, pulling the cell phone from his pocket. "I lose all sense of decency. Last week I was a respected member of the community. Now I'm on the front pages as 'her unidentified companion.' How low I've sunk. Who's 1-5-1-7-0—?"

"That's Jessica," Julie interrupted. "Why?"

"Because she put 911 behind her callback number." He quickly dialed the number, and Jolie pulled down the sun visor to check her hair and makeup while he said hello and then mostly listened. "All right. Terrific. No, I don't know how that happened either. I'll tell her. Yes…we'll wing it from here. Jade? Good idea. Call her, see what she thinks. And call me back when you know more, okay?"

Jolie flipped the sun visor back into position and looked at him. "Well? You said terrific. What's terrific?"

"You remember the night we were…busy in the living room?"

"What night we were—oh. Yes, I remember. Jess called you about *that?*"

"No, she called me because Mrs. Archer was doing some cleaning in there early this morning and found a sheet of paper beneath one of the couches."

"The vanishing-bride file," Jolie said, putting a hand to her mouth. "We missed a page?"

"Apparently." Sam nodded. "Mrs. Archer gave it to Jessica and she just remembered it now. She'd folded it and shoved it in her pocket and just now decided to look at it. Do you want to guess what's on the page?"

"Sam, don't do that. Tell me."

"The page was an electronic airline ticket to Toronto. The Toronto trip is part of our case." He put his hand on the ignition key. "Do you want to try to think up some questions while we drive over to see David Pearson?"

Jolie nodded, her heart pounding as she truly believed, maybe for the first time, that they were actually getting somewhere. Toronto. She had an answer. She just needed to know the question. "I will. But, Sam? First could you go inside and get me a glazed doughnut? I can smell those dough nuts all the way out here and I haven't had a good Philadelphia glazed doughnut in five years. Besides, I don't think we're going to eat much of a lunch at David Pearson's house, do you?"

Jolie was still licking the last bits of sugar from her fingertips as Sam brought the Jeep to a halt outside of David Pearson's home. He got out and went around to open her door for her. "Ready?"

"You should kiss me. I bet I taste like sugar."

"I'll bet you do," he said and leaned in to check

for himself. "Hmm, yes. Sugar. We'll have to name our first child Sugar."

"I will not! What a ridiculous name."

"Didn't an actress name her kid Macintosh a couple of years ago?"

"Close. She named her Apple. But that's not happening with us. Look, Sam. Who do you think owns that huge black boat?"

"Looks like a lawyermobile to me," he said as they walked up to the door and he knocked on the thick wood. "I'm not up to *Lara's Theme* again today. Get ready, Jolie. I had a feeling this was going to be an ambush. The lawyermobile proves it."

Once more they were escorted down the long gallery hall and out onto the large rear patio.

"At least she's dressed today," Jolie muttered out of the side of her mouth. "You weren't up to *Lara's Theme*, and I wasn't up to Nipples On Parade. Who's that other guy? The younger one? Timothy? He looks scared, doesn't he?"

"Timothy, yes. Angela's brother. Now, Jolie, today your role is that of big-time Hollywood star. Play it to the hilt, okay?"

"I *am* a big-time Hollywood star, Sam. Jeez," Jolie said and then lifted her chin slightly, deciding on a persona that was part Jodie Foster, part Julia Roberts in *Erin Brockovich*. It seemed like a good mix. She smiled a Jolie-Jodie-Julia smile and graciously allowed herself to be introduced to Timothy Lutton and Horace L. Rampart, Esquire.

Then she stared at Timothy Lutton very pointedly from behind her dark glasses. He couldn't hold his own gaze steady. Jolie thought if she were a shark, she'd be smelling blood in the water. She decided to make Timothy her personal project.

"I'm afraid I've brought you here on false pretenses, Sam," David Pearson said, pushing at the bridge of his glasses. "Mother insisted—that is, we've decided that, um, that should you and Ms. Sunshine choose to pursue, that is, if you and Miss Sunshine do not...I'll let Horace tell you."

"Ms. Sunshine, Mr. Becket," Horace Rampart said, reaching into his briefcase and pulling out something that looked at least semiofficial. "We— Mrs. Pearson here, and Angela and David, of course, along with Mr. Lutton, since his name has been mentioned—are prepared to file papers ordering you both to cease and desist from bothering any one of them. In fact, I plan to file a request that you not be allowed within one hundred yards of any of my clients, under penalty of law." He smiled. "This is dependant on your cooperation, which we hope for today. Mrs. Pearson has agreed that everyone here will answer any last few questions you might have concerning one Cathleen Hanson, but that is all. If, after today, you attempt to contact any one of my clients, the papers will be filed with the court. Not the sort of publicity you'd want, Ms. Sunshine, hmm? Or you, Mr. Becket."

"Don't presume to know what I want, Mr. Rampart," Sam said coldly, and Jolie took a quick peek at him from behind her sister's sunglasses. "And you, Mrs. Pearson. Do you really want to get into a public pissing match—my lawyers against your lawyers, and with international media watching it all? This is what we'll do—we'll sit down, we'll ask our questions, you'll answer them. And maybe that's all we'll need. But if it isn't, yes, we'll be back. Every December and June until we're all old and gray. Count on it. And since Ms. Sunshine here seems to have the press following her everywhere she goes, we probably won't arrive alone."

Jolie wanted to hug him. He was wonderful! She also had been watching everyone, and the body language told her that now they had two softer targets: Timothy Lutton and David Pearson. No wonder both Angela and Mother Pearson wore pantsuits; it was to camouflage their brass ones....

"I have a question for you, David," Jolie said when the charged silence became awkward. Well, nothing about this confrontation was pleasant. The standoff and stare-down just before the gunfight at the OK Corral had probably been more cordial. "What do you think of Toronto?"

He tilted his head as he frowned at her. "Toronto? I don't know. I've never been. Why?"

"No reason," Jolie said, holding her smile. Darn. He didn't look guilty. None of them had looked guilty when she'd said *Toronto*. "Will you please tell me how you and Cathleen met?"

David looked first to his mother, as if for permission.

"Go ahead, David. The sooner you answer their ridiculous questions, the sooner they're gone."

"Very well. I met Cathleen when the company she was working for at the time catered an affair at the club. She dropped a tray and I bent down to help her and—how does this aid anything? Cathleen left. That's all there is to it." He turned to his mother. "You drove her away."

"David, stop that whining," Mother Pearson ordered, and the fire that had flickered in David's eyes for a moment was snuffed out. "The girl wasn't worthy of the name Pearson. It couldn't have been more obvious that night."

"Yes, that night," Sam said, stepping closer. Nobody had asked them to sit down. "Let's go back to that night, if you don't mind. You argued, David?"

Again David looked to his mother. Jolie didn't know which of them she most longed to slap silly. "I got drunk. I don't know how. I only had two drinks, I swear. But I could barely see straight. I knew I couldn't drive. Cathleen told me to go home with Mother and she'd take a cab. Tim here, he offered to drive her, but Cathleen said no. That's the last I saw her. That's the last any of us ever saw her."

"But, Angela, you talked to her after that, didn't you?" Jolie asked the woman who was already lighting her second cigarette since their arrival.

"Yes, I did. Lock me up—I killed her over the phone. Jesus, when will these people just go away?"

"Angela was nothing but kind to that girl. She even went along to the fittings for the wedding gown, as a maid of honor should. It couldn't have been easy for her, but she did it," Mother Pearson declared rather heatedly. "Not that she had any reason to be kind, what with that gold digger stealing David right out from under her. Ah, but every man is entitled to one mistake, I suppose. He corrected it."

"And yet he endowed a scholarship in Cathleen's name just this year," Sam said. "Guilt, David? Or do you still love her?"

"David! Tell me you did no such thing!"

"I…uh…" David looked from Sam to his mother and then back again. "Yes. Yes, Mother, I created a scholarship in Cathleen's name. She'd been going to night school, hoping to become a nurse. It's a nursing scholarship. I just…I just wanted to do something so that people would…so that people would remember her name."

"Oh, Christ, I need a drink," Angela said, heading for the portable bar set up near the pool. But she stopped quickly enough and turned around at Sam's next question.

"Mr. Lutton, you poured a foundation for a parking garage on Chestnut Street within a few days of Cathleen's disappearance, didn't you? Convenient."

"And what's *that* supposed to mean?" Angela asked, taking hold of her brother's arm.

"This is all dangerous and pointless speculation. I think everyone is done answering questions," attorney Rampart said smoothly.

"Isn't there a rumor that Jimmy Hoffa was buried in one of the end zones in the Meadowlands?" Jolie asked, believing the question to be positively inspired. "But if you own your own concrete company...?"

"I didn't kill her!" Timothy Lutton, a smaller, paler reflection of his older sister, spoke for the first time. "I know what you're implying, but I did not kill her. She left. On her own. She left, I swear to God!"

"Timothy, shut...up," Angela warned tightly. "Just because someone asks a question doesn't mean you owe them an answer."

"Not that I asked a question, but I sure do have some now," Jolie said, suddenly feeling all-powerful. Cathleen Hanson made her all-powerful. The woman deserved better than she'd gotten.

Teddy made her feel all-powerful. He deserved better than he'd gotten, too. "Did my father ask these same questions? Did you all get tired of hearing those questions? Did you all finally have enough and go to his house late one night and invite yourselves in? How long did it take you to figure out he was drunk and fairly helpless? And then there was the gun. Right there, right on the desk. That's not why you went to the house. You went there to ask him to stop visiting you, to stop pushing at you. But there was the gun. How simple it would be to just pick up that gun. There were enough of you to overpower him. Or maybe it was just you, Timothy?"

"I did not! I wouldn't do that! I wouldn't kill anybody! She—"

"You're trying to get us thrown out, aren't you?" Sam said quietly as Angela pulled her brother away, furiously whispering in his ear. "Keep it up, sweetheart. I see an Oscar in your future."

"Look at the two of them, Sam," Jolie said. "He knows something. And she knows he knows it. He's the weakest link, isn't he? Teddy has been wearing him down for twelve long years. Quick— what else can we ask him?"

Sam's cell phone rang again and he grabbed it. "Court's number. Jessica was going to call Jade and tell her about the electronic ticket. Stall while I answer this."

"Stall? How do I stall?"

Sam flipped open his phone. "I don't know. Can you tap dance?"

Jolie made a face at him and turned around to face Mother Pearson. "You never liked Cathleen, did you?"

"I made that obvious, yes. She wasn't one of us. She would never have been comfortable in our lifestyle. You wouldn't be either, Miss Sunshine, in Mr. Becket's. A wise woman would know that. I offered her money, but she wouldn't go. I offered her more money, and she still wouldn't go. And then, in the end, she left on her own. With my necklace and my son's ring. She wasn't just greedy, she was stupid. She pawned that jewelry for well less than a quarter of its worth."

"You offered Cathleen *money?*" David Pearson took a step away from his mother. "She never told me that. How could you do that? We loved each other. I was *happy.* For the first time in my life, I was happy! Didn't you want me to be happy?"

"David, not now," Mother Pearson said, reaching out to stroke his hair as if he were three years old. "We'll talk about this later. Privately."

"No, I think we'll talk about this now. No wonder Cathleen wanted to elope. But I wouldn't listen. I wouldn't hurt you that way. Didn't you always say that the day your only child married would be the happiest day of your life?"

Mother Pearson shook her head. "Yes, and it was, the day you married Angela. Sometimes you're so like your father. *Thick*."

Sam rejoined their merry little group, although he was the only one with a smile on his face. "I've got news, everyone," he said as if he was about to announce that he'd just won the lottery. "Good news. Well, for some of us."

Angela and Timothy rejoined the group, Timothy still looking more than a bit worn around the edges.

"That was Jolie's sister on the phone just now. Jade Sunshine. She worked with her father in the Sunshine Detective Agency."

"Good for her," Angela grumbled, lighting another cigarette but without taking her eyes off her brother, as if ready to pounce on him if he opened his mouth again.

"Yes, and she's very good at what she does. Computer searches. Not to drag this out… We found Cathleen. She's alive and well and living quite openly in Toronto. She's in the phone book."

Jolie watched, fascinated, as Angela Pearson's face went pewter beneath her tan. She grabbed on to her brother's arm. "How can that—what did you do? You *idiot!* Can't you do anything right? What did you do?"

"Angela, as your lawyer, I think it's time you were quiet. And I think it's time you two left," attorney Rampart said, putting his considerable bulk between Jolie and Sam and Angela and Timothy. Mrs. Pearson had already sunk into a chair and was looking at her son, fear naked in her eyes.

"You…you found Cathleen?" David asked Sam. "In Toronto? She's in Toronto? What's she doing in Toronto? You'd mentioned Toronto. She's really there?"

"Working as a registered nurse, yes," Sam said as Jolie slipped her hand into his. She wanted to yell, to jump for joy, to hug everybody in the world. But she knew this wasn't over yet. Teddy had found Cathleen, had hoped he'd found her, but he hadn't considered the case closed. Not yet.

"I—I have to go to her. I have so many questions for her. Please, do you have an address?"

Angela left her brother where he stood and grabbed at her husband's arm. "David, no! You're married to *me,* darling, remember?"

"You never liked her. You were never kind to her, not in any way. I'm going into the house now to get my passport. No matter what happens when I see Cathleen, I don't want you to be here when I get back. Let go of me, Angela."

"My cousin has his company jet at the airport, David," Sam said. "I think Jolie and I would like to offer you a ride, through him, as we're also going up there as soon as possible. Aren't we, Jolie?"

"Oh, yes. Yes!" Finally Jolie wrapped her arms around Sam, hugging him tightly. "I didn't know how much I wanted to hear this news until I heard it. Something good, Sam. Finally something *good*."

"Thank you, Sam." David turned to his mother, his spine somehow straighter than it had been a minute earlier. "Will Cathleen tell me that you finally succeeded in buying her off? Or did you just scare her away?"

"David, I had nothing to do with it," Mother Pearson said, her penitent look not fitting her well, Jolie thought, but appearing genuine. "Yes, I wanted her to go. I was glad when she was gone. But, like you, I never knew why she finally decided to leave."

Which left Angela, didn't it? Jolie walked over to where she was standing watching her husband walk toward the house and away from her. "You did it, didn't you? You and your brother."

"Go to hell," Angela said, reaching into her pocket for her pack of cigarettes and coming up with an empty pack. She threw it into the pool. "I don't know what that bitch is going to say, but it will all be a pack of lies. Timothy! I'm out of cigarettes! Timothy!"

But Timothy Lutton was also walking away. Leaving his sister just as David Pearson had walked away from his mother.

Jolie chased after Timothy. "What happened, Timothy? We're going to find out when we get to Toronto and talk to Cathleen. Don't you want to get your version of the story in first? What did Angela want you to do?"

"I told David we'd wait out front for him," Sam said, catching up to them as they walked down the wide gallery hall for what Jolie knew would be the last time. "Timothy? Tim. Were you involved? And did you or your sister go to see Teddy Sunshine the night he died?"

Timothy was wiping at his eyes now as he shook his head. "Why did I do it? Why do I let her talk me into things? So what if the company went under? I *hate* the concrete business. I've always hated it."

"Tim, concentrate," Sam said as Jolie tried to figure out what the man was talking about— Cathleen so many years ago or her father now. "Did you go see Teddy Sunshine the night he died?"

They were outside again now, standing next to the Jeep. "No," Timothy said, his expression incredulous. "Do I look like somebody who'd kill anybody? I never went near your father, Ms. Sunshine. He scared the snot out of me. I never met with him unless Angela was with me. Otherwise he would have…otherwise I would have told him years ago, just to make him go away."

"So what happened, Tim?" Jolie asked him gently. "Back then, the night before the wedding. What did Angela ask you to do? She asked you to take Cathleen home, didn't she? What else did she ask you to do?"

CHAPTER SEVENTEEN

"IT WAS JUST LIKE A scene from a movie," Jolie told them all as she sat cuddled next to Sam on the couch. They'd been gone for three days, taking the time for some long talks and privacy of their own in Toronto, and now everyone was gathered in his living room once more.

Later she would give Jessica that promised exclusive television interview at her network's station in Secaucus, and then she and Sam would be gone once more, this time to California to get ready for the night of her premiere and another round of interviews.

"As a matter of fact," she continued as Jessica and Jade took seats on the facing couch, Matt and Court standing behind them, "I wouldn't be surprised if it all did become a movie of the week or something."

"There won't be any charges filed," Matt said, shaking his head. "Statute of limitations kicks in on the whole deal. Conspiracy to murder? How do you prove that anyway? It's he said, she said—and, in the end, Cathleen left on her own."

"I don't see David pushing for anything except a quick divorce, frankly," Sam told them as he wound a lock of Jolie's hair around his finger. "I had a talk with him this morning." He looked at Jolie. "Did I tell you that he called, sweetheart?"

"No, you didn't," she said, smiling into his eyes. There was happy, and then there was deliriously happy. She'd probably even passed beyond delirious and was into sappy-happy. But she didn't care. "What did he say?"

"Hey, you two," Jessica interrupted. "Before you start at the end, go back, start at the beginning. Matt told me what he knows, but now you guys tell me from the get-go. Then I'll decide what I want to ask you on the air, okay?"

"Now who's giving orders?" Jade asked as she picked at a corner of the bandage on her left hand. "And can we speed this up? I've got another clinic appointment in an hour. It was like a movie, you said, Jolie. Go from there."

"Always giving orders," Sam whispered in Jolie's ear, and she laughed.

"All right. From the beginning. I know we raced in and out of here, grabbing our passports. Timothy told us the truth—or at least his version of it—and Cathleen pretty much confirmed it when we spoke with her. And Matt knows this all now, too.

Cathleen was pregnant. Angela found out when she went with her to the last fitting for her bridal gown the afternoon of the rehearsal party, and all her hopes that Mother Pearson could buy Cathleen off when she took one last shot at it later, at the party, went down the drain. In fact, Mother Pearson might even forgive Cathleen for being a waitress if she got a grandchild out of the deal. So Angela went to plan B. Right, Sam?"

"Plan B, as Jolie calls it," Sam said, "was put together quickly that same day. Angela was to get David too drunk to drive, which she managed by slipping sleeping pills into his drink, and then Timothy would offer to take Cathleen home. And kill her."

Jolie leaned forward on the couch. "And Angela thought he did kill her and buried her body in Fairmont Park, I think it was. But you'd have to meet Timothy."

"No, I don't," Jessica said. "A grown man and he still answers to *Timothy?* I think I've already got a good mental picture. Go on. What did Timothy really do?"

"He told Cathleen the truth," Jolie said, sighing. "Can you imagine? Cathleen told us he cried and begged her to leave, because if she didn't, Angela would find a way to really kill her, sooner or later. Having met Angela, I'd believe that one. Especially if I had a baby to protect."

"Wait a minute, wait a minute," Jade said, waving her hands in the air. "Back up. How did Timothy get to Cathleen if she didn't let him drive her home?"

"Ah, that's where the midnight phone call from Angela comes in," Sam said. "She called Cathleen and told her that David and his mother had had a huge fight and the drunken David took his car and drove off in a temper and had an accident. She told Cathleen to go down to the street and wait for Timothy to pick her up and take her to the hospital."

"But he was really supposed to drive her somewhere and kill her. Nice woman, that Angela. Not just murder, but both mother and unborn child. Okay, I'm clear on that now, thanks," Jade said and went back to poking at a corner of her bandage. She'd told them that the healing burns now itched incessantly.

"You've really got her riveted," Sam joked to Jolie, who only rolled her eyes.

"Anyway, since some of us are getting bored, the upshot was that Cathleen wasn't all that hot to stay and go through with the wedding. David was a wimp. Her child would have to be brought up in a house with Mother Pearson around. Not to mention Angela. So when Timothy offered to clear out his account at a local ATM and drive her to the bus station, she went. She took the necklace off, gave it and the ring back to Timothy to give to David when he sobered up, bought a ticket to Toronto and that was that. She thought she'd effectively called off the wedding and had no idea Teddy was looking for her."

"But Angela thought Timothy had killed her because that's what he told her, so she put on a blond wig and pawned the diamonds the morning of the wedding. After all, Angela planned to marry David and she wanted those diamonds for herself," Jolie ended, clapping her hands together. "Leaving us with the grand reunion three days ago."

"Now *that's* what I want to hear about," Jessica said, holding a pen poised over one of her notebooks. "You said it was like a movie?"

Jolie felt herself tearing up again at the memory. "We stood across the street from the building where Cathleen has an apartment, with Sam trying to get David to build up the nerve to go over, knock on her door—when Cathleen walked down the street. She was carrying a big paper grocery bag, and David called out her name, and she stopped where she was and turned toward the street, and David took two steps into the street—"

"And nearly got run down by a bus," Sam interrupted, grinning.

"Hey, now *that's* romantic," Jessica said, popping a pecan into her mouth.

"It is to me," Jolie said, bristling. "Where was

I? Oh, right. David called her name again, and Cathleen said his name—we couldn't hear her, of course, not with the bus, but I saw her lips move—and she dropped the grocery bag. Oranges all over the pavement. David started running. Cathleen held her arms out to him. It was…it was wonderful."

"We weren't there when David met his son," Sam explained, "but we did meet them later, which was when Cathleen gave us her side of the story. Jolie wants to think there's a huge happily ever after in the works, but I think David has some heavy lifting ahead of him. Angela can't fight a divorce, not without having it come out that she tried to have Cathleen murdered, but I don't know about Mother Pearson."

"I do," Jolie said, believing every word she said. "He has Cathleen now and he has young David, as well, to hold over Mother Pearson's head. You know—play nice, Mother P, or you'll never see your grandson. Even Angela knew what a grandchild would mean to David's mother."

"So we've got one happy ending," Jessica said, closing her notebook. "And Teddy had already solved the case. He just didn't live long enough to go to Toronto and see Cathleen so that she could fill in the blanks for him about Angela and Timothy. Also—at least to us—proving yet again that Teddy didn't kill himself. Not when he was about to meet Cathleen. Which kind of ruins the happy ending a little—again, at least for us. Now what?"

"Now we get back to work, of course," Jade said, getting to her feet. "Court, don't we have to leave now? I'm hoping Dr. Reardon will tell me I won't need all this heavy bandaging anymore after today. Then you can go home and I can drive myself anywhere I need to go."

"I'm not going anywhere, Jade, not as long as you insist on playing at private detective."

"I *am* a private detective," Jade said as she and Court walked toward the foyer. "And I don't need a babysitter."

"Young love—ain't it grand," Jessica said on a sigh as she, too, got to her feet, smoothing down her navy-blue on-air suit. "Come on, Matt, drive me to the studio and I'll treat you to the grand tour. Jolie? Six o'clock okay?"

Jolie nodded and then watched Jessica lead Matt out of the living room. "He seems to follow her willingly enough."

"While planning ways to murder her, sure," Sam said, sliding his arm around Jolie's shoulders and pulling her close. "I already told Court that everyone can still stay here while I'm out in California with you. You father's house isn't ready for occupancy yet anyway. Plus, this way Court can keep an eye on her. And now you're frowning."

"I won't be here to help them anymore," Jolie said, sighing. "And you know they're not going to give up. Especially now that one case is solved, even if we didn't really solve it."

"Still, we make a good team, Ms. Sunshine," Sam said, kissing her temple. "God," he said, pulling back a fraction. "I just thought of something. I'm going to be Mr. Sunshine, aren't I? Out in La-La Land. You're going to have to be good to me, you know. *Very* good to me."

Jolie took hold of his hand and stood up, urging him to his feet. "We have about an hour before I have to get ready to leave to meet Jess. I could start being good to you now, just to keep ahead of the curve?"

Sam smiled. "Exactly what did you have in mind, Ms. Sunshine?"

She whispered in his ear and then stood back and looked at him, raising her eyebrows. "Well?"

"I'll meet you upstairs in five minutes, *Red*. First I'll call Jess and tell her we might be a little late…."

* * * * *

Watch for Jessica Sunshine and
Lieutenant Matthew Denby!
Their story, MISCHIEF BECOMES HER,
is coming in November 2008 from HQN Books.

REQUEST YOUR FREE BOOKS!

2 FREE NOVELS
FROM THE ROMANCE/SUSPENSE
COLLECTION PLUS 2 FREE GIFTS!

YES! Please send me 2 FREE novels from the Romance/Suspense Collection and my 2 FREE gifts (gifts are worth about $10). After receiving them, if I don't wish to receive any more books, I can return the shipping statement marked "cancel." If I don't cancel, I will receive 4 brand-new novels every month and be billed just $5.49 per book in the U.S. or $5.99 per book in Canada, plus 25¢ shipping and handling per book plus applicable taxes, if any*. That's a savings of at least 20% off the cover price! I understand that accepting the 2 free books and gifts places me under no obligation to buy anything. I can always return a shipment and cancel at any time. Even if I never buy another book from the Reader Service, the two free books and gifts are mine to keep forever.

185 MDN EF5Y   385 MDN EF6C

Name _____ (PLEASE PRINT) _____

Address _____ Apt. # _____

City _____ State/Prov. _____ Zip/Postal Code _____

Signature (if under 18, a parent or guardian must sign)

Mail to The Reader Service:
IN U.S.A.: P.O. Box 1867, Buffalo, NY 14240-1867
IN CANADA: P.O. Box 609, Fort Erie, Ontario L2A 5X3

Not valid to current subscribers to the Romance Collection,
the Suspense Collection or the Romance/Suspense Collection.

Want to try two free books from another line?
Call 1-800-873-8635 or visit www.morefreebooks.com.

* Terms and prices subject to change without notice. N.Y. residents add applicable sales tax. Canadian residents will be charged applicable provinâal taxes and GST. This offer is limited to one order per household. All orders subject to approval. Credit or debit balances in a customer's account(s) may be offset by any other outstanding balance owed by or to the customer. Please allow 4 to 6 weeks for delivery. Offer available while quantities last.

Your Privacy: Harlequin is committed to protecting your privacy. Our Privacy Policy is available online at www.eHarlequin.com or upon request from the Reader Service. From time to time we make our lists of customers available to reputable third parties who may have a product or service of interest to you. If you would prefer we not share your name and address, please check here. ☐

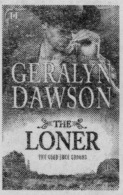

Kasey Michaels

77127	EVERYTHING'S COMING UP ROSIE	___	$6.99 U.S. ___	$8.50 CAN.
77059	STUCK IN SHANGRI-LA	___	$6.99 U.S. ___	$8.50 CAN.

(limited quantities available)

TOTAL AMOUNT	$ _____
POSTAGE & HANDLING	$ _____
($1.00 FOR 1 BOOK, 50¢ for each additional)	
APPLICABLE TAXES*	$ _____
TOTAL PAYABLE	$ _____

(check or money order—please do not send cash)

To order, complete this form and send it, along with a check or money order for the total above, payable to HQN Books, to: **In the U.S.:** 3010 Walden Avenue, P.O. Box 9077, Buffalo, NY 14269-9077; **In Canada:** P.O. Box 636, Fort Erie, Ontario, L2A 5X3.

Name: _____
Address: _____ City: _____
State/Prov.: _____ Zip/Postal Code: _____
Account Number (if applicable): _____

075 CSAS

*New York residents remit applicable sales taxes.
*Canadian residents remit applicable GST and provincial taxes.

HQN™

We *are* romance™

www.HQNBooks.com

PHKM0508BL